Carrier Daze

Carrier Daze

Tales from the USS Oriskany and
USS Lake Champlain

DICK MALTZMAN

CARRIER DAZE
TALES FROM THE USS ORISKANY AND USS LAKE CHAMPLAIN

This is a memoir, but the names of characters have for the most part been changed, dates of incidents are estimated, and dialogue in this memoir are either the products of the author's imagination or are used fictitiously.

iUniverse books may be ordered through booksellers or by contacting:

iUniverse
1663 Liberty Drive
Bloomington, IN 47403
www.iuniverse.com
1-800-Authors (1-800-288-4677)

ISBN: 978-1-4917-3438-4 (Softcover)
ISBN: 978-1-4917-3437-7 (Hardcover)
ISBN: 978-1-4917-3436-0 (eBook)
ISBN: 978-1-4917-5123-7 (Audio)

Library of Congress Control Number: 2014908746

Printed in the United States of America.

iUniverse rev. date: 12/17/2014

Table of Contents

This book is dedicated to my three sons,
Jeffrey, Forrest and Reed,
who pestered me constantly while they were
growing up to put down on paper the many stories which I
regaled them with concerning my experiences in the Navy. Of
course, they were young and naive and believed the stories.
This book is also dedicated to the love of my life,
my wife Charlene Maltzman,
without whom I would not have the humor to see
these events as they are described herein. While the events
described happened at or about the times described, I have taken
the liberty of changing many of the names of the personnel
involved to protect the innocent and the not-so innocent!

Part I

Getting There

Chapter 1

TAKING WING

Let me be perfectly clear, I am no hero. I look both ways before crossing streets. In the time I will be talking about I also had an abysmal fear of heights, and generally didn't take chances in life. I considered myself at that time, and still do today, to be one of those safe and sane people. I would never think of driving if I was drunk, and in the days of which I am speaking religiously stopped at five scotches if I was behind the wheel. And at that time I viewed flying in an airplane as only slightly less dangerous than ski jumping.

Now today one might wonder how anyone could fear flying, but the scene is not today—this is the 1950s, not that long after the end of the Second World War, and an age when the only planes that flew with a jet engine were military. Commercial aviation might not have been in its infancy, but it certainly was barely out of short pants, and no one in my family had ever considered flying anyplace if they could help it. My parents traveled incessantly, but went by ship if they couldn't get there by car or train.

In the spring of my freshman year at Stanford I heard that I had passed the competitive exam to become a "Regular" midshipman in the NROTC, the initials for the Naval Reserve Officer Training Corps. I saw this as a great opportunity, not because I wanted to fight for my country or wear a swash-buckling uniform, but for the simple reason that I really didn't want to fight anyone just then. I much preferred Stanford to a foxhole in Korea. In 1951 there was something called a police action taking place on the Korean Peninsula that looked a lot like a war to my naive view of world geopolitics. And in 1951 there was also something called the draft, which called up young men of military age to fight in that police action. As you

3

have probably surmised by now, I was of military age at the time of which I am writing, and the NROTC came complete with a four-year deferment.

Then there was the money. The NROTC at that time had, and they may still have today, something called the Holloway Plan that paid much of a Regular NROTC midshipman's college expenses (tuition, books and $50 a month in the 1950s) in a program designed to augment Annapolis and provide a larger pool of Regular (as distinguished from Reserve) Naval Officers for the U. S. Navy. The only hitch was that as a "Regular" NROTC midshipman I would have to serve three years of active duty and five years in the Navy Reserve after graduation and go on three summer cruises, during which I would be paid as a seaman apprentice. There was also a similar program for "Contract" NROTC midshipman, who didn't get any help with collage expenses or a monthly stipend during the school year, served only two years of active duty (but six years in the Reserve) and went on only one summer cruise, during which they were also paid as a seaman apprentice. As a Regular midshipman I would be commissioned on graduation from Stanford as a regular naval officer. A Contract midshipman would be commissioned as a reserve officer.

It also seemed to me a lot more civilized to defend one's country from the comfort of a ship surrounded by water than from a foxhole filled with water. But probably the most significant aspect of my desire to accept the NROTC appointment was my fear of flying. If God had meant me to fly, I believed I would have been born with wings and covered with feathers. I had no intention of ever voluntarily setting foot on an airplane, and what I liked about the Navy was that it went places by sea in things they called ships. While I couldn't fly, I could swim.

Thus it was that as a Stanford freshman I found myself in the early spring of 1951 being interviewed for a Holloway Plan NROTC scholarship by the Commandant of the Stanford NROTC program, a Marine Colonel. After listening to his pitch about what a great career the Navy had to offer to regular naval officers, I asked if I would have to fly if I became a naval officer.

"Of course not," the Colonel responded, "You don't have to fly in the Navy unless you want to."

So I signed up and became a Regular NROTC midshipman.

Of course, the colonel lied!

Or perhaps he didn't understand my question. He might have thought I meant, "fly" like being a Naval aviator, but I meant fly like getting on an airplane to go someplace.

The true depth of my perception of the colonel's apparent perfidy became obvious to me on my second summer cruise. They sent me not to sea, but to Corpus Christi, Texas, for three weeks of naval air indoctrination. When that was over, they then had the audacity to fly me and my fellow midshipmen in Navy transports from Corpus Christi, Texas, to Little Creek, Virginia, for three weeks of Marine Corps indoctrination.

The first thing they made each midshipman do at Corpus Christi was to go up in an SNJ, a single engine two-seater training plane with two open cockpits, one behind the other. The pilot sat in the front cockpit, the passenger (me) in the back cockpit. It looked to me like a remnant from World War I, not World War II. They required everyone to take at least one flight in the SNJ. If you didn't like it after that, you could refuse to go up again or trade your future flights with other midshipmen more "gung-ho" for flying, but one flight was mandatory for everyone, even someone like me who considered myself immune from flying based on a Marine Colonel's perceived promise.

Unfortunately, the Marine Colonel wasn't there at Corpus Cristi to back up my story, and the people in command there demanded that I take at least that one flight. As that choice seemed slightly better than the draft notice I was sure I would receive if I refused completely, I took my first flight.

The pilot assigned to me was a friendly guy, who wanted to show me everything that the plane could do. It could do loop-the-loops. It could do power dives. It could do spins.

And I showed the pilot what I could do. I could throw up, and did. Repeatedly!

When I finally landed, I was greeted by the news that one of the other planes that had gone up with us that afternoon had lost a wing doing a loop-the-loop, and both the instructor and the midshipman in the plane were killed. I opted not to take any more flights.

—◦◦◦—

When my three weeks of air indoctrination finished, it was time to fly to Little Creek, Virginia. My first experience had only amplified my fear of flying, and as the big day grew closer I grew ever more nervous. I told anyone who would listen about the nice Marine Colonel back in San Francisco who assured me that in the Navy you didn't have to fly unless you wanted to—and I didn't want to. I offered to go by train at my own expense, or by bus, or hitchhike—anything but fly. They were sympathetic but emphatic; I had to fly. They were also callus enough to assure me that I would love the flying experience once I got used to it.

On the day of my departure from Corpus Cristi, they lined up all of the midshipmen by platoons in a big hanger. The platoons were lined up for boarding alphabetically by the schools represented in each platoon, and the schools were assigned to platoons in general alphabetic order with two schools to a platoon.

My platoon consisted of midshipmen from Stanford and USC. At the exit to the tarmac was a lieutenant with a clipboard. By some strange mischance, which will be described later, I happened to be the platoon leader for the combined Stanford/USC contingent for the Corpus Christi portion of our cruise. When it was our turn, the lieutenant with the clipboard directed me to take my platoon to the third aircraft parked on the left. The third aircraft parked on the left was an R4Q, a Navy transport affectionately known as "the flying boxcar," and less affectionately as the "flying coffin," or just plain "aw fuck you" as a play on its R4Q official Navy designator. The Air Force used them, too, and called them the C-120. It was built by Hughes Aircraft out of plywood and looked something like a giant (and fat) P-38 left over from the Second World War, with two large booms coming back from the engines which supported the tail structure while the cargo and passenger superstructure hung there in between supported by its high wing.

When I learned that I was going to have to fly, I read up on everything I could find on the different types of planes that the Navy flew to transport people or things. In the course of this research I discovered that the R4Q/C-120 had the worst accident record of any plane then flying, thus the nickname "flying coffin."

The next plane past the R4Q to which the Stanford/USC platoon was assigned was a DC-4, not the newest plane but at least one that commercial airlines still used in the 1950's. Furthermore, the DC-4 had the range to fly non-stop to Little Creek; the R4Q did not and had to stop at Pensacola for refueling. I had also discovered in my research that takeoffs and landings were the most dangerous part of air travel. Therefore, one of each seemed a hell of a lot better than two of each.

So as platoon leader I marched my platoon right past the R4Q to which we were assigned and right onto the DC-4 parked next to it. I figured, rightly, as it happened, that the lieutenant would assume that I was an idiot who couldn't handle simple instructions, or couldn't count, but rather than chase after us would probably just assign another platoon to the still empty R4Q.

I was more right than I had any reason to be. After we landed in Little Creek we discovered that an R4Q had crashed on takeoff from Pensacola, and all but one of the 48 midshipmen aboard had been killed. It contained the University of Utah and University of Texas midshipmen, who had been behind my platoon waiting to board in Corpus Cristi. I, of course, don't know which platoon actually went into the R4Q I had skirted in favor of the DC-4, but I have thanked God ever since that it wasn't mine.

Thus ended my confrontation with airplanes—at least for a while. When I was commissioned an ensign after completing four years of NROTC—by this time I had already completed two years of law school at Stanford—I received orders to report to the 12th Naval District for further transportation to the Western Pacific, there to report to my first duty station, the USS Oriskany (CVA-34). The Oriskany was an Essex class attack carrier, and was affectionately known to its crew as the "O-Boat." While it was designated "CVA 34" and many of the higher numbered CVAs were commissioned before the end of World War II, the Oriskany had not been completed by VJ Day and at the war's end had been mothballed. At the advent of the Korean War she was rushed back into commission with a number of improvements, which were later incorporated in all of the Essex class carriers, and she saw extensive duty in Korea.

Thus it was that shortly after graduation and being sworn in as an ensign in the Regular Navy I reported to the 12th Naval District offices in the Federal Building in San Francisco, where they gave me enough shots to protect me from everything except bullets, a bus ticket to Travis Air Force Base, and a ticket for a MATS, or Military Air Transport Service, flight to Japan.

Of course, I demurred. I advised them of that wonderful Marine Colonel who had assured me that I would never have to fly if I joined the Navy. They, of course, assured me that the good Colonel never meant that I wouldn't have to fly MATS. I offered to go by ship, but they insisted I go by air.

"What type of planes does MATS fly?" I asked.

"The latest super constellations or DC-6B's." I was assured.

"Is MATS safe?" I enquired.

"MATS is run by the Air Force. It has the finest safety record of any airline aloft, civilian or military," they lied.

I actually had several weeks before I had to leave for Travis to make sure my shots took affect. I filled that time with a round of parties to say farewell to my Stanford friends and my then girl friend, who just happened to be an admiral's daughter. Her father was in charge of all the Naval air forces for the Hawaiian Islands and, when she wasn't at Stanford, she lived with her parents on Ford Island in Pearl Harbor.

The night before my impending departure we were up partying much of the night. The next morning I took her to the Navy's Mars flying boat at Alameda and saw her off to Hawaii and I embarked on a bus for Travis Air Force Base. There I turned in my ticket and a copy of my orders and spent the rest of the day waiting nervously for a flight, my stomach churning like a washing machine while I stared at the wall clock ticking ever so slowly toward flight time

At about six that night they called my flight and I lined up to board with the other passengers. My legs were shaking I was so nervous. Past the airman taking tickets I could see the silver super constellation parked on the tarmac that was hopefully going to take me to Japan. As I moved up the line, I was getting more and more nervous. This was not just a flight; this was a flight half way around the world.

Then, just as I almost reached the door, they were calling my name over the public address system. They wanted an Ensign Richard Maltzman to report to something called the "Courier Desk," and immediately. And they were emphasizing that "immediately." I was saved! As I was the only Ensign Richard Maltzman that I knew of, they had to be referring to me! I looked around at the other poor souls boarding that flight, and I was sure they were doomed. After my experience at Corpus Christie, I was sure that they would not make it to Japan on that plane. This was like the R4Q I had walked past in favor of the DC-4. I literally skipped out of line and ran to find this "Courier Desk" to which I had been directed by divine intervention.

At the Courier Desk an Air Force major of diminutive size with red curly hair and a bushy red handlebar mustache greeted me. The major advised me that I was the junior officer on that Constellation flight to Japan and had been drafted to be a courier officer to escort fifty-two crates of cryptographic equipment to an admiral in Japan.

"On what kind of airplane will I be flying?" I asked.

"The latest Douglas cargo plane," the major responded.

"Ah," I thought, "It must be the latest DC-6B with a cargo configuration." A little knowledge is a dangerous thing.

The major gave me a 45-calibre pistol, which I had not the slightest idea how to use, and an Air Force sergeant, complete with a sub-machine gun, which I later discovered the sergeant didn't know how to use, either. The major then proceeded to take me out a back door into a hanger to show me my cargo, reminding me as we went that there was an annual softball game at Leavenworth Penitentiary between the disbursement officers with sticky fingers and the courier officers that lost boxes of crypto gear. I informed the major that I hated softball and had no skill at the sport, but the major seemed neither amused nor reassured.

The fifty-two crates were olive green, and stacked up on a flat bed trailer being pulled by a jeep. The major and I counted the crates and checked off the serial numbers and I signed for them. Then the major directed me to get in the jeep with the sergeant and a driver and the four of us drove out onto the tarmac, pulling the fifty-two olive green crates behind us.

Thoughts of flying prior to this had only engendered fear in me. Now I felt something new stirring within. Panic! The field was alive with planes, some taking off, some landing, and some just sitting, with or without their engines running. The noise was deafening! At the far end of the runway, waiting to take off, was the biggest plane I had ever seen. It was a B36 bomber, with eight reciprocal engines and four jets hanging from its huge wings, all of which were very much on. It made such a roar as it sat there that it sounded like the voice of God. And it was directed at me, telling me not to fly and to get the hell out of there!

I asked the major, "Where is the airplane I'll be flying in?"

"Over there," the major said, pointed to a large structure with two huge, gaping doors that stood ajar.

"In that hanger?" I asked.

"That's no hanger, son, that's your airplane!"

Escape from the speeding jeep was impossible, but the thought crossed my mind as the jeep and my fifty-two olive green crates crossed the tarmac toward the Douglas Globemaster C124 that was to take my cargo and me to Japan. By the standards of the time, the C124 was huge. The fuselage was two decks high, and the wings stuck out from the middle of the plane like two small diving boards. The four Pratt & Whitney R-4800 engines looked like tiny toys. Neither the wings nor the engines looked large enough to lift the monster. Two huge cargo doors in the front of the plane stood wide open, ready to engulf me, the jeep and its entire load of olive green crates, but the major ignored the ramp and had the driver drive the jeep and the cargo around to the belly of the airplane.

When we drove under the great plane, the major stood up in his seat and circled his hand over his head, apparently signaling to someone in the cockpit. Immediately two great hatches, like giant bomb bays, opened on the bottom of the plane and a large platform was lowered on wires suspended from each of its four corners. Almost simultaneously, the two doors in the front of the plane began to close. Two airmen then proceeded to load my fifty-two olive green crates of crypto gear on the platform. The major next instructed one of the airmen to remove two cots from the back of the jeep and set them up on top of the load. The major, the sergeant and I then climbed on top of the load, and the major again circled his hand over his head. This time the platform started rising into the bowels of the plane.

To me it was like entering the body of a huge whale. Standing on the crates, we rose into the belly of the beast until our heads were only inches from the roof. Running the length of the roof along the spine of the aircraft was a single wire held in place every six feet or so by hook eyes.

"This plane doesn't do worth a damn if it has to make a forced landing at sea," the major said reassuringly. "The two doors in front cave in and the plane falls apart. It's very important, therefore, that you jettison the load before you crash (the logic of this statement made no sense to me). See this wire?" and the major pointed to the wire running down the spine of the aircraft along the roof, "if it looks like the plane is going down one of you has to pull this wire which tells the pilot to jettison the load."

"But wait a minute," I demurred, "we're standing on the load. One of us would have to be standing on the load to reach the wire."

The major looked rather puzzled, as though he had never thought of that before, hesitated a minute, and finally said over his shoulder as he climbed down off the crypto gear, "Don't worry, the pilot will give you time to jump off before he dumps the load."

I looked at that wire and thought for a minute. Then I turned to the sergeant and said, "Leavenworth be damned, Sergeant, that is one wire that we're never going to pull."

The sergeant, who was also standing there staring at the wire, just slowly shook his head in the affirmative.

"Sarge," I asked, "Do *you* play softball?"

———◦◊◦———

The takeoff and the landing were both uneventful, and that was all I remember of that first leg of my flight to Japan. It was eight hours to Hickham Field in Hawaii, our first stop, and I conked out on the cot the minute we took off. The combination of partying all night and worrying all day had done me in.

After landing at Hickham, one of the pilots, a Major, came back to tell the sergeant and me that the landing had broken something called the strut on the left landing gear and we would be "stuck" in Hawaii for several weeks. "Check in your gear with the courier office and give us a call at the BOQ (Bachelor Officers' Quarters) every morning about 0700 starting in two weeks," he told us. "It certainly won't be fixed before then."

It turned out to be three-and-a-half weeks, all of which I spent with the admiral and his daughter on Ford Island. My girlfriend was delighted to see me, but the admiral was ecstatic. He was a bridge fanatic, and his daughter, in an attempt to get the admiral to accept this strange ensign-like creature that she had brought home, had told him of my slight skills at the game. It was enough. He had me punishing the tables with him at the officers' club from the moment I arrived. I had a reputation at Stanford as a bridge shark, and after I bid and made a couple of difficult slams, the admiral wanted to have my orders rewritten to his own staff (apparently good bridge players were hard to find on Ford Island), but with the territory came the daughter, and while I liked her just fine, my idea of adventures on exotic Pacific Islands did not include Ford Island. Assuring the admiral that a capital ship would be better for my career in the Navy (the admiral was pleased with that one), I stuck to my course, even though it obviously meant some more flying to get to Japan.

When they advised me on my morning call three and a half weeks later that they were finally ready to leave on the next leg to Wake Island, I said my goodbyes to the admiral and family, checked back in with the Hickham Field Courier Desk and received back my fifty-two olive green crates, my sergeant with the sub-machine gun, my 45, and our cots, and proceeded to sleep all the way to Wake Island. Again the landing seemed uneventful, but after we had taxied to a stop the pilot, the same Major who had talked to us at Hickham Field, came down and again told the sergeant and me that they had now broken the strut in the right landing gear.

"My God!" I asked the major, "Are we going to be stuck here for three-and-a-half weeks?"

"No," he replied, "They should have the strut fixed by morning."

"How come it took three-and-a-half weeks at Hickham and they can fix the same thing here overnight?" I asked.

"First," the major replied, "this is not a military installation; it is run by Pan Am and they are a hell-of-lot more efficient. Second, you're not the only one with friends in Hawaii. It took a good case of Scotch Whiskey to get them to take that long at Hickham."

I was learning something about the military that they did not teach at Stanford, and I had yet to even find the Navy.

Wake Island did not have a courier officer on duty to whom I could hand over my load of olive green crates, so that night the sergeant and I took turns sleeping and guarding our precious cargo with the sergeant's sub-machine gun. In the morning, true to the pilot's words, the plane was ready and we were off to our final destination, Atsugi Air Force Base outside Tokyo.

Again, as soon as the plane took off I climbed onto my cot and went to sleep. This time, however, as I had actually slept some the night before, I got up after several hours. Having nothing better to do, I asked one of the enlisted men on the flight crew if I could go onto the flight deck. The enlisted man replied that he was sure it was okay and directed me to the stairs and door that led to the flight compartment. I climbed the stairs and entered, not knowing exactly what to expect, but feeling certain that I was in for a real treat.

The scene was impressive, if not awe inspiring. The Globemaster had a huge cockpit that sat on the top of the plane, with the pilot and co-pilot's chairs at the front with two more rows of identical chairs, but without controls, immediately behind. Along the right wall were the flight engineer's chair and a wall full of equipment and the radio operator's position with an equally impressive wall full of equipment.

On the other side, not to be outdone, were the Navigator's chair and his wall full of equipment. At the rear of the compartment were three tiers of bunks, laid out like three sides of an octagon in terraces, with three bunks to a terrace. In other words, there were nine chairs to the front of the compartment and nine bunks at the rear, immediately next to the door. As I looked at the scene, an ominous feeling came over me. There was something wrong. The nine chairs were really very impressive—each one fitted out in wonderfully soft black leather—but they were all empty! On the contrary, all nine bunks, also in black leather, were full of sleeping men.

A rather loud voice started shouting into my subconscious from that little pit of fear I carried with me whenever I even thought of flying, and it said: "WHO THE HELL IS FLYING THIS THING?"

But on further inspection I breathed a slight sigh of relief. As I entered the cabin and got a better angle, I realized that there was a tuft of blond hair sticking over the top of the pilot's chair, the front left. I approached the pilot's chair with trepidation.

"Sir, may I sit in the copilot's chair until he needs it?" I inquired.

The Pilot's chair swiveled around. Blond hair spoke, "Sure, Sir, but you don't have to call me 'Sir,' I have to call you 'Sir,' Sir. But just make yourself at home."

There was a message there, but in my state of panic it was slow to sink in. Equally slow to sink in was that blond hair was not the pilot I had talked to at Hickham Field and Wake Island. I sat down, and the first thing that caught my eye was that the blond headed occupant of the number one chair, as the pilots seat is called, was reading a book.

As I was white as a ghost and in a visible state of panic already from all the other empty chairs, the sight of the pilot paying no attention to the controls and reading a book did not give me much comfort. It seemed only logical to me that if the Air Force wanted all those chairs and all that equipment in the cockpit, there must be a reason for it.

"Is it all right for the pilot to be reading a book while he's flying the plane?" I asked timorously.

"Pilot!" blond hair replied, "I'm not the pilot, Sir, I'm the radio operator. Major Henderson back there is the pilot. He's asleep right now, but we're on automatic pilot and there's nothing out here anyway. I'll wake up Major Henderson if something comes up."

Something almost came up right then—my breakfast. It was also at about this instant that I realized that blond hair appeared to be no more than 18 years old and his uniform bore an uncanny resemblance to those that enlisted men wore, even though the difference is difficult to detect in the Air Force. I immediately came to the logical conclusion that I had been put on this plane as part of God's greater plan; I was the designated lookout.

So I looked. I looked straight ahead. I looked to the left. I looked to the right. I looked up. I looked down. Fortunately, I didn't see anything but a few clouds in any direction but down, but down was distinctly unusual. There was the ocean, exactly where you would expect it to be. But there was a straight line cutting right across the ocean from as far to the right (north I assumed) as I could see and ending almost immediately beneath us.

Now I had heard of the International Date Line, and I knew we had to cross it, but I never really thought it was something you could actually see. So I kept the fear and my breakfast down long enough to ask the airman cum pilot what the line was.

He was as perplexed as I was. "Gosh," he said, "I don't know. I never saw anything like that! Major Henderson told me to wake him if I see anything unusual, and I guess whatever that is, it must be something unusual and I'm definitely seeing it."

So the radio operator woke the pilot, and everyone else as well, and they all came forward to see the wondrous sight that I, a brand new ensign, had discovered.

"I know what that is," said Major Henderson, "those are snorkeling submarines. I used to fly Liberators over the Gulf of Mexico during the Second World War, and I would recognize them anywhere. We had better report this."

Whereupon, much to my relief, both the pilot and the copilot got back in their chairs and every one else grabbed a chair except for the obviously extra man who sat on one of the bunks. While I was now without a seat, I had a terrific standing room only position to watch the unfolding drama. Or I could just lie down on one of the bunks and cry myself to sleep.

The pilot, who until that time had been communicating in a normal voice with no trace of any discernible accent, now developed a Texas twang as he spoke into his microphone, "Wake Island Tower, this is

MATS R276492 reporting at longitude (something-or-other) and latitude (something else), we have an unknown number of submarines proceeding at snorkel depth on course one-eight-zero degrees almost immediately beneath us."

And we flew on. The line was rapidly dropping behind us when the plane got a response from Wake. In the world's slowest Texas drawl, Wake's tower now responded: "MATS R276492, this is Wake Island Tower, please return to location of your submarine sighting, reduce altitude to 500 feet, and get all details you can observe. If anyone on board has a camera, use it. There are no friendly submarines in your vicinity."

There was a momentary silence in the cockpit as the full impact of what Wake Island was saying sank in. Then Henderson, in an equally slow voice, but still with the twang, responded, "Wake Island Tower, this is MATS R276492 . . ." Then his voice exploded and the words tumbled one on top of the other ". . . YOU'VE GOT TO BE OUT OF YOUR FRIGIN MIND! THIS IS A GLOBEMASTER CARGO PLANE. WE'RE AS BIG AS THE GODDAMN GOODYEAR BLIMP, AND NOT MUCH FASTER. YOU COULD KNOCK US OUT OF THE SKY WITH A BEE-BEE GUN. I AM NOT RISKING THIS PLANE AND ITS CREW . . ."

"Don't forget its valuable cargo of crypto gear!" I interjected.

". . . AND ITS VALUABLE CARGO OF HIGHLY CLASSIFIED MATERIAL ON SOME WILD ASS EXCURSION TO COUNT RUSSIAN OR CHINESE SUBMARINES."

Then it was the plane's turn for the radio to erupt. Whoever was on the other end didn't shout, but the tone of his voice seemed to indicate that he didn't need to shout: "Ahhh, MATS R276492, this is General Wheeler, Commanding Officer Wake Island, speaking from Wake Island Tower, this is an order, repeat, an order! You are to return to the scene of the sighting of the previously reported submarines, reduce you altitude to 500 feet, and report back to us immediately exactly what you see. If you have any cameras aboard, you are to take photographs."

Then General Wheeler's voice exploded, "DO YOU READ ME MATS R276492?"

Henderson's voice was now quite a bit quieter when he tried to reply, "Wake Island Tower, this is MATS R276492, but General Wheeler, sir, what if . . . ."

The radio erupted louder than ever: "MATS R276492, *THIS IS GENERAL WHEELER*, DO YOU READ ME?"

Henderson responded, in barely over a whisper, "Wake Island Tower, this is MATS R276492, yes sir, read you loud and clear, proceeding back to intersect point and will investigate sighting at altitude of 500 feet. Over and out."

And so MATS R276492 returned to the scene of my eagle eye spotting of the submarines. However, my eagle eyes were not very popular on the flight deck at that moment. By now everyone was not only up, they were very alert indeed. Major Henderson told everyone to look for clouds to duck into if the submarines began to surface. At this point, the flight engineer announced that he was concerned about the accuracy of the equipment on the aircraft. He thought that the altimeter had been acting strangely lately. He opined, and Henderson agreed, that the altimeter was really at 500 feet when it read 2,000 feet.

With this technical clarification taken into consideration, they returned to where the submarines would now be, based on the navigator's calculations, and reduced their altitude to "500 feet" as indicated by the altimeter reading "2,000 feet."

There they found eight submarines cruising in formation at snorkel depth. If they weren't U.S. or British, and they weren't, they apparently had to be Russian. Henderson made one pass, reported his sighting, and climbed out of there as fast as the plane's puny little wings and tiny little engines would carry it.

When the plane rolled to a stop at Atsugi Air Base later that evening, two black limousines drove onto the tarmac to take away everyone on the crew for debriefing about the submarines. They would have taken me, too, but I had my fifty-two olive green boxes to deliver, an armed sergeant and my 45. It was kind of like a standoff at the OK corral.

The next day I ran into Major Henderson at the BOQ (Bachelor Officers' Quarters, although married officers without their wives along were welcome to stay there). He told me that Naval intelligence had told him that what we had seen was the first reported sighting of a Russian wolf pack in the Pacific.

———⟨ɷɷɷ⟩———

In spite of the success of the flight, my adventure in trying to find my ship was not over. I spent some three weeks in the BOQ at the United States Naval Base at Yokosuka waiting for word of where the Oriskany was and when I could join it. Once they went so far as to put me in an old P2V flying boat to fly me to the Oriskany, which was reportedly in Southern Kyushu.

The Navy had found a new way to scare me half to death—a seaplane! The plane raced across the surface of the water in Tokyo Bay, bouncing hard on every wave. It was just rising on its point, with a steady "thup, thup, thup" that I thought would tear the plane apart, when the pilot suddenly cut power and returned to the pier. They heard on the radio, just as the plane was about to lift off, that the Oriskany was no longer in Southern Kyushu.

Of course, I could make no plans as I waited for the Navy to find the Oriskany, as I never knew when I would have to leave. Finally they told me that my ship was at Okinawa, but I would have to wait to reach her as a typhoon was bearing down on Okinawa. So the next day I made plans to go to the beach with a young nurse I had met at the PX. We agreed to meet at the Yokosuka train station at 10 a.m.

That, naturally, was a mistake. I should never have assumed that I could rely on the Navy or a typhoon. At about three the next morning, an enlisted man came to my room to tell me that I was leaving in an hour for Atsugi AFB for a flight to Okinawa.

"But there is a typhoon heading towards Okinawa!" I protested. "You can't fly me there."

But this was the military, and an hour later I was on my way to Atsugi. I had a new roommate that day in the Yokosuka BOQ, so I gave him a description of the nurse and told him to meet her at the train station and take her to the beach. I never heard from him or the nurse again, and do not to this day know whether he ever did meet her, whether they are now married, or whether the nurse is still to this day waiting for me at the train station in Yokosuka.

When I arrived at Atsugi, the first thing I saw was the headlines on the "Stars and Stripes": "TYPHOON HEADING TOWARD OKINAWA", and in smaller headlines, "FLEET FLEEING STORM."

When I got to the ticket counter (yes, you even need tickets on a MATS flight), I flashed the Stars and Stripes to the attendant and assured him that they should not be trying to fly me to Okinawa.

"Don't be ridiculous," the attendant assured me, "we have the finest aerologists in the world. They never would let you fly to Okinawa if a typhoon was heading there."

They finally loaded me and about 300 other unwary victims of Atsugi's aerology department into another Globemaster, this one equipped with two decks of "bucket seats", a webbing contraption that they tied you into. It was not unlike the way they hung convicted criminals on the dungeon walls of medieval castles. Or meat. The analogy was not lost on me when they served me k-rations for breakfast.

But they took off, and instantly everyone in the plane fell asleep except, hopefully, the pilot. How the military was able to accomplish this was a complete mystery to me. They put more people than I thought humanly possible into seats that are as uncomfortable as anything ever conceived of short of the torture racks of the inquisition, and everyone falls instantly asleep. Again, it is probably the fear factor at work. The last thing I remembered before sleep overwhelmed me was the sight of Mount Fuji passing by the right side of the airplane.

The first thing I saw once I woke up was the sight of Mount Fuji passing by on the left side of the airplane.

I asked an attendant why we were passing Mount Fuji twice, and the attendant replied that they had to return to Atsugi, it seems a typhoon was bearing down on Okinawa.

After they landed they drove me to the Atsugi BOQ to wait for the typhoon to pass and flew my Globemaster to Korea—with all of my and everyone else's luggage. That caused another delay while the Air Force diligently (?) tried to put my luggage and me at the same place at the same time.

This they eventually accomplished, and they finally flew me to Okinawa in an uneventful flight, and from there the Navy flew me aboard the Oriskany on a World War II torpedo bomber called a TBM that had been converted to carrying cargo and passengers to the carriers. These flights were called COD flights, with "COD" being short for carrier onboard delivery. I had a great seat for the flight, right behind the pilot, and right on top of eight other passengers who, by this time, I outranked. I watched with fascination as the TBM approached the carrier at its landing speed of 65 knots. The carrier was doing about thirty knots into a twenty-five knot wind, which gave the plane a closing speed of slightly faster than I could walk. When the plane actually touched down, it seemed as simple as coming down in an elevator.

I had landed aboard the Oriskany, I had found the Navy, and I loved flying!

Chapter 2

DISCOVERING YOU'RE NAVAL

Well, it would be rather an overstatement to say that I found the Navy when I landed on the Oriskany; the Navy had certainly found me long before that.

My first year as a midshipman at Stanford had been almost uneventful. We spent the year studying something euphemistically called seamanship under an inspiring lieutenant commander named Phillips of unquestionable quality, and my Stanford first year class came in first in the nation on the Bureau Final, a single exam given to each class at each of the 52 Naval Science programs throughout the country at the end of each year's work. The only really eventful moment in my first year involved my own experience with the Bureau Final.

I had another four-hour final in the morning of the same day the Bureau Final was to be given at 4 p.m., and I never quite got around to studying for it. Commander Phillips (both lieutenant commanders and commanders are generally addressed as "Commander") had told my class that anyone who wished to look at last years Bureau Final was welcome to do so as he had one in the office. I finished my other final at noon, had lunch, and with only two hours to study for a whole year's work in NROTC, decided to take Commander Philips up on his offer.

I walked over to Phillips' office and asked to see last year's exam. Phillips remarked that he was impressed by my diligence—I was the only one in the class that had taken him up on the offer and Phillips gave me the prior year's exam, complete with answers, to study. It was a multiple-choice exam of 150 questions and I read it over observing the answers. Then I walked over to the lecture hall and took the current year's Bureau Final. It was exactly the same exam—only the order of the questions had been changed—and I received one of the few perfect scores, a "4.0" in Navy parlance, in the country. This came complete with a letter of commendation from the Bureau of Naval Personnel and an invitation to see Commander Phillips in his office.

"Congratulations," he said, "For a solid "B" student you really aced the Bureau Final."

"Yes, Sir, thank you, Sir," I replied.

"Of course, you may have had a little advantage. I just noted that the Regs. say that no one is to be shown last year's Bureau Final, and I showed it to you. Do you think that gave you a leg up?" Phillips asked.

"Yes, Sir, I think it did." I replied.

"What do you think would be a fair grade for you in view of what has transpired? A 4.0 Bureau Final should get you an A in the course."

"Well, Commander I would be very pleased with a B+."

I was very pleased with the B+.

—⁓—

When June came after that first year of NROTC, I went off on my first Summer Cruise aboard the U.S.S. New Jersey, a real, full-fledged battleship, complete with nine 16-inch guns

Once a midshipman completed his first year as a 4th class midshipman, he graduated to 3rd class. The Navy is very logical in some instances. Third class "middies" on their first summer cruise wore the same uniform as a seaman apprentice, i.e., no indicia of rank whatsoever. The only two things that distinguished middies from real seaman apprentices were the midshipmen's sailor caps, which had a blue ring around the upper edge, and the fit of the midshipman 3rd class' uniform—it didn't. The average 3rd class midshipman's uniform looked as if Omar the tent maker had manufactured it. My uniform was no exception

The New Jersey left Norfolk, Virginia, late in the afternoon of a brilliant day in early July. Midshipmen were bunked throughout the ship randomly and not by school, so there was an immediate opportunity to make new friends from other schools. I wound up sandwiched in a stack of four enlisted men's bunks in the second bunk from the top. Above me was Bill Sundquist from Harvard and immediately below him Harland Small from the University of Pennsylvania. The former became my immediate buddy; the latter—not so much.

Besides the cramped quarters and the new people, two things were to have a lasting impression on me that first night at sea. The first of these was my receipt of a copy of the ship's newspaper. It was a two-page mimeographed sheet that was little more than a write-up of the ship's daily plan. The other was my first duty watch. I was assigned as a lookout high atop the ship's superstructure. It was my first experience with a "mid-watch" which starts at midnight and ends at 4 AM, or 0400 in Navy speak. On that first night out, the shoreline was still visible in the distance when I checked in. Overhead the sky was clearer than I could remember since a small child at camp in the New Hampshire mountains, but over the shoreline a thunder and lightning storm was lending its theatrics to the moment. It was so quiet, in spite of the constant hum of the ship, and so beautiful, that my love of the sea was fixed forever at that very instant.

The two-page newspaper, however, had some short-term ramifications. I considered myself a journalist of sorts, having been editor of my high school newspaper and a sports desk editor on the Stanford Daily, and I thought that a ship the size of the New Jersey, with thousands of men, could do a lot better than the two-paged mimeographed sheets I had received. So the following day I went hunting for the ship's newspaper office and found it in short order. The paper was put out by a couple of journalists 3rd class with a chief journalist in charge of the operation. The ship's Communications Officer, a Lieutenant Commander Nichols, was their boss.

When I entered the office where the paper was "published," the two journalists 3rd class were drinking coffee and holding a bull session with their chief. I introduced myself, and suggested that, with almost 800 midshipmen on board, this would be a good time for the Navy to show its stuff and one way it could do that would be to put out a better paper, one with world news coverage and tips on how to get around and what to do and buy at the ship's destination ports, Portsmouth, England, and Cherbourg, France.

They thought that was a good idea. Out of all those midshipmen, there had to be dozens with journalism experience, and my plan was to beef up the staff and put out a really significant paper. I felt that I could put together a staff that could put out the entire paper so that all the ship's company would have to do was supervise. That idea they really liked.

They immediately took me under their wing and went out looking for Lieutenant Commander Nichols to see if he would approve the idea. They found him in short order, I introduced myself and outlined my idea, and Nichols approved the plan for a midshipmen run newspaper on the spot, subject only to his getting the approval of Commander Marchand, the officer-in-charge of all the midshipmen on the cruise. This he promptly obtained.

I let out the word in the ship's paper the following day that the New Jersey was looking for midshipmen with journalism experience to work on the ship's paper. By the end of the following day I was turning away applicants and had a whole newspaper staff at my disposal. Nichols gave me and my cohorts access to the wire service for current news and sports, we used the extensive ship's library and volunteers from among the ship's company officers to get insights into our ports of call and London and Paris, the obvious destination spots from Portsmouth and Cherbourg, and within days the New Jersey's daily was massive, once reaching 32 pages, complete with cartoons from some of the more talented middies and photos off of the wire services.

———◦◦◦———

But it was this experience that caused me to run into the abuse of power that can, albeit very infrequently, be an ugly aspect of a military experience. In this case it took the form of Midshipman Chief Master-at-Arms Billy Joe Manrod, a 1st class midshipman from Vanderbilt who was actually *majoring* in Naval Science. Manrod was a tall, handsome young man who carried himself with true military bearing. He looked, *and acted,* much like a young General MacArthur. He was undoubtedly the most powerful midshipman on the ship. He regularly strode though the New Jersey, cigar clenched between his teeth, a phalanx of sycophants in tow, and his pencil poised and his clipboard at the ready to put anyone that displeased him on report.

Unfortunately, I wound up displeasing him greatly. We did a little parody of him in the ship's paper and called the comic-strip character "Ramrod." Manrod was upset by this "lack of respect," and I had not yet learned the adage that you don't screw around with a 600-pound gorilla. However, several days later I came to appreciate that adage when I finally had the opportunity to meet Manrod personally.

On that auspicious occasion I was sitting topside reading during normal morning cleanup drill before breakfast. Every midshipman had a cleanup duty station except those that worked on the paper. I had gotten them excused because they were working from 1600 on after the normal work day ended to put out the paper for the next morning's delivery before breakfast.

At the time of this meeting the "smoking lamp was out throughout the ship" while the New Jersey took on fuel from a tanker. That meant NO SMOKING! Bill Sundquist, my Harvard friend from the bunk above, was sweeping down the deck around where I was sitting reading a novel when along marched Manrod with his ubiquitous cigar.

"What the hell do you think you're doing sitting here on your ass reading during cleanup drill, (expletive deleted)?" he queried of me politely.

Now when a 1ˢᵗ Class Midshipman, especially one of Manrod's rank and demeanor, came along, a 3ʳᵈ Class Midshipman was supposed to leap to his feet and stand at attention, just as I would have to do if an officer came by. However, I didn't jump to my feet and therefore obviously was not standing at attention, a great mistake, as I was shortly to discover. Instead, I continued sitting where I was and replied, "I don't have cleanup drill duty because we work late putting out the paper. Check with Commander Marchand if you have any questions."

"Yeah, I've heard about you, you're that smart-ass Maltzman, aren't you?" He asked.

At that point Sundquist said, "Pardon me, Mr. Manrod, but I think the smoking lamp is out throughout the ship."

At that, Manrod turned to Sundquist, flicked his ash onto the deck where Bill had just swept, and said, "You mind your business, Sundquist, and I'll mind mine." You couldn't go incognito as a midshipman as your last name was stenciled on your blouse.

Then he turned to me and said, "And as for you, "Maltmouth", I don't want to see your fat ass above decks during cleanup again. Have you got that?"

I finally got the message and leaped up, snapped to attention, saluted, and replied in my loudest voice short of a shout, "YES, SIR, MR. RAMROD, SIR!"

Now Manrod went from apoplectic to ballistic. "WHAT DID YOU CALL ME?" he shouted

"RAMROD, SIR, BUT I LISP!" I replied.

That did it. I had just offended that proverbial 600-pound guerilla, and so had my friend Sundquist, apparently based on guilt by association. That afternoon both Sundquist and I found ourselves on report. Not for insolence to a superior officer, that would have allowed us an opportunity to tell our side of the story, but for leaving clothing around outside of our respective lockers.

This was strange, as both of us were put on report for leaving out the identical item, and both of us were sure that we had locked up everything in our lockers when we left our area after breakfast.

That afternoon we had mast in front of Commander Marchand and each of us received five demerits. That was nothing; really, you could get up to 35 demerits without washing out of the program. But 35 demerits was the death knell for a midshipman.

The next morning Sundquist and I went on report again. This time we each had allegedly left out one rubber sandal. By that night we had ten demerits, in spite of our protestations of innocence.

The next day it was one pair of socks each. At mast that day we protested that the identity of these items made it clear that someone was entering our lockers and removing the items for the purpose of putting us on report. We suggested that Mr. Manrod had a personal antagonism against us and must have the keys to our lockers, which he did.

Manrod replied that if he were going to do that he would never select identical items to remove from each locker—that would be stupid. He claimed that this had to be a plot on our part to flaunt regulations and show that a couple of smart-ass middies could beat the system. He also opined that we probably wanted out of the program and figured this was an easy way out.

Manrod finished by volunteering: "And if you don't mind my observing, sir, I don't think it would be much of a loss to the Navy if these two washed out."

Commander Marchand was clearly troubled. He liked what I was doing for the paper and I believe he liked me, but he didn't know what was going on.

When Bill and I reached 30 demerits each, it was obvious that if we didn't do something we were going to be out of the program before we ever made our first landfall. With that in mind, we decided to do a pilgrimage to Mecca, or at least the closest thing to it on the New Jersey, a trip to

Manrod in the Midshipman Chief Master-at-Arms office, after we finished our normal duty day.

Manrod's office was on the main deck at the very aft of the superstructure, immediately below and behind the rear 16-inch gun mount. We found Manrod alone in his office with the door open. He was sitting in a chair, writing a letter on a small wooden barrel, when we knocked and asked permission to enter.

"What do you (expletives deleted) want, aren't you getting your demerits fast enough?" He asked.

"Mr. Manrod," I said, "I am sorry that I was disrespectful to you that day on the 05 level when I was reading during cleanup, and Mr. Sundquist is sorry that he ever met me. Neither of us wants to flunk out of this program, and we are prepared to do whatever it takes to convince you of that and get you or whoever it is working for you off our butts."

Manrod appeared to me to be enjoying this immensely. "You little sanctimonious bastards," he replied, "wimps like you will make the lousiest Navy officers in the world. Do you think for one minute that I could look myself in the face in the morning if I let scum like you become regular Navy officers? I owe it to everyone in the program to screen out misfits, and I'm screening you bums out. You can whimper all you want to Marchand, but he is going to believe me over you every friggen time. What do you have to say to that, wise ass?"

Unfortunately for Manrod, I did have something to say. I was sitting opposite Manrod on the other side of his barrel, and while Manrod was berating us, I was reading the letter Manrod had been writing. Working on the newspaper at Stanford had taught me the art of reading upside down and backwards while the typesetters were putting the paper to bed. Manrod's letter was easy as it was only upside down, and he, unfortunately for him, had a very clear handwriting. We had interrupted Manrod in the course of writing a letter to his wife. That was certainly an exemplary thing to do if you are married, but Navy regulations prohibited midshipmen from being married.

"My God!" I exclaimed with dramatic emphasis to my shocked demeanor, "the letter you're writing starts off with the salutation, 'My dearest, darling wife:' could it be that Midshipman Chief Master-at-Arms Manrod, that soul of virtue and vehicle for the enforcement of all regulations naval could be married in violation of the strictest naval proscriptions? Oh, please Mr. Manrod, tell us its not so! Tell us you're not a hypocrite!"

I was about to add: "It would be so devastating to our respect' for you if that proved to be the case!" but I never got a chance to finish my soliloquy.

Manrod leaped to his feet, grabbed up the letter and crumpled it in his hands, which had suddenly started shaking violently, and screamed at us, "You've got nothing on me. You don't have any evidence. It's your word against mine and they'll believe me 'cause I'm the kind of naval officer they want. The Navy doesn't need creeps like you. Now get the hell out of my sight and don't let me ever see you bastards again!"

When we walked out of Manrod's office and into the sunlight, Bill was really upset. "Now you've done it," he said, "he'll hang our butts so high they're going to need a telescope to see us from the ground. Even if it's true, why did you have to tell him that?"

"Bill," I replied, "he was going to cut us up into little pieces and feed us to the sharks. Maybe he'll think better of having to confront us at mast next time now that he knows that we have something on him. We certainly can't be any worse off than we were before. You know I'm not the type that would extort the bastard, but he and that pea brain of his do not know that. At least we've given him something to worry about."

I was so right! From that moment on, Bill and I couldn't get on report if we tried. We kept getting written up for a while by Manrod's henchmen, but someone kept pulling the report chits before they ever got to the mast list. I suddenly realized that I now had the power, and it was my turn to abuse it.

The battleship had dial telephones throughout the ship connecting every compartment and office. All you needed was the ship's telephone directory and you could dial anyone. I got the numbers of the Midshipman's Office and the Master-at-Arms Office and would call Manrod at all hours of the day and night. When Manrod would come on the line, I would do a Peter Lorry imitation and say: "Ramrod, you're a God damned son-of-a bitch!" Then I would immediately hang up.

The last time I did this I didn't quite hang up fast enough and heard an anguished cry on the other end, "For God's sake, leave me alone, I can't take any more of this!" That stopped me. My stomach started to turn and I realized that I had been just as bad as Manrod had been, if not worse. Manrod may have been an (expletive deleted), even a pompous (expletive deleted), but he was down and I was still kicking him. I never gave Manrod the time of day again.

—◦◉◦—

The final proof that I had found the Navy before the day when I landed safely on the Oriskany's deck came in the form of my second-year Naval Science instructor at Stanford, Lt. Klaus Bormann. "Santa," as he was humorously called by the class behind his back, or "Martin," his more derisive behind-the-back nickname, was a piece of work. He was well over six feet and 230 pounds, and had a voice that sounded like the character "Lennie" in the original movie version of Steinbeck's, *Of Mice and Men*. When the first day of class started in that second year, he introduced himself with the following speech:

"Haw, haw, haw, it's really funny that I should be teaching here at Stanfud (he always pronounced it "Stanfud"). When I graduated high school in 1940 I was a hell-of-a fullback and Clark Shaughnessy (the football coach at Stanford in 1940 and the inventor of the T-formation) wanted me to come to Stanfud so bad he could taste it, but they said I wasn't smart enough to come here so I had to go to Oregon State and look it, here I am teaching at Stanfud, haw, haw, haw!"

But the joke was on me and the rest of my class at "Stanfud." Santa had apparently been drafted by the Navy in 1942 and played football with Frankie Albert and company at St. Mary's Preflight until he washed out of the academic part of the program, and had to finish up the war playing for Great Lakes Naval Training Station. He ended the war as a chief and somehow got a commission when he elected to stay in. It was probably a reward for a touchdown or two.

In any event, they apparently assigned him to "Stanfud," as a direct result of his football. Rumor had it that Lt. Bormann was telling old football stories to his chief while serving as officer of the deck (OOD) on a destroyer when the destroyer came within inches of being run down by the aircraft carrier Wasp. The admiral on the Wasp demanded that whoever had the conn on that destroyer had to be out of his fleet by nightfall. So they sent him to Stanford/Stanfud where the only damage he could do would be indirect.

Actually, his teaching style was not that bad, basically because it was nonexistent. Gunnery was the second year subject, and Santa would get up at the beginning of every hour, announce what the lecture was about, and proceed to make a statement. The statement was almost always wrong, but he was usually so wrong that anyone who had prepared would obviously know it. Then he would turn to Chief Watson, a chief gunnery mate assigned to the Stanford program and who attended all the lectures, and say, "Isn't that right, Chief?"

On Santa's better days Chief Watson would say, "Well, that's partially right, Lieutenant, but you might want to give the boys a little more information so that they'll be able to get the right answer on the Bureau Final."

On his worse days, which were by far in the majority, the chief would simply say, "I'm afraid that's not quite the way it is, Lieutenant."

In either event, Bormann would then say, "Chief, why don't you come up here and tell the boys the way it really is. You know all this stuff."

Fortunately for the class, the chief did, and he taught us a solid course in Gunnery.

Stanford had the ability to attract the children of famous people and one of Bing Crosby's sons, Gary, was a Contract NROTC student in my class. No big deal! The other students and the faculty and administration treated Gary and the children of other famous people who attended Stanford just like any other student. Gary was not flashy, belonged to a fraternity, and had a reputation of being a pretty good guy. He only had two apparent dislikes; the first was discipline, the second was NROTC, and not necessarily in that order. He fit right in with most of the class.

The Stanford NROTC midshipmen were required to come to NROTC classes in uniform, and we had two—blues, which consisted of midnight blue pants and midnight blue shirts with a naval officer's cap with a narrow gold band and black plain toed shoes, and khakis, which consisted of khaki pants and shirt and brown plain toed shoes. The hat was the same; we just changed the colors of the cover by the season. In winter the midshipmen were the "black shirts" and in fall and spring the "brown shirts."

Bormann would usually have the class line up for inspection at the opening bell. At the beginning of the year, when the uniforms were khakis, Crosby kept showing up in penny loafers instead of the required plain toed brown shoes, and after a couple of warnings, Bormann said to him, "Crosby, how come you don't wear regulation shoes? I should give you demerits for that."

Crosby answered, "Mr. Bormann, if I could afford another pair of shoes, I would buy them, sir, but the Navy doesn't issue shoes, just the rest of the uniform."

"Oh, come on, Crosby," Bormann replied, "Anyone can afford a pair of plain toed brown shoes. All you got to do is go down to Thom McCann's. You can get a good pair of shoes for under twenty bucks, I know you can."

"Oh, Mr. Bormann," said Crosby, "If I had twenty bucks I would run right down to Thom McCann's and buy a pair of regulation shoes, but I just don't have the money."

Of course, the rest of us were near busting a gut. Everyone on campus knew who Gary was, and while he didn't flaunt his father's money, after all, he was Bing Crosby's son!

At this, Santa really became Santa, reached into his wallet and pulled out a twenty dollar bill. He handed it to Crosby and said, "Here, Crosby, take twenty bucks, pay me back when you can, but get yourself the proper shoes."

"Oh thank you, Mr. Bormann, I'll run right down to Thom McCann's as soon as class is over," Crosby replied.

Two days later, at the next inspection, Crosby still had on his loafers. The only difference was that he no longer made any attempt to shine them. He never got regulation shoes and never paid Santa back the $20.

While Crosby was getting indebted to Bormann, Bormann was getting indebted to me. The Korean War was running full tilt at this time, and every university in the country ran regular blood drives. Stanford always came in with about 350 pints of blood, and several of the middies in my class gave blood regularly. I was not one of them. It wasn't giving the blood that bothered me, it was the needle.

After the Winter Quarter blood drive that year and the usual 350 pints, plus or minus, a student named Ken Schechter came into the Stanford Executive Committee, or ExCom, the chief governing body of Stanford's student government, and asked to speak. I happened to be a member of ExCom at the time, so was present when this occurred. He was a very quiet, soft-spoken man, but he told of his experience in Korea as a Navy pilot flying off an aircraft carrier. Shrapnel over North Korea had blown out his cockpit and plastic from the canopy had shattered into his face, blinding him. His wingman had actually talked him down to a safe landing while Ken was literally flying blind. They made a movie out of his experience called "*The Men of the Fighting Lady*", which most of the ExCom members had seen, and he told them how, after he finally got down, it took over 60 pints of blood to save his life. He was appalled that a school the size of Stanford could only produce 350 pints of blood with the Korean war going on, and asked us to let him head the next blood drive. He promised that if ExCom appointed him to run the drive, he would get the students and staff to give 5,000 pints of blood, over three times what any other school in the country had ever given.

That was a challenge, and a story, that ExCom and I, who happened to also be on the *Stanford Daily*, couldn't resist. Ken proceeded to take over the Spring Quarter blood drive with a vengeance. I was so turned on by him that I volunteered to run publicity for the drive, and Ken appointed me its vice-president in charge of publicity.

By my second year in NROTC, I was a junior by University standards, as I had not joined the program until my second year at Stanford. By then I had worked my way up the ladder on the *Stanford Daily* to Sports Desk Editor and was also a feature writer with a regular "*Bull Session*" column and was also a regular contributor to the campus humor magazine, the *Chaparral*, and a member of its support organization, the *Hammer & Coffin Society*.

But it was in my capacity as vice-president in charge of publicity for the blood drive that I asked Lt. Bormann one day to poll the class to see how many would give blood in the upcoming blood drive.

"Maltzman, do you really think that you clowns are going to get 5,000 pints of blood?" Bormann asked.

"Yes, Sir, Lieutenant, I believe we have a really good shot at it," I replied.

"Haw, haw, you don't need to ask for hands, I can tell you who'll give blood. McNulty and Collins, they'll give blood. They always give blood, but the rest of these guys would faint if they got a mosquito bite—forget someone stickin' a needle in 'em."

"Oh, I don't know, Mr. Bormann, there's a lot of enthusiasm for this blood drive among the guys," I responded.

"I'll tell you what, Maltzman, I'll give you a buck for every pint you get over one thousand if you give me a buck for every pint you get under a thousand."

"You've got a bet," I said, and we shook hands on it.

Then, with a sarcastic smile on his face, Bormann turned to the class and said, "OK, you guys, anyone that's gonna give blood in the blood drive stand up."

The entire class stood as one.

I wrote my *Bull Session* column the next day in the *Stanford Daily* and it contained a plea to help me get rich off "the good Lieutenant" Klaus Bormann, my NROTC instructor, and I related the story of our wager.

The blood drive was a great success! Ken Schecter roamed the campus telling everyone who would listen of his experience in the Korean War and how those 60 pints of blood saved his life. Blind in one eye and with very thick glasses that allowed some vision from the other eye, and with handsome good looks and a magnificent speaking voice, he was a very hard person to ignore, and he wasn't! The Stanford community gave 4,680 pints of blood that spring, a record for a college that probably stands today. Some of the co-eds got so wrapped up in the campaign that they put irons under their skirts to try and pass the minimum 100-pound weight limit.

The good lieutenant wound up owing me $3,680, which he refused to acknowledge or pay. Now my column in the *Daily* lamented the lack of honor among today's Navy officers and how the good lieutenant was welching on a bet. Still he wouldn't pay. The class would hound him about paying up his debts, but still he wouldn't even discuss the subject with me or anyone else, or acknowledge the wager other than to say: "Don't worry about Maltzman, I'll take care of him!" That sounded pretty ominous to all of us; who knew what that meant?

Then came the Bureau Final. As mentioned earlier, my class had come in number one in the nation the year before, thanks in part to my "miraculous" 4.0, and the class was anxious to repeat. Thanks to the chief, our class was reasonably well prepared when they closed the doors and handed out the exams. I opened my exam, I had not had the opportunity to read last year's exam this time, and read the first question. It was:

"The ring that sets the timing fuse on a 5 inch shell is:
     (a)   The middle ring;
     (b)   The blue ring;
     (c)   The top ring;
     (d)   The bottom ring."

My problem with the question was that it didn't say if you were looking at the shell from the top or the side, and I made the unbelievable mistake of asking Bormann for clarification. Looking at the question as a whole it was fairly obvious that they were talking about looking at it from the side, the way the shell had been illustrated in the textbook, but I hadn't read the textbook and my question took Bormann by surprise, and Chief Watson wasn't there.

"Well, Maltzman, that's a good question," Bormann replied. "I guess there could be two right answers. Or there could be no right answers. Maybe on a given question leaving all of the choices blank is the right answer. On another question, maybe marking them all right is correct. It don't say here that there has to be one right answer to each question. These questions can be pretty tricky."

With the experience of a year listening to him give us the wrong answers to every question, why any of the class listened to him is a mystery, but listen we did, and that was the way everyone answered the Bureau Final. Everyone, that is, except Gary Crosby, who arrived late to the final in his scuffed penny loafers and never heard Bormann's brilliant words of instruction. Gary Crosby was the only one in the class that passed the Bureau Final. He got a B.

But then Lieutenant Bormann paid all debts. He gave Crosby an unsatisfactory fitness report and flunked him out of the program for wearing penny loafers to class and not repaying the $20 he owed, and gave me an A, which I didn't deserve, and the highest fitness report in the class, a 4.0, which I *really* didn't deserve, for not paying the $3,680 he owed me. Lieutenant Bormann couldn't know that the one time he really was Santa Claus he probably saved my life and the lives of all of the other regulars in our class. Getting the 4.0 got me the post of Platoon Leader for the first half of our next summer cruise, our flight training at Corpus Christi, Texas. Had I not been Platoon Leader, I would not have been able to march my Platoon past the R4Q that probably crashed and onto the DC-4 that didn't. Thus, Lieutenant Bormann became the most important instructor in my career, Naval or otherwise.

Part II

The USS Oriskany (CVA-34)

Chapter 3

THE LANDING OF THE
LEGAL EAGLE

As soon as I climbed out of the cockpit and stepped out onto the flight deck of the Oriskany, I heard someone calling my name. I turned and saw a tall, sandy-haired lieutenant looking around among the new arrivals.

"That's me," I replied.

The lieutenant approached with a huge smile and a big handshake. "Gawd," he said with a Texas drawl, "am ah glad to see you, Mr. Maltzman. Name's Hewitt, I'm the Legal Officer. I hear from the Captain's office you've had a couple o' years o' law school under your belt. Right glad to hear that. I'm due to get out and my relief is overdue. How'd you like to be Legal Officer until my relief arrives?"

"Gosh, Mr. Hewitt, sounds great," I replied, but with my usual naiveté continued, "But I wonder if I'm qualified; I missed 29 out of 30 questions on the Uniform Code of Military Justice portion of last year's Bureau Final." Two years of law school were apparently insufficient to understand the nuances of "Naval Justice" without at least taking a little time to read what it was about, which I had not done.

Hewitt's smile waned a bit, and some of his color drained, but he was quick to reply: "Hey, no one's perfect! Anyone can do this job, but don't tell the Exec about missing those 29 questions; I've been spending the better part of a week trying to sell him on letting you be the Legal Officer when you're not a lawyer yet. The Captain hates anything legal and even refuses to perform Captain's mast, so the Exec is under a lot of pressure to keep the legal ends nice and neat."

At this, Hewitt grabbed me by the arm, told some sailors to deliver my bags to my JO (for "junior officer's") bunkroom, and dragged me off to meet the Exec.

The Executive Officer, or the "Exec" as he is universally referred to, is the second in command on a ship, and on the Oriskany, and probably on most Essex Class carriers, his stateroom and office are immediately adjacent to the entrance to the Wardroom.

The Exec of the Oriskany, Commander Collins, was a large, rotund man from South Carolina, with a fatherly face that alternated between jolly and worried. On his first meeting with me it was about 70% worried and 30% jolly.

"Welcome aboard, Mr. Maltzman, Mr. Hewitt here tells me you've had two years of law school at Stanford before you got commissioned. Think you know anything about the Uniform Code of Military Justice?"

"Well, Sir, I studied the UCMJ in NROTC," I replied. In the Navy, the first thing they teach you is to talk in abbreviations. I also thought it was probably better if I didn't mention my 29 wrong answers. I had been a very good law student, made law review at Stanford, but law school and law review left little time to study NROTC. As I had been a sophomore when I started NROTC instead of a freshman like most of the other midshipmen, I had the opportunity to do one year of graduate school before I was commissioned. Furthermore, in 1955 Stanford let a limited number of students start law school their senior year, giving them a "pre-law degree" after their first year of law school. When the Korean War ended, I decided to take that fast track and start law school my senior year, hoping to get a year's deferment and the opportunity to finish law school before I went into the Navy. My deferment never came through, but in my last year of NROTC and my second year of law school I had very little time for anything but law and law review and tried to fake the UCMJ portion of the Bureau Final by applying the logic I had learned in law school. It had not yet dawned on me that logic and Naval justice might not be compatible.

The Exec approved my appointment as interim Legal Officer until JAG (the Judge Advocate General's office) filled the billet with a JAG officer, who would be both a full lieutenant and an attorney, and Hewitt left the ship that night on the same TBM that had brought me to the Oriskany.

The Legal Office on the Oriskany consisted of the Legal Officer and two clerk-typists, Wood, a yeoman 1st class and Shirley, a yeoman 3rd class. Both knew how to transcribe proceedings using a device called a steno-mask, but neither knew shorthand. The steno-mask was a tape recorder with a soundproof mask that fit over the yeoman's nose and mouth. He talked into it and just repeated whatever anyone said during a court-martial proceeding without others being able to hear him. Later he would transcribe his own words.

For my first few days as Legal Officer there was very little for me to do. The ship had been to sea for some time, and Hewitt had cleaned up all the baggage of the last duty stop before he left.

My first opportunity to play lawyer occurred when an airman named Miller came to me with a complaint that someone had stolen his wallet containing $150 he had saved to buy a camera. In 1955, $150 was big bucks, particularly for an airman. Miller told me it had been very hot, and he had taken to sleeping in a workstation that was open to the outside between the flight deck and the hanger deck and was much cooler than his regular berth. He had placed his wallet in a padlocked drawer in the work area just before going to bed, but apparently had failed to make sure the padlock was secured. In the morning when he got up and went to retrieve his wallet he immediately knew something was wrong. When he went to open the lock he noticed that it had been placed on the hasp from the left side. Miller claimed he always placed the lock in the hasp from the right side.

With this as my only lead, and having read too many Perry Mason novels when I should have been studying Naval Science, I went to Miller's compartment, a large interior space below decks where he and his division mates were supposed to sleep and where they kept their belongings, and inspected each of the lockers to see how many sailors in the division hooked their locks from the left instead of the right. Probably because most people are right handed, very few hooked their locks onto the hasp from the left. Next I assembled all the men in the compartment and questioned each one separately in my office while the rest remained in line outside. I asked them about their whereabouts the night before, when they went to bed, when they got off watch, etc. I asked each one how much money he had in his possession, and none admitted to having as much as $150, or anything close to that, on their person or in their lockers.

Then, as each rose to leave, I asked him to place an open padlock on a locker located in the office, to observe which way they performed the exercise. Unfortunately for my scheme, there seemed little consistency between the way they placed the lock on the locker in the office and the way they placed their locks on their own lockers in their compartment. But my tactic paid off in another way. I had placed my two clerk-typists in Miller's compartment to observe what happened as each man returned from questioning. One of the men questioned, an airman 3rd class named Schraper, went right to his locker, opened his lock and turned it around without even bothering to open the locker.

With nothing else to go on, I waited to see what Schraper took with him on liberty. Miller, the airman who had lost his wallet, acted as my spy and notified me the minute Schraper started getting dressed to go on liberty. I then alerted the officer of the deck, who waited for Schraper to get on the gangway. As enlisted men had to wear their uniforms when they went on liberty and their names were stenciled on their blouses, he was easy to spot. At a signal from the OOD, the Marine guard situated at the bottom of the gangway lowered his rifle and stopped him. I then came down the gangway from the OOD's station with two other Marines I had commandeered and asked Schraper how much money he had on him for liberty. He replied that he had $25.00. I asked for his wallet and he pulled it out. It contained only $14.00.

"Gosh, Sir, I guess I was wrong," he protested.

Not being burdened in the Navy by such niceties as search warrants, reasonable cause and the like, I had the Marines take Schraper back aboard ship and the Marines searched him. They found $180 in his sock.

Ships of the Navy have various ways they can perform punishment. On most ships a person caught violating regulations or committing a crime would go up before the Captain in what was known as Captain's mast, probably a leftover from the days of sail. There the Captain, pursuant to Article 15 of the UCMJ, the Uniform Code of Military Justice, would hear the charge against the man and the sailor's side of the story and either mete out punishment there and then if he thought the man was guilty, release him if he thought he was innocent, or direct the matter to a court-martial. At Captain's mast the Captain could inflict at maximum confinement to the ship for up to 30 days or up to two weeks in the brig, and in addition to either of these punishments, the loss of up to two weeks pay.

Alternatively, the Captain could order either a summary court-martial or special court-martial aboard the ship or could direct the accused to a general court-martial at a facility that had general court-martial jurisdiction. That would always be a land-based facility with a JAG office.

A general court-martial was a big deal, and could inflict any punishment authorized by the UCMJ, including long prison terms, loss of rank, loss of pay, a dishonorable discharge, and even the death penalty for crimes such as treason or murder. It had a JAG officer as judge and a jury of at least five officers. A special court-martial was similar but much less formal and could be held aboard ship. The senior officer on the court-martial board presided, not usually a lawyer, the Legal Officer would usually, but was not required to, sit in for instructions to the court-martial board on legal issues, and there had to be at least three officers on the panel, but as both the prosecution ("trial counsel") and the defense counsel had one peremptory challenge, the special court-martial tribunal appointed by the Captain, or in the Oriskany's case, the Exec, almost always consisted of five officers. The trial and defense counsel were usually not lawyers but were generally line officers. The trial counsel had to advise the defendant of his rights, which included the right to be defended by anyone aboard the ship, so theoretically the defendant could be defended by a chief or enlisted man, but I had never seen that happen. The maximum punishment a special court could mete out was six months confinement, six months loss of pay and a bad-conduct discharge, referred to euphemistically as "six, six and a BCD."

A special court-martial, like a general court-martial, was required to follow the rules of evidence and was subject to review, first by the Captain as the convening authority, and then by the admiral in charge of the Carrier Division. Serious cases would go to JAG and, if the ship was not operating in a Carrier Division, as when it was in port stateside, review would be by JAG in all cases.

Then there was the summary court-martial. This was a one-officer court where the officer appointed to the court served as judge, jury, trial counsel and defense counsel. The accused did not have the right to bring counsel. The summary court officer had the power to call and swear in witnesses, and the maximum punishment that could be meted out was one month in the brig, forty-five days loss of pay and the reduction of one grade in rank. A summary court-martial did not have to follow the rules of evidence, was very informal, and was only subject to review by the convening authority, i.e., the Captain.

As I mentioned, the foregoing applied to most ships—but not the Oriskany. On the Oriskany, the Captain did not like to be bothered with Captain's mast or anything legal, so the Captain had merely delegated the responsibility for Captain's mast to the commanders of the various Air Groups aboard. While not authorized in any Naval Regulation I had ever seen, he also directed the Exec to have an "Exec's mast" to screen out ship's company offenders such as Schraper and, if the Exec felt they were guilty, give them either a summary court-martial or a special court-martial, but lets not have any Captain's mast. This kept the court-martial boards on the Oriskany very busy.

Unfortunately, I had a problem with Schraper. While everyone was convinced he was guilty, the only evidence I had was that Schraper had $180 on him when he went on liberty, and Schraper was now claiming that he won the money in a poker game. Gambling aboard ship was probably not permitted by Navy regulations, but it certainly was a far different offense than grand theft.

I expressed my concerns to the Exec prior to Schraper's Exec's mast, and the Exec promptly solved the problem.

"If we give Schraper a special court-martial," the Exec said, "and he gets convicted it could get reviewed all the way up to JAG, and we really don't have a lot of evidence that would hold up to JAG scrutiny. From what you tell me I'm not sure we even have enough evidence to convict him, period. I'll hear him out at mast, and if I think he's guilty after that I'm going to give him a summary with Lieutenant Commander Farrell."

As I was unfamiliar with Farrell, the Exec explained to me that LTCD Edward Farrell was a "mustang," the naval euphemism for someone who has worked his way up from enlisted to officer rank. He was an engineering officer and had an unblemished record as a one-man summary court-martial board; every single person ever sent to Farrell had been convicted within fifteen minutes and had received the maximum sentence. Farrell's policy was very simple: "I started as a seaman apprentice, worked hard, kept my nose clean and look where it got me. You should have done the same thing. Maybe a month in the brig and loss of 45 days' pay will kick a little sense into your head!" And, according to the Exec, that was the net result of every one of the summary courts he had conducted to date. It was no surprise, then, when I discovered that Farrell had a nickname among the enlisted men: the "Hangman!"

Farrell was as good as his nickname, and after a bad performance at Exec's mast, the Exec sent Schraper to Farrell and Farrell gave him a month in the brig and a loss of 45 days' pay after a fifteen minute "trial."

—◦◦◦—

But Schraper was just the beginning of my legal "trials." Four days after we pulled out of Yokosuka, my first liberty port on the Oriskany, I was called into the Exec's office late one night and told that the ship had a serious problem. Chief Warrant Officer 2nd Class Sam Hills, a big, burly engineer with the potbelly sometimes associated with that craft apparently had a drinking problem. I was told he had already passed all of his requirements for CWO 1st class and was about to reach that lofty height, but earlier that evening he had failed to report to his duty station. On investigation he had been found drunk and asleep in his cabin with a Bogans (blood-alcohol level) of .03, enough to kill most normal people and certainly enough to slow down the typical CWO, even big, burly types. As the ship had been at sea for four days, the officer-of-the-deck reached the rather logical conclusion that Hills must have been drinking aboard ship, a heinous offense according to U.S. Naval Regulations, albeit one observed more in the breach in those days by officers aboard aircraft carriers. To support this obvious conclusion, the investigating officers had found a number of empty whiskey bottles strewn around his cabin.

A CWO is a bridge between commissioned officers and enlisted men in the Navy, and a 1st class CWO was as high as you could go without getting a commission. They were former chiefs that had obtained great skill in specialized callings and, to a large extent, ran the technical aspects of the ship, if not the entire Navy.

The Exec had already notified the Captain, who took a personal interest in the matter and wanted it resolved aboard ship, not farmed out to a higher shore authority. The Exec informed me that the onus was on me, as the Legal Officer, to make sure nothing went wrong with the court-martial. He also made it clear that if I screwed up, the Captain would blame the Exec for appointing a non-lawyer as Legal Officer and letting Hewitt off the ship. It was at about this time that I started regretting that

I missed those 29 out of 30 UCMJ questions on the Bureau Final. I was busy racking my brain trying to remember the one question I got right.

While Naval Justice may not always be particularly fair, it at least is swift, and the Exec convened a new special court-martial board to try Hills immediately. He appointed the commanding officer of the Marine Corps detachment on board, Captain Zach Anderson, to be trial counsel and his second in command, 1st Lieutenant Harrison ("Harry") Richardson, as defense counsel and placed five relatively senior officers on the court-martial board headed by the Gunnery Boss, Commander Slater.

Before the trial started, the Exec again warned me that the Captain was taking a personal interest in this case and wanted to be personally kept posted on the progress of the trial. In other words, I was to sit in on the trial and make sure there were no screw-ups.

The trial started at 0900 the next morning and lasted until 1830 (6:30 p.m.) that night with only a short break for lunch. My two yeomen, taking turns using the steno-mask, recorded the whole proceeding. Normally the transcript would not be started until after the court-martial was completed as there was no appeal of an acquittal, so no record would be needed should that be the result. If there is a conviction, then the transcript is typed up for the Captain to examine after it is first approved by both the trial and defense counsel. The Captain is, in effect, the first appellate level. If Hills was found guilty and the Captain approved the verdict, it would then go to the admiral commanding the carrier task force for his legal officer to review and, if a serious enough offense, which any trial of an officer or CWO would almost certainly be, it would go back to JAG for a final review.

After both sides rested, everyone left while the court-martial board deliberated. While they were deliberating, I went to the Exec with Richardson and Anderson in tow to report on the progress of the trial. We found the Captain with the Exec, and the Captain grilled all of us about every detail of the case, practically demanding from us a promise that there would be a conviction. Finally, he turned to me and ordered me to have a verbatim transcript of the proceedings on his desk before 0800 the following morning.

"Pardon me, Captain, but that will be impossible." I responded. "My yeomen transcribing the case have been working since 0900 this morning transcribing the proceedings. I can't ask them to do any more today."

The Captain turned several shades of red, I thought his eyes would bulge out of his head, and he gulped once or twice, and then said, "0800 tomorrow morning!" He then stormed out of the room.

The Exec, easy-going and Southern as he was, looked up at me through his bushy eyebrows and said, "Dick (we were now on a first name basis, at least in one direction), you have a lot to learn. When the Captain gives you an order, you have only one response. That's 'Aye, aye, Sir!' You don't make excuses 'cause the Captain doesn't give a damn about your excuses. Just 'Aye, aye, Sir!', that's all, just 'Aye, aye, Sir!' Of course, you can't fulfill the order, that's basically understood, but you try damn hard and you get it to him as fast as you can. But you never argue with the Captain, you just say 'Aye, aye, Sir!'"

I at least had the wit to come back with the perfect answer: "Aye, aye, Sir!" I replied.

About then Wood, my senior Yeoman, came in with word that the deliberations were over and the court had come back with its verdict. The court had spent only thirty minutes to reach its conclusion. The Exec and the rest of us ran up the ladder to the room set aside on the Oriskany for a court-martial and stood at attention as the court returned from the deliberation room. Hills stood at attention as CDR Slater faced him directly and reported a guilty verdict. He then asked if any party had anything to add for the penalty stage of the court-martial. As neither side had anything further to add, the board left the room for all of one minute. They then returned and announced that they had decided that the punishment would consist of loss of two months pay, confinement to ship for two months (practically the balance of the Oriskany's WesPac cruise), loss of one thousand numbers on the Chief Warrant Officer Promotion list, and a letter of reprimand in his jacket. What that really meant was that Hills would not make CWO 1st class in the 20th Century and we were still in 1955.

Richardson, Anderson and I proceeded to report the results to the Captain, who again reiterated his demand for a transcript in the morning, to which I responded with a smart "Aye, aye, Sir!" and then retired. The others went to the wardroom for a late dinner while I grabbed some sandwiches and headed up to the legal office to get my Yeoman to their typewriters. Much to my pleasant surprise, Wood and Shirley were already at work on the transcript; they knew the old man better than I did and while one of them had been doing dictation, the other had been typing up what he had already transcribed.

As they appeared to have things well under control, I retired to Harry Richardson's room where a post court-martial party was under way. In his two-man state room immediately across the hall from the wardroom on the 02 level and separated from the Exec's cabin only by the ladder (a euphemism for a steep stairway) that led up to the hanger deck, Harry, Captain Anderson and all five members of the court-martial board had gathered to celebrate the end of the ordeal. Each officer on board had a desk and a safe, and Harry had opened his safe and pulled out a bottle of gin and someone had brought in a fruit juice concoction made up by the wardroom stewards nicknamed "jungle juice." Add the vodka and you had a "Kickapoo joy juice" that could put a glow on Li'l Abner.

By midnight the party was getting into high gear. I had been up to the legal office several times to check on progress, and was in the process of mixing myself another drink when there was a knock on the door.

"Must be the Exec!" I joked with a broad grin and reached over and threw open the door without thinking about the glass in my and everyone else's hand and the open bottle of gin on Harry's desk.

It *was* the Exec! Dressed in white pajamas covered with hearts, he held a glass in his hand, although it was empty, and said in his soft, South Carolina drawl, "Can ah join your party fellows, I need a drink bad!"

My staff got the Captain off the Exec's and my back by getting the transcript to the Captain before 0800 the next morning. If he was pleased, he didn't show it. He just sat there with his poker face and read the transcript while I sat there. Finally, after about half an hour he dismissed me, telling me to keep myself available in case he had any questions. He had none, however, and later that day the Captain called in all of the officers involved with the court-martial and commended everyone. While the system called for the transcript to be reviewed and signed by both the trial and defense counsel before it went to the Captain, I had bypassed that process by making three copies of the transcript and allowing everyone to review it simultaneously. Now the trial and defense counsel signed off, the Captain then signed the transcript, and I, as the Legal Officer, forwarded it off to the admiral.

The admiral's legal officer, a full commander, reviewed the transcript and was equally impressed. He commended the Captain on the efficiency of the legal staff on the Oriskany and forwarded the transcript on to JAG.

Unfortunately, JAG didn't think as much of my and the court's efforts as had the Captain and the admiral's legal officer. It seems no one bothered to enter into evidence the date when the ship had last been in port, and while everyone knew the ship had been at sea for four days when Hills got himself bombed, reading the transcript wasn't very instructive. The case was reversed and Hills' record was expunged, but by that time three months had passed, I was no longer legal officer, the Captain had forgotten all about the case, and Hills had already served his confinement period, which at least kept him sober for a while. By the time the decision came down, Hill's promotion to CWO 1st Class had also come through. No harm, no foul.

Chapter 4

FAST FRIENDS

In spite of the long delays on my flight across the Pacific, I was the first ensign of my graduation year to arrive on the Oriskany that fall. Initially I found myself very much the outsider, the new boy in town. Everyone else had established relationships, and that went from card games to bull sessions. The flyers, usually referred to as "airedales" or "brown shoes," as they hardly ever wore their blue uniforms aboard ship, were the most accepting of new people, possibly because they had such a high turn-over rate from attrition, and they weren't part of the permanent ship's company in any event.

Two of the pilots became my first friends on board. Their names were Bill Lockhart and Jim Turner, and they were both recently minted lieutenants permanently attached to one of the squadrons on board. Their squadron was home based at NAS Moffett Field in Mountain View, California, about 40 miles south of San Francisco. Each squadron on board was assigned temporary duty on board a carrier when it deployed, but would return to its NAS (Naval Air Station) when the carrier returned to its homeport of Alameda NAS, California.

Turner and Lockhart had been friends at Cal before going to Pensacola and, for some inexplicable reason, latched on to me. Maybe it was because I had gone to Stanford, Cal's archrival, and they felt sorry for me. At that time Stanford had not beaten Cal in the "Big Game" since before the Second World War. Whatever the reason, I was soon eating with them in the Wardroom on a regular basis, when I wasn't on watch, and going on liberty with them at each port we visited.

Turner and Lockhart flew the Douglas AD-6 Skyraiders, a propeller driven ground support aircraft that had done tremendous work in the Korean War. An Air Group is formed each time an attack carrier deploys and usually consists of four squadrons, each performing a different function, plus some miscellaneous support aircraft. It is commanded by Commander Air Group ("CAG"), a very senior commander, to whom each of the squadron commanders reports. Pilots and the non-flying officer staff of the Air Group, the "brown shoes", augmented the ship's officers, nicknamed the "black shoes."

In any event, Turner and Lockhart latched on to me and tried to show me the ropes, or at least give me enough rope to hang myself. On one occasion when the Oriskany returned to its 7th Fleet homeport of Yokosuka, Japan, they dragged me off to Tokyo for a weekend of rest and recreation, known affectionately as "R&R," at one of the many hotels then run by the military for just that purpose. The experience was very enlightening for a brand new ensign.

I cleared my weekend pass with the Exec, still pleased with my performance in the Hills affair, and Turner and Lockhart had to check out with their squadron commander. When the three of us went looking for him, we were told he was with the other squadron commanders in CAG's cabin. When we got to CAG's cabin, we found all four squadron commanders with CAG, sitting on the floor around a cocktail table. Each was wearing a Japanese style ceremonial robe. On the table was a beautiful Noritaki tea service and each commander had his own Japanese teacup either in his hand or in front of him.

Turner and Lockhart asked their boss for permission to go ashore for the weekend, which was promptly granted, but conditional on their first joining the five commanders for a cup of tea. I was also invited to join in the tea party. I wasn't much of a tea drinker and was concerned that we would miss our train to Tokyo, but Turner and Lockhart enthusiastically agreed, and CAG ceremoniously poured a clear liquid from the large tea pot into three small Japanese tea cups, those little cups without handles, and then pushed two sugar bowls toward the three of us, picked up their lids, and asked, "Olives or onions?"

The clear liquid was, of course, gin with a hint of vermouth, but on a U.S. Navy ship where liquor was technically prohibited, this was a naval aviation version of the Japanese tea ceremony.

While Turner and Lockhart were not shocked by the tea party, we were all shocked when we arrived at the R&R hotel in Tokyo to find that the bar was closed to everyone except "Field Rank Officers" until 1930 (7:30 p.m.). As it was then 1700 (5 p.m.) and we were a very thirsty lot, already primed with our "Japanese tea," Turner and Lockhart were not of a mind to wait. They were lieutenants and I was a brand new ensign. "Field rank," they informed me, "means major or above in the army, which equates to a lieutenant commander or above in the Navy."

Turner and Lockhart grabbed me and pulled me into the little commissary in the R&R hotel where, for $2.00 each, they purchased three pairs of silver oak leaves, the insignia of a lieutenant commander. I was reluctant to participate in this endeavor, but who was I, a young, newly minted ensign, to hold out against the impressive persuasion of two full lieutenants who risked their lives daily flying AD-6's off an aircraft carrier? When I suggested to my two companions that I might look a little young for a lieutenant commander, they assured me that they had flown with full commanders that looked younger than I did. With that, they took off my gold bars, tacked on my new badge of rank on my shirt collar, saluted me, and marched me into the bar. As it was very hot and humid, khakis were the uniform of the day and jackets were not required, so we left them with their telltale insignias of rank in our rooms.

It was a terrific bar, with a jazz band playing in one corner, a bar loaded with Navy and Army nurses for whom the "Field Rank" proscription appeared not to apply, and beautiful wood paneling that reminded me of a London pub. We moved in quickly and started up a conversation with several of the nurses and had several rounds of drinks when a large hand dropped on my shoulder and a familiar voice said from behind my back, "Well, well, Commander, fancy meeting you here! I hadn't heard about your recent promotion, I'm *very* impressed indeed!"

It was Commander Nelson, the navigation officer and third in command on the Oriskany. His office was immediately adjacent to the signal bridge, my combat duty station, and he, unfortunately, knew quite well who I was and what rank I had been a few short moments before.

"I'm surprised you could reach this elevated rank without more knowledge of navigation, Commander," he continued, "I would think that you would want to come and see me for some special instruction in the fine art of navigation in view of your unusual promotion."

"Oh, yes sir," I replied, "That sounds like a wonderful idea. I would love to stop by Monday morning, or at your convenience, to get some special instruction, I know it will be very beneficial."

"I'm sure it will be," he whispered, "and if you're lucky, maybe this little incident can just remain between the two of us. I'm sure your friends here," raising his voice and turning to Turner and Lockhart, "are not any stronger in the memory department than they are in the brain department."

"Yes, sir!" was about the cleverest thing I was able to get out of my mouth. Nothing more than that slight dressing down would come to Turner and Lockhart, or anyone else who risked his life flying off carriers, but I was black shoe and did not fall in that elevated category. Pissed as Commander Nelson appeared, in my gut I realized that he was doing me one hell-of-a favor. "Rest assured, sir, I'll be there first thing Monday morning. I am really looking forward to some special assignments," I lied as a newly minted ensign cum lieutenant-commander.

"How does twenty hours of special assignments sound to you?" asked the commander with a very strong emphasis on the "you."

"Twenty hours sounds a hell of a lot better than some other things I can think of," I replied.

"A hell-of-a lot better," said Commander Nelson, "now let me buy you a drink, Commander."

And he did.

The third thing I remembered about that weekend was our return to Yokosuka. We missed the last train. That was de rigor for a pair of party animals like Turner and Lockhart, so we decided that the three of us would share a taxi back. In those days there were three types of taxis roaming the streets of Tokyo and Yokosuka, each type being known by the price they charged for a given distance—100 yen, 200 yen and 300 yen.

The difference was both size and quality. The 300 yen cab was the size of a modern compact, at that time a big car by Japan's standards but still a small piece of junk by American standards. The 200 yen was a compact car by anyone's standards, but at least it could still be described as an automobile. The 100 yen was a sewing machine on wheels in which three passengers could barely fit. If they had springs, they must have come from a mattress factory. There certainly was no insulation, and if you ever were in an accident in one you would be a statistic.

Turner and Lockhart insisted that we had to take a 100 yen cab the 35 narrow, winding miles to Yokosuka, and they went through four cabs until they found one that would do the trip for 3600 yen total, $10 at the then exchange rate.

That was a ride I could never forget. Our driver had to have been the one kamikaze pilot that survived WWII and regretted it. The car had no ventilation and the windows did not roll down. It was near 90 degrees out with humidity to match, and the combination of heat, humidity, overcrowding and fear produced enough steam to keep the windows constantly fogged. Lockhart, sitting in front, took off his shirt and undershirt and used the latter to clean the front window so the driver could see. The driver apparently had nothing else with which to clean the window, and didn't seem to care if he could see or not. After all, at sixty to seventy miles per hour down streets wide enough for a bicycle, who needs visibility?

When we made it safely to the gates of Yokosuka Naval Base, we were so glad to have arrived in only three pieces that we each gave the driver 1500 yen and all of my companions' earlier negotiations were for nothing.

The fourth thing that I remembered from that event was the 20 hours of navigation assignments that I was very glad to receive and actually finished.

My fifth lesson regarding the antics of Lockhart and Turner didn't occur until two and a half months later when the Oriskany was about to arrive at its homeport at Alameda NAS. Turner had not flown off with the rest of his squadron for some reason and he was frantically tearing his room apart when I walked in.

"What are you looking for?" I asked.

"My wedding ring," he replied, "if I can't find it my wife will kill me!"

My jaw dropped. I had been buddies with Turner and Lockhart for three months, we went on liberty constantly, we now knew just about every Navy nurse in the Yokosuka area, and not once did Turner ever tell me that he was married or mention his wife. On the other hand, all of our socializing with those lovely ladies had been totally innocent.

"You're kidding," I replied, "you never mentioned a wife. You can't be married."

"Lockhart's married, too, and has two kids," was Turner's response, "but that lucky son-of-a-bitch found his wedding ring. Mine has to be around here someplace."

Turner wasn't kidding. He eventually found his ring—it was hidden with the picture of his wife that he now dutifully placed on his desk. When the ship tied up at Alameda NAS, his wife was there on the dock to meet the ship and Turner made a point of introducing me as the "new ensign he and Lockhart were attempting to educate on some of the finer points of navigation." Apparently he had written her about the youngest commander in the Navy, who was thinking of taking up navigation as a specialty.

Chapter 5

THE WRECKER GOES TO SEA

Difficult as it was to make friends with the other ship's company officers when I first reported aboard, all that changed once the flood of new ensigns started to arrive. I was no longer alone in the strangeness of the Navy and this huge ship, and the new ensigns were all assigned to the same forward Junior Officer bunkroom to which I had been assigned and where we immediately flocked together as a community of outlanders.

One of the new ensigns was Ron Reicher, a farm boy from Nebraska. Reicher had played halfback for the University of Nebraska before that school had started its football dynasty, but still weighed in at about 215 pounds on a 6'2" frame. He was a great guy, soft spoken and very polite, but he was hard as nails and could bench press a guy twice my size without half trying. He hated his first name, Ronald, and his nickname on the football field had been "Wrecker," and Wrecker he became in the Oriskany lexicon. One thing I learned young; you don't call a guy who can bench press someone twice your size by a first name he doesn't like.

Tough as he looked and was, Wrecker had one weakness, *mal-de-mer*. When he first reported aboard he suffered from chronic seasickness, with the emphasis on chronic and sick. At the time he reported the ship was tied up at the pier at Yokosuka. He walked up the gangplank, saluted the flag, saluted the officer of the deck, handed in his orders and threw up; and not necessarily in that order.

Now a 48,000 ton aircraft carrier doesn't move much at sea, but when tied up in port it doesn't move at all, except, apparently, in relation to the amount of movement you get on a farm in Nebraska.

For the first five days after he reported aboard, the Oriskany remained tied up in Yokosuka and Wrecker spent most of his time tied up emotionally in his bunk. The new ensigns could not convince him to get out of bed, and this huge guy was so frightened he actually shook whenever he tried to get up, even to go to the can. For those first five days the stewards or we brought him food from the wardroom and he subsisted principally on sandwiches, bouillon soup, and an occasional bowl of corn flakes.

This was a major problem for a naval officer. All of the new ensigns, including me, tried to talk to Wrecker and convince him that it was all in his head, but he would hear none of it.

"If the Oriskany hits a big wave on Tuesday, you don't feel it until Thursday," I lied, but Wrecker ignored me and just uttered a groan at the mention of "big wave."

Finally, the huge ship got underway and, contrary to Wrecker's expectations, he did not appear to get worse. The other JOs kept telling him that he would get accustomed to the movement of the ship, which we still hadn't felt as we were not yet in open water, but we could tell from his eyes that he didn't believe us. Still, there certainly didn't seem much difference between the way the ship felt at sea and the way the ship felt tied up in Yokosuka. At least not yet, and we JOs didn't have the heart to tell Wrecker that it could only get worse—this was as good as it got as we had yet to feel the first swell.

By five o'clock that first day at sea Wrecker was beginning to come around. Some of his old cockiness seemed to be trying to break out, and he actually got out of his bunk and put on his uniform. This didn't seem that bad! Of course, he didn't leave the bunkroom yet, but at least he was dressed. That was a major victory, of sorts.

By six o'clock, the other JOs and I had convinced Wrecker that he should try dinner in the wardroom. Very unsteadily we showed him the way to the wardroom to which he had not yet visited and led him into the outer wardroom, which was set up like a clubroom with comfortable leather chairs and gaming tables for card games. The inner wardroom was many times the size of the outer wardroom and was set up with row after row of tables and chairs, with room to feed about 250 officers at one time. As there were almost 400 officers aboard with the Air Groups, we ate in two shifts, the early sitting at 1700 (5 p.m.) and the late sitting at 1815 (6:15 p.m.) at which the Exec usually presided. You didn't have to sign up for a particular sitting because of the way the watch sections and duty sections worked; you just came to one or the other and there was almost always room for everyone.

After the second sitting the stewards would fold up some of the tables, put in more chairs, and there would be a movie in the inner wardroom for the officers. There were also movies in the Warrant Officers' wardroom, the Chiefs' wardroom and on the hanger deck for the enlisted men and anyone else that wanted to see that specific film. Even officers went to the hanger deck if they had missed a movie in the wardroom that they wanted to see when it was shown there. New films were constantly delivered to the ship with almost every mail or equipment delivery and they generally rotated first to the Officers' wardroom, then the next night to the Warrant Officers' wardroom, etc.

Wrecker was feeling shaky after the trip down from the bunkroom, so we sat down for several minutes in the outer wardroom while he gathered his strength for the trip into the inner wardroom for the second sitting at 1815. At our prompting, Wrecker practiced deep breathing. Then we went in, took positions behind seats at the table closest the door, and stood waiting for the Exec to enter—a ritual that was done nightly at the second sitting before we could sit down.

The Exec came in seconds later, but before we could sit Wrecker grabbed my arm and said, "I'm not going to make it!" With that he ran for the door.

Had any of us been thinking, we would have realized that Wrecker probably didn't know where the wardroom was in relation to the rest of the ship, and he certainly didn't know the location of the head closest to the wardroom. At least one of us JOs should probably have followed him out, but dinner looked pretty promising that night, what Wrecker was probably about to do didn't, and our little cordon of new ensigns stayed where we were, leaving Wrecker to his own devices.

—◊◊◊—

As Wrecker entered the outer wardroom, he realized that not only wasn't he going to make it to the head, he had no idea where the head (a.k.a "bathroom") was in this part of the ship. Directly in front of him was the galley, so he dashed in, meaning only to ask directions, but then there were all those thick smells of greasy food and . . . .

"Not going to make it" now took on a meaning all of its own, and it dictated events. Realizing that he had neither the time nor the ability to ask any questions, Wrecker headed for the nearest garbage can, lifted the lid, and proceeded to throw up over the entire supply of fresh coffee for the wardroom mess.

As we were on our way out on a three-week exercise, Wrecker's *mal-de-mere* had taken on a new dimension. Somehow the officer's mess continued to serve fresh coffee for the next three weeks, but all the new ensigns from the forward JO bunkroom, after Wrecker told us what happened, switched to tea on the spot and never went back to coffee until we were sure that a certain garbage can was empty.

Chapter 6

GETTING IN THE HABIT

Shortly after my arrival on board, the Oriskany stopped in Hong Kong for a little R&R. I was standing duty as the In-Port JOOD (Junior Officer of the Deck) just before midnight, when the enlisted men had to be back on board (there was no time limit for officers). In Hong Kong the Oriskany anchored in the bay and ferried people back and forth on motor whaleboats for the enlisted men and officers' motorboats for the officers. Motor whaleboats were large, open boats with hard wooden bench seating on which you could crowd several hundred men. The officers' motorboat was a large enclosed cabin cruiser with a bridge between its forward and aft cabins that could hold about 50 officers with some degree of comfort. Seating in each cabin on the officers' motorboat was in the form of padded seats that ran around the circumference of each cabin.

Of course, officers were always free to ride back in the whaleboats, and on this night an officer came on board sandwiched between two surging masses of inebriated enlisted men. He had a large bundle that looked like a white laundry bag thrown over his shoulder and was clearly two sheets to the wind. I was alone on the quarterdeck with one of the chiefs while the senior OOD (Officer of the Deck), a gunnery officer named Bill Hawkins, was in the OOD's office writing out the log and waiting for our relief.

The officer with the laundry bag saluted shakily and asked permission to come on board.

"What's in the bag, Lieutenant?" I asked. The officer was in uniform, which was rather surprising as most officers went ashore in civilian clothes.

"A Rug," he replied.

Then the rug giggled and the enlisted men on either side of him roared with laughter.

"WHAT THE HELL HAVE YOU GOT IN THERE?" I yelled, but the bag toting officer was gone, heading for the nearest down ladder.

"CHIEF, STOP HIM!" I yelled.

"Who?" replied the chief who at that moment was busy with several drunken enlisted men.

"That guy, that lieutenant with the laundry bag that just came through. He's got someone in it."

"Hmmm, that's bad," said the chief, "you can get in trouble if something' like that happens on your watch. You sure there was someone in it?"

"Of course I'm sure," I replied, "his damn laundry bag giggled. Laundry bags don't giggle unless someone is inside giggling."

But by this time I had stopped the flow of drunken sailors coming up the gangway, additional boats were attempting to disgorge drunken sailors at the foot of the gangway, the lieutenant with the laundry bag had disappeared down the closest ladder, and pandemonium was on the verge of breaking loose on the quarterdeck.

"Well, Sir, I think we better get these guys off the gangway first and then you can talk to the OOD about this problem of the giggling laundry bag." replied the chief skeptically.

When the gangway was finally cleared I cornered Hawkins and told him what I had seen and that while the officer looked somewhat familiar to me, I didn't know his name and wasn't sure I could recognize him. "There was an awful lot going on just then!"

"Can you describe him at all?" Asked Hawkins?

"Sure, not a real large guy, no bigger than me—well, maybe a little bigger. He had aviator wings and I think he was JG. Pretty sure he's not ship's company but from one of the squadrons." I replied.

"Damn it," said Hawkins, "I sure don't want to write anything about this in the Log. Are you absolutely sure there was someone in that bag?"

"I heard someone giggling in a high pitched voice and it looked like the bag was moving—it sure sounded like there was a person of the female persuasion in there."

"Dick, if you are absolutely sure we can go to the Exec and do a lock-down and search the ship from stem to stern. We'll make an awful lot of enemies in the course of that type of thing, and I'd hate to do it unless you are ABSOLUTELY SURE!"

"Well," I replied, "I guess it is always possible that one of the other sailors crowding around—it was pretty crowded up there—giggles with a high pitched voice, and I guess its always possible that he had something very flexible in that laundry bag that looked like it could be a person."

"Now you're talking," said Hawkins, "I hear you saying you're not absolutely positive it was an officer with a girl in a bag that came aboard while you were standing watch—because if that was the case you should have stopped that from happening and I would have to write that up in the Log and report it to the Exec. Of course, if we don't report it and we are wrong and there was someone in that bag, some airedale is going to get into big trouble if he gets caught, but who is going to know when exactly he came aboard and who was standing watch?"

"Yeah," I replied, "I might have just been hearing things, and no sense in getting all worked up about it."

"I agree completely," said Hawkins, lets just forget the whole thing.

And forget it we did. I must admit I kept my ears open to see if I heard any funny noises coming out of any of the officers' rooms as I went about my business the next day, but I heard nothing. Apparently, however, I was right and one of the flyers had smuggled a stark naked hooker aboard in that laundry bag. He and his roommate or roommates, some bunkrooms are bigger than others, then had to figure how to keep her concealed and get her off the ship. To our great surprise we later learned they did get her off and how they did it.

Apparently the little incident on my watch was on a Friday night. On Sunday the ship was having an open house for the U.S. Consul in Hong Kong and the American community there. The importer of the young lady and his friends decided they could keep her under wraps until then and sneak her off as a visitor on the following Sunday. However, there was at least one problem. In importing the young lady they had neglected to import any clothing with her. Not even shoes.

There were, of course, other less revealing logistic problems. Sneaking food up to her turned out to be not a problem, there seemed to be a number of people in the importer's squadron ready and willing to accommodate her in that regard. That, of course, produced a number of creditable sources for the tale I am about to reveal.

They also had to keep out the Filipino stewards who made up officers' rooms and figure out a way to get her signed in on Sunday so when she left the ship, assuming they could find her some suitable clothes, the count would be right, but that turned out to be not so difficult either. On the day in question one of importer's support group just walked up to the sign-in sheet to look at it and wrote in a pseudonym for the young lady.

The biggest problem by far was the clothes and how to make her look like she fit in with that crowd. So Saturday one of the importer's friends went into Hong Kong to buy the young lady an outfit, complete with shoes. In a stroke of genius, the duty shopper pulled off a tour-de-force and found a store catering to religious clothing. He bought her a complete nun's outfit, even to black, sensible shoes. Dressed as such, they snuck her off the ship that Sunday without anyone noticing. As the story was later related, however, it turned out that the shoes were way too big and she was practically falling out of them as she hobbled down the gangway to the waiting officers' motorboat.

—◦◦◦—

The story, of course, came out after the fact, but almost everyone except Hawkins and I thought the young flyers that claimed to have pulled off that stunt were making the story up. However, that very Sunday night at dinner seated at my table were several airedales I didn't know. They were in a very gay mood indeed, and I started staring at one of them—I thought he was the guy with the giggling duffle bag. I introduced myself, brash ensign that I was, and his name turned out to be Collin Weed. I thought it was him, but I wasn't sure and certainly had no intention of raising the subject. He was accompanied by three or four of his friends, all of whom introduced themselves.

We happened to be seated that night with the boat officer in charge of one of the officers' motorboats used that day to take the VIPs to and from the ship. "Damndest thing happened to me on the four o'clock run," he told us, "I got propositioned by a bloody nun. Can you believe it, a bloody nun? What in the hell is this world coming to."

There was no immediate response, but then Weed broke the silence. "Yup, it's enough to give a man religion."

Weed and his friends then burst out laughing. They didn't calm down for several minutes. When the story eventually leaked out I certainly understood why.

Chapter 7

ENSIGN BENSEN BAGS A BIRD

I have to be honest; I was not an eyewitness to every one of the stories in this book. My good friend and Stanford and NROTC classmate, Tom Timberlake, told the following story to me. Tom was the source of at least one other story that started on the Oriskany and ended on the USS Hornet, CVA-12, the carrier to which Tom was assigned at the same time that I was assigned to the Oriskany, but more about that later.

One of the last of the new crop of ensigns to report on board the USS Hornet to which Tom was assigned was Ensign Benjamin Benson III, of the New York and Newport Bensons, direct from four years at Yale and ninety days at OCS without passing go and without collecting his $200. But then, he didn't need $200. Ben was alternately called Double Ben or Triple Ben by the various groups on board, and it was clear from the outset that there were certain aspects of naval officer life that he took to with great relish. He delighted in ordering Filipino stewards around, they were so much like the help he had at home, and he fully appreciated the deference that was supposed to be given to him in his status as an officer and a gentleman. He had not, however, learned in his short time in the service that deference in the Navy really had to be earned.

He wasn't long in catching the eye of the Captain. Double Ben was assigned to Gunnery, a good starting spot for a line officer. His general quarters' station was in the Mark VII gun director. The Mark VII sat high in the island superstructure of the carrier with an unobstructed view in all directions. It tied into the radar and could lock onto an incoming target. Once it had a target locked on it could lock one or more of the five inch and/or 40 mm guns onto the target with the appropriate angle of deflection to reflect the relative location of the gun, the speed of the approaching hostile and the angle of deflection from the Mark VII director. However, once you locked the guns with the director, as you moved the director you moved all guns that were locked onto that director.

A Benson never waited to be told. Once he received his assignment and had some free time, he immediately searched out the Mark VII and inspected it. It was terrific, and its entrance hatch wasn't locked! There was a great console seat from which you could look out the slits on the front of the director. In this way, you could sight the guns manually if your radar failed, or you could use the director for sighting if you were shelling a shore installation, although 48,000 ton aircraft carriers wouldn't normally be expected to be shelling shore installations. However, the Oriskany had done just that in the Korean War.

Well, Double Ben dropped into the seat of the gun director and examined the console. There was a large red switch that was obviously the "on-off" button. A Benson doesn't wait to be told how to do something, so he experimented and turned it to the "on" position. Immediately lights came on and motors started to hum. This was great fun! Then there was this control stick. Ben touched it and the director made a slight move. So he touched it harder and it moved more. In the distance, or at least it seemed like a distance, there was a klaxon horn sound. Actually, the klaxon was on the Mark VII and sounded whenever it moved to warn anyone in the vicinity to stand clear. However, with the door closed the sound was very much muffled, and Benson had put on the earphones that came with the location, but neglected to turn them on. But they made great ear plugs!

Benson now had the gist of the thing, so he started swinging the director left and right, then all the way around, then up, then down. Man, was this fun. It was like a carnival ride at Coney Island. Next there were all those buttons. Fantastic! You pushed a switch and the red lights went to green. He started pushing the switches and swinging the director, and man was he having a ball.

Down on one of the five inch gun turrets Seaman 1st class James Hinshaw wasn't having quite as much fun. He had been assigned to paint over some rust on the top of the turret. First he heard the sound of a klaxon horn, and while trying to work through where the sound could be coming from, suddenly the gun mount he was riding started jerking back and forth under him. Before he could reach for the paint, Hinshaw and the paint bucket went sailing off in opposite directions, the paint right onto Hinshaw and Hinshaw off in the direction of the barrel of the gun and the Pacific Ocean gleaming directly, and far, below. He clutched the barrel just before being thrown rapidly over the side, all the while screaming for all he was worth

Hinshaw wasn't the only one screaming. The Captain of the Hornet, while not in the same imminent peril as Hinshaw, and definitely not covered in paint, was screaming loud enough to drown out air operations had they been underway. Ben had also locked on the aft five inch gun to the Mark VII, and while it had no one on it or in it at the time, its gun barrel had an arc of swing that encompassed a portion of the flight deck. A portion that, unfortunately, happened to be occupied at that instant by a parked Banshee fighter-bomber. The gun, controlled as it was by Benson's wildly swinging Mark VII, caught the Banshee just right, knocked it off of its landing blocks, and shoved it over the starboard side of the ship into that same Pacific that Hinshaw was clutching desperately to avoid.

The Captain, alerted by this time that something was very much amiss, had grabbed the 1-MC public address system and was screaming for whoever was operating the Mark VII gun control system to cease and report to the quarterdeck, immediately. Over and over he screamed, and around and around went the Mark VII and all the guns to which it was locked. Unfortunately, the earphones made very good ear plugs. All the earphones did was serve to drown out the noise of the gear inside the Mark VII, the klaxon, and the sound of the 1-MC. Several brave souls tried to get into the Mark VII to alert Benson that the Captain wanted him, but as long as it kept swinging around it was impossible to get a handhold on the entrance hatch.

Benson finally stopped the device long enough for one brave seaman to leap onto the hatch and open it. Inside, the grinning Benson was clearly having a ball. He hadn't had so much fun since his first roller-coaster ride. When told, however, that the Captain wished to see him, and on the double, Benson was puzzled. He had no idea why that great man could possibly want to see him, except possibly to commend him on showing the initiative to learn the use of the Mark VII even before the first drill.

By this time the Captain had sent a squad of four Marines to bring Benson to the Bridge, which was fortunate, as Benson had not the slightest idea of how to get there. As he was being escorted to the bridge, he failed to notice the paint covered, shaking enlisted man named Hinshaw being led past him to sickbay.

On the bridge the Captain was not a happy man. When Benson was led onto the bridge, there facing him were the Captain, the Exec, the ship's Navigator, and the Hornet's Gun Boss. The Exec introduced Benson to the Captain.

"Captain, this is Ensign Benjamin Benson, new on board this week right out of OCS, and he appears to be the young man who climbed into the Mark VII and locked on the guns."

"Yes, Sir!" replied Benson, "I was familiarizing myself with the equipment, Sir, in anticipation of my duty assignment during general quarters."

"Young man, you're an idiot," said the Captain in a barely controlled voice that kept getting louder with each syllable, "DO YOU KNOW WHAT YOUR LITTLE PLAYING AROUND UP THERE DID? YOU KNOCKED ONE OF THE BANSHEE'S OFF THE FLIGHT DECK AND INTO 3,000 FEET OF PACIFIC OCEAN! DO YOU HAVE ANY IDEA WHAT ONE OF THOSE PLANES COSTS?"

"No Sir, but not to worry, Sir," replied Benson, bringing himself to his full height of 5'8" and snapping off a perfect imitation of a Marine Corps salute, "have them send the bill to my father, he'll be happy to pay it."

With that, having rendered the four senior officers opposite him speechless, he thought the matter resolved, and Benson turned and started to leave.

"WAIT A MINUTE, MR. BENSON," shouted the Exec and the Gun Boss in unison, "YOU DON'T LEAVE UNTIL THE CAPTAIN TELLS YOU TO LEAVE."

Benson swung around, again snapped his snappy salute, and replied "Aye, aye, Sir!"

Now the Captain looked at Benson, then to the Exec, then to the Gun Boss, then back to Benson. "Can you type, son?" asked the Captain in a quiet, resigned voice.

"No, Sir!" snapped Benson, again with the snappy salute.

"Can you speak without saluting?" asked the Captain.

"Yes, Sir!" came Benson's response, again with the snappy salute.

"Do you know Morse code or semaphore?" the Captain asked.

"What is that, Sir?" came back Benson, this time with a rather hesitant hand motion that might have passed for a salute in some very relaxed military service.

"How about putting him into Communications?" said the Captain looking over towards the Exec, "He can't screw things up too much down there, can he?"

"Well, Captain, I sure as hell would hate to have to recommend this man for a security clearance, but he would find it difficult to sink the ship from the radio room."

"It's decided then," the Captain said, "he has all the qualifications for Communications—he can't type, he can't think, he doesn't know code and he's an obvious security risk."

At that they all laughed except Benson, who had no clue as to what that was all about, and Benson was finally told that he was dismissed. It was a shame that Benson never learned what the joke was. Unfortunately, Tom Timberlake was in Communications and did.

Chapter 8

THE RING KNOCKER

Aircraft carriers are the biggest ships in the Navy. But to the big brass, aircraft carriers are not the "real Navy." The "real Navy" is battleships, cruisers and destroyers, with maybe an occasional submarine thrown in for color. Those are "Fighting ships!" Carriers contain almost four hundred officers who live by a different book—particularly the airedales. They hide booze in their safes and drink on board, wear the wrong colored shoes that are usually scuffed, and pride themselves on their casualness in an organization that prides itself on spit and polish. And the airedales infect everyone they touch, and particularly the ships company officers, who usually wind up also hiding booze in their safes and drinking on board, wearing the right colored shoes, but usually scuffed, and trying to be casual.

Someone up there at the Bureau of Naval Personnel ("BuPers") had apparently decided that such an environment is a bad influence for young Annapolis graduates, and therefore populates the ranks of the ship's company junior officers on aircraft carriers with reservists and regulars from the 52 NROTC programs and OCS graduates, but seldom anyone from the Naval Academy. Thus it was with the first twenty-eight ensigns that reported aboard the Oriskany that fall. However, the twenty-ninth arrival, and the one that completed our ranks, was an actual "ring knocker," i.e., an Annapolis graduate. Every Annapolis graduate buys the traditional class ring, and every senior officer, all of whom seem to have gone to Annapolis, looks for that ring when he meets a junior officer. Even if you bought a class ring when you graduated from Harvard or Stanford, or any of the fifty other NROTC schools, a senior officer with fading eyesight could spot the real thing a mile away.

The ring knocker who finally showed up in my class of ensigns was Carlton Kincaid, an improbable name for a more improbable guy. Within ten minutes of his reporting aboard we all knew that Carlton had graduated near the very top of his class, his father was a general in the Army, and that it was some huge mistake that he was on a carrier instead of a cruiser. "Cruisers are the real Navy," he assured his new compatriots, "Carriers are the bull-shit Navy." But not to fear, he assured us, he would show us how to do things right.

And show us he did. He showed us on liberty that he couldn't drink. He showed us aboard ship that he couldn't think. And later, when we returned stateside, he showed us that he couldn't even see. But more of that later.

His route to becoming a legend in his own time started one morning about six weeks after his arrival. The Oriskany was leaving Yokosuka for the last time and heading stateside. Its relief was the Coral Sea, a larger carrier than the Oriskany, complete with a new admiral taking over as ComCarDiv-3 (Commander, Carrier Division Three). Its orders were to anchor outside the harbor exit and wait for the Oriskany to disgorge the pilot. Pilots are provided by every port to guide ships coming in and out. The pilot is in charge of the ship while entering and leaving harbor, even a U. S. Navy ship, and the pilot is accompanied by a pilot's tug that transports him to and from the various ships coming and going. The orders for the day were for the Coral Sea to anchor outside the entrance channel and wait for the pilot taking the Oriskany out of the harbor to come aboard and take the Coral Sea in.

At Yokosuka, the deep channel used for large capital ships like aircraft carriers entering or leaving the harbor runs along a finger of land that juts out from the mainland and serves as the northern protective barrier for the harbor. The land runs along the port side of the ship when exiting the harbor, and on this day I was at my usual "putting-to-sea detail," the signal bridge, immediately behind and slightly below the real bridge where the Captain, OOD and JOOD were located. Carlton had been promptly made Junior Officer of the Deck (JOOD) for our putting-to-sea detail on the assumption that, being an Annapolis graduate, he would perform just that much better than one of those NROTC or OCS types at such an important task.

Being of a curious nature, I was anxious to see our relief, and took advantage of the 36 power binoculars mounted on gimbals on the starboard side of the signal bridge. There was an identical pair on the port side. Through the huge glasses I got my first look at the Coral Sea through the early morning mist. She was a huge ship, quite a bit larger than the Oriskany, and was pointed at right angles to the Oriskany at "2 o'clock" when she first emerged through the mist and materialized in my glasses. I was euphoric as I looked at our relief carrier, the reason why we were now able to go back to our homeport of Alameda. But through my euphoria I sensed something was wrong.

I remembered very little from my NROTC days, but the best instructor I did have was the one that taught us seamanship my first year, and I remembered being told you could tell if you were on a collision course with another ship if the angle of reckoning between your ship and the other ship remained constant—and I was *not* moving the binoculars to keep the Coral Sea in view. Then I noticed that the Coral Sea didn't have anchor balls up. A ship at anchor hoists four huge balls into its rigging to let other ships know that it is not underway. The Coral Sea was heading straight for the Oriskany and, if she missed us, she would plow straight into the rocks that ran along the channel on the port side of the Oriskany.

I immediately hit the 1-MC and shouted to the bridge, "Bridge, signal bridge, the Coral Sea does not have her anchor balls up, appears to be underway, and appears to be on a collision course."

The only response was four blasts on the whistle, the sign of imminent danger, four bells to announce that the ship was in full reverse, and the bosun of the watch screaming over the public address system: "COLLISION ALERT FORWARD, COLLISION ALERT FORWARD! THIS IS NO DRILL! THIS IS NO DRILL! ALL HANDS TO COLLISION QUARTERS!"

At this, the flight deck below became literally alive. Hundreds of men working in the forward area of the flight deck started running aft as fast as they could go. It was a mass exodus of frightened men who were clearly concerned that a collision at sea with the Coral Sea could be injurious to their health and safety.

On the bridge, however, Ensign Kincaid was faced with a far different dilemma, as he related what happened next to all of his JO buddies when the incident ended. At Annapolis, he told us afterwards, they had drilled into him that when a ship with an admiral passed, the bridge should command all hands to stand at attention and face starboard, if the admiral's ship was passing to starboard, or port, if the ship was passing on the port bow. But the Coral Sea apparently looked to him like it would pass, if it passed at all, dead ahead. He told us he was unsure whether to command the bosun to use the 1-MC to call "Attention to Starboard!" or "Attention to Port." He had never heard that there was something called "Attention Straight Ahead!" This was a problem that apparently strained even an Annapolis graduate from near the top of his class.

At times when you are not sure of the proper course of conduct, he told us that Annapolis directs you to seek guidance from more experienced officers. So Carlton approached the officer of the deck, a seasoned JG named Woody Thevenot, who was only about one degree from apoplexy at that particular moment. Most of what subsequently transpired, considered unbelievable coming from Carlton, was subsequently confirmed by Woody.

"Sir, should we call 'attention to starboard' or 'attention to port;' there's an admiral on board the Coral Sea?" Carlton inquired.

"GET THE HELL OUT OF THE WAY!" Woody replied in his most military manner.

Kincaid refused to be rebuffed and decided, in good Annapolis tradition, to take his problem up the chain of command to a higher authority. He went to the Captain, who at that moment was transfixed partway between a catatonic fit and a state of prayer.

"Sir," he said in his best military bearing, and accompanied by a very polished salute, "should we call 'attention to starboard' or 'attention to port'; there is an admiral on board the Coral Sea."

He repeated the question three or four times to the Captain. Finally, the Captain slowly turned and saw Carlton for the first time. His voice was soft and understanding. He simply said: "Get the hell away from here and stay out of the way!"

Frustrated at every turn, Kincaid resorted to further Annapolis training. At Annapolis, Kincaid claimed, they teach you that when an officer is confronted with a situation where it is impossible for him to determine what his commander wishes him to do, he must innovate.

So Kincaid analyzed the situation. The Coral Sea was approaching rapidly. It must have looked to Kincaid on the Bridge, just like it looked to me on the Signal Bridge, that if it did hit, it probably would hit more on the starboard side than the port side. Yes, it clearly was slightly to the starboard side.

So Kincaid went up to the bosun of the watch and ordered him to call "Attention to starboard!"

There was no response from the bosun.

He repeated the order.

Still no response.

There was no time to argue, the Coral Sea would be on us momentarily. A terrible gaff would happen if "Attention to starboard!" was not called immediately.

Innovate! Kincaid had to innovate. He grabbed the bosun's whistle from around the neck of the surprised petty officer and proceeded to pipe the appropriate tune for "Attention to starboard" over the 1-MC, the ship's public address system (Annapolis training was thorough indeed), and followed that with his own commanding baritone: "NOW ALL HANDS, ATTENTION TO STARBOARD! ATTENTION TO STARBOARD!"

From my vista on the Signal Bridge, directly aft of the Bridge, all I could see were hundreds of men in full gallop heading from fore to aft when the 1-MC came on with that intriguing command. Of course, discipline in the Navy is drilled into everyone. But so is common sense. To a man, hundreds of fleeing men paused in mid-stride for what looked like a simultaneous micro-second, contemplated for the briefest instant what was being asked of them, and then continued running to the rear of the ship as fast as their legs could carry them—in contravention of a direct order!

The Oriskany came to a halt about 100 feet from the Coral Sea's port side elevator, and the Coral Sea stopped a couple of hundred yards short of the rocks, and everyone who knew what was going on was soaked in sweat and limp as a dish rag. Except, of course, for Kincaid, who was elated that he had done the right thing, and done it on his own. There was no question now that more of the Coral Sea was to the right of the Oriskany's centerline, and therefore starboard had been the right call. He clearly had been correct.

The Captain was a little more sanguine about it. He merely turned to Woody, gestured toward the beaming Kincaid and said, "Woody, tell the gun boss to get that idiot off the bridge during putting-to-sea detail."

So they changed his putting-to-sea detail, but Carlton considered it his first of many promotions.

—◆◆◆—

If Carlton wasn't much fun on the bridge, he was even less fun on liberty. That was because he was in love. He longed desperately for a little girl back at Annapolis. He spent his every spare minute, which wasn't much as he was on a mission from God to read every operations manual ("Op Manual") aboard ship, writing her, or rereading her occasional letters.

"She doesn't write much—she isn't the writing type," he explained.

Her name was Elizabeth "Lollie" Beauchamp, and she had red hair and worked behind the counter in a small diner close to the gate at the Academy in Annapolis. Lollie came from a very poor family, he confided to us, but was very religious and very beautiful. All the Annapolis Midshipmen were allegedly in love with her, but she had eyes only for him, and had been his date at the graduation ball.

As he pined away for her, his plans began to formulate. He told us he was going to ask her to marry him. He would be her ticket away from the poverty of her childhood. She would be an officer's wife, and probably some day an admiral's wife, because if there was one thing Carlton had an oversupply of, it was confidence in his career opportunities

He held off his proposal until the ship arrived back at Alameda, its homeport, and then called and popped the question. He was on cloud nine. She had accepted without even taking time to think it over, and told him to wire her some money, get an apartment, and she would quit her job in the diner and come right out to California.

The next day Carlton was on the streets looking for a place they could afford, and his first day out found a very cute furnished cottage on Telegraph Hill. He took us all to see it, and we all agreed he had made a great find. It was on a little wooden walking street on the cheap side of Telegraph Hill. It had charm, a fireplace, and a view that made its $80 per month rent a bargain anyplace in the world. It was right below the Shadows, then my favorite restaurant in the City, and shared the same view of Oakland, the Bay Bridge, Treasure Island and the San Francisco wharves. It was very small and nestled on the east side of the hill, but it was a great place for a honeymoon year.

So Carlton wired Lollie the money for the ticket, bought a second hand car, and waited expectantly for her arrival. Within several days it was all arranged; she was arriving Saturday on a TWA Super Constellation, and Wrecker, Carlton, Collin Sommers, another new ensign from the U. of Texas and I loaded into my 1955 turquoise and white Chevy hardtop, which was the class of the cars we had at our disposal, for a trip to San Francisco International Airport to meet the intended Mrs. Kincaid. The plane was due to arrive at 5 p.m., and the entourage was there an hour early at Carlton's insistence.

This was, of course, before the days of the concourse and the jet way, airport security and all the things that go along with airport security. It was even before commercial jets, and Carlton and our entourage were there on the tarmac to meet Lollie when she came down the moveable stairway of her Super Constellation.

"There she is!" Carlton yelled, and there she was. At the top of the stairway stood a woman with henna red hair that clearly came from a bottle, a dress so tight it left nothing to one's imagination, and a walk that advertised all of her ample wares. To round out the picture, she was chewing gum.

From the top of the stairway she looked to the others and me like she had long since seen the sunny side of thirty, but what did we know? As she got closer we were pretty sure of it. Before she could reach the bottom Carlton was charging forward, and grabbed her in an embrace that forced me to look away as Lollie ground her groin into Carlton's.

When they finally came up for air, Carlton said, "Lollie, let me introduce you to some of my friends. This is Wrecker, he played ball for Nebraska, and this is Sommers, he's from Texas, and this is Dick, he's the legal officer and is from around here and knows 'Frisco real well." Then to us he continued, "Isn't she great, guys!"

Lollie looked at the three of us, all standing there bug eyed and mouths agape. Somehow, in spite of their mad embrace, the gum was still in place and she was chewing a mile a minute.

"Hi, boys, glad to meet ya!" she exclaimed, with a shrug of her shoulder and a wiggle of her hips. Then she took a good look at Wrecker, and she stopped chewing. Her eyes took him all in, lingered a bit at his groin, which was somewhat distended at the moment, and continued, "Just call me Lollie, 'cause I'm an all day sucker!" And with that her head went back and she let out a laugh that drowned out the noise on the tarmac.

Carlton roared with delight. He clearly didn't have the foggiest idea of what Lollie was alluding to. The rest of us ensigns were unable to even muster a polite smile. While we all considered Carlton a pompous ass, he was our pompous ass, and the thought of what he was getting into, literally, was more than any of us could stomach. Wrecker, Sommers and I looked at each other, and our looks were looks of disbelief. This was the virginal little girl that Carlton was going to take from her life of poverty and make an admiral's wife? God help him! She was pure and simple, all right. But pure and simple what was the question.

Carlton took five days leave and they left the next day for Reno to get married. That was Sunday. Monday morning Carlton was back on ship. He refused to answer any question about why he came back early, where Lollie was, or what happened except that he admitted that he was now married, but something had happened on their wedding night that so shocked him that he couldn't stay with Lollie. He had left her that very night and returned to the ship, leaving Lollie in Reno where she was apparently content to spend her honeymoon even without the bridegroom.

Carlton was disconsolate. He moped and brooded and picked at his food, and he didn't even try to read his beloved Op Manuals. There was nothing that could be done for him; he was inconsolable! We were all concerned, and several of the JOs went to see the Protestant Chaplain to see if he would talk to Carlton. This he did, at great length, and after several weeks of around the clock counseling from the Chaplain, Carlton and Lollie were reconciled and moved into that lovely little apartment behind Telegraph Hill.

It was shortly after the reconciliation that Carlton finally found lasting fame on the Oriskany, and literally his place in the sun. It was a Monday on a beautiful September day in San Francisco. San Francisco has an amazing climate. You freeze all summer in a cold, foggy overcast with brisk winds coming off the ocean and with temperatures in the mid 50's. Then September comes and with it what passes for summer in that beautiful city by the Bay. And this was one of those great days. The drill for the day was that the ship was leaving port on a two week cruise to qualify air groups from Moffett Field and other Naval Air Stations in central California.

Embarkation time was 9 a.m., and by the time they tossed off the mooring lines from the Oriskany's pier at Alameda NAS, the sun was out, it was shirtsleeve weather, and the bay was calm as glass. Woody Thevenot was again at the con, with the Captain on the bridge with the San Francisco Bay pilot as the Oriskany steamed out of port. I was at my usual putting-to-sea detail on the signal bridge, slightly below and to the aft of the main bridge.

The 1-MC actually serves a dual purpose when a message comes from the bridge—it is an intercom for selected locations and a public address system to all locations, depending on which mode is selected.

Aircraft carriers carry a number of small boats used to shuttle personnel around. On Essex class carriers, as I mentioned earlier, there are two officers' motor boats in addition to at least two motor whaleboats, a Captain's gig and, when the admiral is aboard, the admiral's barge, these latter two being elaborate and luxurious cabin cruisers to ferry the serious brass.

But when a carrier goes out from its homeport for a short cruise and intends to return to that same port without any stops in between, it doesn't bother to load its boats and the other vehicles that it usually carries. Instead, they are left behind. In the case of an officer's motorboat, it is left in the care of the coxswain and bosun mate assigned to that boat.

So it was on that beautiful Monday in September that, after the Oriskany set sail, a car raced onto the pier and out jumped Ensign Kincaid. He briefly kissed his bride farewell, ran to the Oriskany's number one motor boat, leaped aboard and gave his first order as an officer in charge of a United States Naval vessel: "Catch up with the ship!"

The coxswain knew an order when he heard it, took one look at Kincaid and replied, "Aye, aye, sir!"

With that, the bosun cast off the lines and its Number One motorboat was in hot pursuit of the Oriskany.

Now, in the Navy, if your ship sails without you it is called "missing movement." It is very serious, like in special or general court-martial serious, and it shouldn't be any easier if you are an officer. There are probably only two more serious crimes as far as the Navy is concerned: one would be selling secrets to the enemy, like the Russians or the Chinese; the other would be the unauthorized commandeering of a naval vessel, like, for instance, the Oriskany's Number One officer's motorboat.

By the time I had been alerted by the bridge that we were being chased by one of the motorboats, Kincaid had climbed in front of the windshield of the motorboat's bridge and was standing on the front cabin. The bosun was out there with him and was holding onto the windshield with one hand and Kincaid's belt with the other while the coxswain steered the boat. Kincaid, erect as a ramrod, as they had taught him to be at the Academy, was signaling to the ship in semaphore.

Unfortunately, they didn't teach me semaphore at Stanford, and even though I was assistant Signals Officer, I didn't know Morse code or the flags. That's what you had enlisted men for. But even enlisted men didn't learn semaphore any more. In the modern Navy, if you are close enough to signal with arm waggles you're too damn close. However, the signals chief knew of an air division chief that allegedly knew semaphore, and he was immediately called to the signal bridge over the ship's 1-MC, now acting as a public address system, to see if he could read what Kincaid was trying to communicate.

I notified the bridge of our predicament, but within minutes the air division chief came storming up to the signal bridge and I turned the 36 power glasses over to him to see if he could read the message. Fortunately, he could—Kincaid was repeating, over and over, "Wait. Missed ship, traffic on bridge!"

I promptly informed the bridge of the source and contents of Kincaid's message, and within a minute the Captain's rich baritone voice came over the 1-MC, again in public address mode: "Now attention all hands! Attention all hands! This is the Captain speaking. The Oriskany has been challenged to an unofficial race out of San Francisco Bay by its Number One Motor Boat, which for the occasion is being captained by Ensign Carlton Kincaid. Ensign Kincaid has advised us through semaphore that he has missed movement 'because of traffic on the bridge.' For the race, the Oriskany will be captained by yours truly, Captain C. L. Westhofen, with Lieutenant Junior Grade Woody Thevenot at the con. NOW ALL HANDS NOT ATTENDING TO AT-SEA DETAIL WILL MAN THE RAILS!"

And man them did they! Fifteen hundred to two thousand screaming sailors jammed the starboard side of the ship while Woody had the Gun Boss extend a yard arm over the starboard side and drop a rope ladder down for Kincaid to climb when, *and if*, he ever caught the ship.

On the bridge, the old man was having a ball. As Woody related to me afterwards, the Captain told him, "Take a few turns off, Woody; we want to make a race of it." Usually the O-Boat steamed out of the harbor doing sixteen knots, but for today it slowed to twelve to give Kincaid a sporting chance. Of course, as the little boat came close, the wake from a 48,000 ton aircraft carrier doing twelve knots turned that glass-like Bay into a frothing inferno.

The motorboat bobbed up and down, and the Oriskany's wake broke over its bow, soaking both Kincaid and the bosun clutching Kincaid's belt.

Once they both slipped, and it looked like they might go into the drink, but they righted themselves and the motorboat inched ever closer to that tantalizing ladder.

As they came up alongside the ship, Woody later told us that the skipper gave him a wink, spun his index finger around several times, and said, "Turn it up a little, Woody."

The two ships matched knot for knot through the Golden Gate and out to the Coast Guard Station below Fort Funston. Then, as the ocean started to add its play to the waves from the ship, the motorboat took one last wave over its bow that soaked everyone on board the little boat and killed the engine. With a "Putt, putt, arrrge . . ." the little boat came down on its bow and was adrift in the water.

Kincaid, who had almost reached the ladder a dozen times, only to have the great carrier lurch forward, just seemed to melt from the onslaught of the waves and his disappointment. Those arms that had been gesticulating for the better part of an hour dropped to his side like lead, as one huge roar came up from the thousands of men lining the rails. Then, a number of them, expense be damned, hurled their caps into the sea, and they floated down around Kincaid like snow in the Rockies. One of the ship's photographers caught the scene with a powerful telephoto lens, and that picture of Kincaid, looking like a drowned rat with despair written on his face and hats flying around him and floating on the surface of the water, was the cover of that year's cruise book.

Three days later they flew Kincaid aboard on a COD flight. The Exec reported it immediately to the Captain, and the Captain's words to the Exec were all over the ship by dinner. The Captain merely looked up at the Exec and said, "So what!" But Kincaid, of course, was a ring knocker, as was the Captain, the Exec, and all the important officers on board. Nothing really happened to Kincaid. The Exec talked to the admiral about the boy and everyone decided that he really wasn't cut out for carrier duty. He probably would be better off on a smaller ship. After all, he had done so well for that brief period of command on the Number One Motorboat.

So it was that several weeks later Kincaid mysteriously got orders to a destroyer escort and left without even bothering to say good-bye to his "friends." But then, Kincaid probably thought of it as another promotion.

Chapter 9

HARRY "THE HOSS"

Harrison Lambert Richardson, III, who I introduced you to at the time of the Hills court-martial, was the Marine first lieutenant on board the Oriskany and second in command of the Marine detachment. Every U.S. "capital ship," such as an aircraft carrier, cruiser or battleship, has a Marine detachment. On the Oriskany, the Marine detachment consisted of 69 enlisted men and two officers, Harry and Captain Anderson, the defense and trial counsel, respectively, in the Hills court-martial.

Harry, or "Harry the Hoss," as he was occasionally called, was from Maine and looked like he was carved from a piece of that Maine granite. About 6'2", Harry was square jawed, with steel blue eyes that pierced right through you and short sandy hair. He had played tackle for the University of Maine, walked with a sort of pigeon toed gait that belied his mobility when he had to move, and was, by almost everyone's standards, a "hell-of-a-nice guy!" He had been in the Marines for some time and planned to make a career or it. He had fought in Korea with the First Marine Division, which had taken the brunt of the Chinese invasion when the Chinese Seventh Army, their most famous fighting unit, hit them at the Inchon Reservoir and they made their famous retreat. The Marines were badly bloodied in that retreat, but they carried out their dead and wounded and did so much damage to the Chinese Seventh Army in the course of the fight that it never appeared in Korea again.

My first contact with Harry was during the Hills court-martial where he was defense counsel. From that time forward we became fast friends, which was very flattering to me as one of the more junior ensigns aboard.

We would often take liberty together and, on one of our liberty stops in Okinawa, Harry conned me into renting a motorcycle with him to race up to the Inn of the Sixth Happiness made famous by James Michener and the movie of the same name. The Inn was located at the very northern tip of the island. It was a hot, mucky day, as were all of the days on Okinawa when it wasn't raining, and Harry and I were dressed in our cotton khaki shirtsleeve uniforms.

I had never ridden a motorcycle before, and the entire concept made me rather nervous, but Harry gave me a few rudimentary tips, pointed out the gear shift, clutch, brake and accelerator, assured me it was just like riding a bicycle, albeit a fat and fast one, and we were off.

We sped out of town. Well, Harry sped, I followed cautiously. Harry would get far enough ahead of me to worry that I would get lost and stop long enough for me to almost catch up. Then he would tear off again.

Once we left the main town the roads disintegrated to dirt ox paths wide enough for one vehicle at best, and dusty enough to force me to keep a respectful distance behind Harry even if I hadn't been scared out of my wits. The road north cut through fields of endless rice paddies, and was elevated about five feet above the level of the water in the paddies. If you have never seen rice grow, the fields are flooded and the rice takes root in the muddy soil, eventually growing until it reaches the harvest stage. The fields in Okinawa were fertilized by use of "night soil," i.e., human excrement collected overnight in slop pails and thrown into the paddies in the morning. Needless to say, the ride through these fields was odoriferous, to say the least.

I would generally keep to 35 miles an hour, fast enough it seemed to me on that dusty, pock marked road, but Harry kept turning around and yelling, "Come on, Smiley (Harry's nickname for me), pour on the gas!" or words to that affect.

At one narrow point in the road it turned slightly to the left into a grove of banyan trees that grew on either side of the road and created what looked like the entrance to a tunnel as the tops of the huge trees merged together. At that very instant as the road curved to the left Harry, now about 200 yards ahead of me, raced into the blackness created by the shadow from the trees.

It was just like a road-runner cartoon. Harry disappears into the entrance of the "tunnel," two hoots sound on a loud horn, and an old bus comes out of the "tunnel" the next instant loaded with suitcases strapped to its roof, taking up the entire road, but without Harry plastered to its grill—the usual finale to a road-runner cartoon.

I immediately slammed on my brakes and pulled over as close as I could get to the side of the road to let the bus pass. It barely cleared me.

I was at a total loss as to how the bus had missed Harry, and raced forward to find out what had happened to the fearless road warrior.

When I entered the "tunnel" and made the half turn to the left, I almost fell off the bike I started laughing so hard. To miss the bus, Harry had merely kept going straight instead of turning to the left. He missed the tree trunks and sped off into space and landed about 15 feet off the road, buried literally up to his ass in a rice paddy—and everything that went with it.

"Maltzman, stop laughing and get me out of here!" he cried. "I swear, I'm going to kill you when I get out of this!"

"Calm down, Harry," I yelled, "talk nice to me or you aren't ever getting out!"

We screamed back and forth at each other for about five minutes, which did have an appropriate effect. An old Okinawan farmer came by at about that time with his water buffalo pulling a wagonload of hemp. He heard the screaming, and stopped. He saw Harry's predicament immediately and indicated to me that he had a solution. Of course, he didn't speak English.

He went back to his load of hemp and started twining the stuff together into rope with an agility that belied his age and knurled hands, and after half an hour, with Harry still cursing from atop his bike, the Okinawan farmer had a sufficiently long piece of rope to reach Harry. He then tied one end to his water buffalo and threw the other end of the rope to Harry, who caught it deftly on the first try and tied it to his motorcycle. The ox-like animal then proceeded to pull Harry and the machine from the brown ooze with ease.

We thanked the farmer profusely and tried to give him some local currency and then some U.S. dollars, but he refused both with a gracious, albeit somewhat toothless, smile. His payment would be the story he could tell at his village that night about the big blond officer in his uniform buried in night soil to his waist.

That unfortunately ended Harry and my little excursion to the Inn of the Sixth Happiness. I tied the rope to the back of my motorcycle and proceeded to pull Harry's muck laden cycle and self back to the rental agency. This time he wasn't screaming at me to hurry.

They weren't particularly happy to see what Harry had done to their machine, but they took one look at Harry and the state of agitation he was in by that time and decided, correctly, not to complain. Fortunately for Harry, the rental agency also rented cars and had a wash rack in back. And that's what they did with Harry; they sent him and his motorcycle through the car wash. Harry elected not to pay extra for wax.

On the way back to the ship I agreed with Harry, after a little prodding, that I would not tell anyone about Harry's little mishap, but Harry was going to have to explain for himself why he looked like a drowned rat.

Chapter 10

TRYING TIMES

My tenure as legal officer was brief. Shortly after we returned Stateside, JAG finally sent out a designated legal officer for the ship and the Exec offered me my choice of new duty assignments. I chose communications, thinking that the communicators at least knew what was going on, and the Exec appointed me assistant signals officer, a job with which I was familiar from my previously assigned going-to-sea detail, and a communications watch officer. He also decided to send Harry and me off to the full seven-week course at Naval Justice School in Newport, Rhode Island, as soon as the next session started in October.

The Exec was as good as his word, and in late September Harry and I received orders to report to Naval Justice School for the session starting at the end of October.

We reported the Saturday before school was to start and elected to room together for the duration. On the weekends, Harry would go north to his family and friends in Maine and I would head south to New York where I had family and friends or north to Boston where I also had family and friends. During the week, however, we both worked hard and tried to do well in the course. I was determined that I was not going to miss 29 out of 30 questions this time around, and I didn't.

I came in number two in the class and Harry number three, only a whisker behind. Number one, however, was reserved for a Marine Captain who had worked his way up through the enlisted ranks (also referred to in the Marine Corps. as a "mustang" just as it is in the Navy) and had never had a day of college. He also drank his way through the school and never cracked a book. Harry had known the Marine Captain before from some prior duty assignment and we helped him bring a case of Jack Daniels up from his car on that first day at the school. Number One had probably one of the great natural legal minds, and for him Justice School was just a little diversion from the real business of being a Marine, but for the life of me I never saw him without a drink in his hand when we weren't in class and never saw him ever appear inebriated.

When we returned to the Oriskany, Lieutenant Bracken, the new legal officer, decided to use his new resources and had the Exec appoint Harry and me as trial counsel, each on one of the two special court-martial boards that the ship maintained.

On most ships that would have meant that we would only have occasional opportunities to use that which we had learned at Newport, as a special court-martial was a serious thing that was seldom used on most ships. However, that was on most ships, and this was the Oriskany with Bracken (read "Queeg" without the ball bearings) as Legal Officer. As Lieutenant Hewitt had told me that first day aboard the Oriskany, the Captain hated Captain's mast, the informal method of punishment used on most ships for minor infractions. More serious matters would be reserved for a summary court-martial or special court-martial.

Without Captain's mast, Bracken would get the Captain to give even minor infractions a court-martial. As Bracken considered the punishment that a summary court could mete out insufficient to put the fear of God (or Bracken, they were interchangeable in his mind) into the men, most got specials. This kept Harry and me constantly busy, especially after we left Alameda for a new cruise to WesPac in late February. Seldom would a week go by after we got into the Orient without at least one special court-martial, and Harry and I would usually both be involved regardless of to which court-martial board it was assigned.

This was so because the trial counsel on a special court-martial board was also the charging officer with the responsibility of calling in the accused, reading the charges to him, and explaining his rights under the UCMJ, the Uniform Code of Military Justice. One of his rights was to be defended by any qualified person of his choosing aboard the ship. That actually included enlisted men, but no one ever asked for an enlisted man to defend him and neither Harry nor I ever bothered to mention that fact to the accused. Instead, the accused would almost always ask the charging officer who was the best defense counsel on the ship. If I were the charging officer, I would always tell the accused it was Lieutenant Richardson, and if Harry were the charging officer he would refer them to me. As a result, in all but a few of the courts-martial tried aboard the Oriskany while Harry and I were on board, we alternated being trial and defense counsel in each trial. Both of our consciences were clear as we each considered the other the best on the ship and we loved the challenge of going at each other. Here was moot court with real stakes.

Our constant combat was made even more convenient when, after our return from Newport, a vacancy occurred in Harry's two-man bunkroom which, as described above, was on the 02 level immediately across from the wardroom and adjacent to the Exec's cabin, and Harry invited me to move in. This I readily did, as the room was far better than any junior ensign could expect, and Harry and I had taken a real liking to each other in spite of our differing backgrounds. Now, when one of us read the accused his rights the other was usually right there to advise the accused to keep his mouth shut. After the accused had left and we could argue about the case, we could really get into the spirit of things. Harry would generally refer to me as a "bleeding heart" when I had the defense and my favorite term for Harry was that he was an "intellectual mushroom" when he couldn't fathom one of my more esoteric legal concepts. When the roles were reversed, the invectives usually were as well.

Harry and I had some glorious battles during the year that followed our return from Newport. In one case, Harry was prosecuting one of his own Marines, a PFC named Turner, for being asleep at a special weapons station deep in the bowels of the ship. His particular guard post was located directly between the forward catapults. On the Oriskany the catapults were huge hydraulic devices that propelled a loaded fighter-bomber from a standing stop to takeoff speed in a distance of about 100 feet. More advanced carriers used steam as the propellant, but hydraulic catapults worked, although less reliably and with a significantly greater noise level.

"Special weapons" was one of those Navy euphemisms, and meant weapons that made very big bangs that were associated with mushroom clouds. When the Oriskany was finally finished in 1950 it had been modified from its original Essex Class configuration to include the capability of carrying nuclear weapons. Subsequently all of the Essex Class carriers were modified with the "Oriskany Conversion" so they could perform the same unthinkable task. None of the junior officers actually knew if we actually carried such devices of mass destruction on the Oriskany, but there certainly were several locations aboard ship that were called "special weapons spaces," and each merited its own Marine armed guard 24-7.

Unfortunately for Harry, air operations had been underway at the time that they alleged Turner was asleep at the particular special weapons space he was allegedly guarding. I took the court to view the scene during similar air operations, and no one could believe that the accused could have slept through the deafening racket made by the catapults. Further, the sergeant of the guard in making his rounds found Turner tilted back in his chair with his hat over his eyes and balancing his chair on two legs with his feet up on the hatchway leading into the area. The officer in charge of the ships dispensary (he was a staff officer, not a doctor) was on the court, and I convinced him (and he convinced the rest of the court) that it was impossible to balance that way if you are asleep.

Admittedly, the sergeant of the guard had first called the accused several times from above, had tried to get his attention on the intercom that connected one end of the hatchway with the other (I entered evidence that it frequently didn't work) and had rattled and then climbed down a clanging ladder to reach Turner without alerting his attention or getting him to lift his cap off his eyes or return his chair to all four legs. The court concluded that Turner wasn't much of a guard, but they were not convinced beyond a reasonable doubt that he was asleep.

Harry, of course, was beside himself. After the trial I took Turner aside and told him that if he ever did something like that again I would personally prosecute him and hang his ass.

About two weeks later the same sergeant of the guard called me in my room to tell me that Turner was asleep on a mess deck table outside another special weapons station that he was supposed to be guarding. This station was off the enlisted mess deck, and he asked me what he should do. I immediately contacted the ship's photography department, and they had one of their photography mates run down to the area with high speed movie film. Next I went to the table on which Turner was asleep and, with the camera running, removed his gun and his hat. Then I woke him up.

This time I prosecuted, Harry refused to defend so the regular defense counsel assigned to my court defended, and Turner got six, six and a BCD (six months in the brig, six months loss of pay and a bad conduct discharge). I was true to my threat and hung his ass.

On another occasion I was playing bridge with the senior medical officer, Captain James, who actually outranked the Captain of the Oriskany in seniority. I was about to defend a Seaman named Ross for being AWOL and was talking about the case when James volunteered that, in his opinion, Ross was crazy.

"Crazy, why do you say that?" I asked.

"Anyone who breaks the rules around this place is crazy," James said. "The rules are so very simple, and if you follow them the Navy will take care of you just fine. If you break them they hang your ass. Everyone knows that, so you have to be crazy to violate the rules."

The next morning I sent Ross to Captain James for a complete physical. I told Ross to tell the doctor his reason for going AWOL, which was the usual silly thing that you hear in these cases. Sure enough, James came back with a written report saying that Ross was crazy and recommending that he be detached from the ship and sent to a shore establishment with mental facilities. When the court-martial came on, I pleaded Ross "not guilty by reason of insanity" and Captain James was my chief witness. Naturally, Ross was found "not guilty by reason of insanity" and shipped off to Letterman Naval Hospital where they kept him for months trying to figure out why he had been sent there in the first place. They finally sent him back to the ship without, according to Ross, their having given him any treatment at all.

I got the next two defendants I represented off the same way, but by my fourth try Harry and the entire court had concluded that if anyone was crazy on the ship, it was Captain James, and my insanity strategy never worked again.

Our most controversial court-martial was Conners, a black airman in one of the air divisions arrested in Po City outside the Subic Bay Naval Base for allegedly pulling a switchblade on some members of a Filipino gang. Harry was the trial counsel and pitched me for the defense, to which Conners agreed and I, as usual, accepted.

Conners was a real anomaly in the Navy. By all odds he should have had no hope for a future in the service, but he had to that point beaten the odds. He had a GCT score (the standardized intelligence test given to each prospective enlisted man when he applies to join the Navy) of 33, the lowest possible passing grade, which made him a marginal admit and someone who usually would be suited only for the most menial jobs with no hope of any significant advancement. But Conners had somehow become a mechanic and had proven himself skilled, reliable, and efficient. He also was in a division with a great deal of racial tension and had acted as an ameliorating force among the blacks, arguing constantly that they had a better deal in the Navy than they ever would get outside and they shouldn't blow it by screwing up, mouthing off or getting in trouble. Indeed, he had never screwed up, mouthed off (except in a positive fashion), or gotten in trouble. Instead, he had worked his butt off studying for the promotion exam and had recently passed his 3rd class petty officer's exam, an unbelievable accomplishment if his GCT of 33 was accurate, which it probably was not.

On the day in question, he had gone on liberty with another black from his division, a notorious "bad ass" named Irwin who had been constantly in trouble. They got themselves into a difficult situation with a Filipino street gang, an altercation followed, and when the shore patrol showed up one of the Filipino's was cut, but not too seriously, and a bloody switchblade was on the ground. Irwin immediately claimed that he was innocent and that it was Conners who pulled the knife. Conners neither admitted nor denied the allegation, the shore patrol screwed up any hope of getting prints off the knife, and Conners was charged with assault with a deadly weapon and possession of a switchblade.

The assault charge was very serious. On most ships it would have been sent to the beach for a general court-martial, but Bracken liked to keep everything at home. "Take care of your own dirty laundry," he would pontificate. So the charges were assigned to Harry's special court-martial board and I got another juicy defense.

At first Conners was reluctant to talk to me. To him it still seemed that I somehow must represent the enemy. I called in Conners' chief and had the chief explain to him that his defense counsel was his friend and that anything he told me was privileged and would go no further. Only then did he loosen up and tell me what really happened, which was exactly what I had already surmised.

It was Irwin, of course, that pulled the knife, but Conners refused to "rat" on a friend. I tried to explain to Conners that Irwin was no friend, Irwin had ratted on him with a dirty lie and he had done nothing.

"I know, Sir, but I got to lead my life the way I think I got to do, and Irwin, he got to lead his life. He shouldn't o' done that, but my mom taught me that two wrongs don't make a right."

Try as I could to convince him that this wasn't a "wrong," Conners refused to get on the stand and tell what had really happened. I therefore was forced to defend him by attacking Irwin and his credibility, and that is exactly what I did.

At the trial, I cross-examined Irwin mercilessly but was really unable to crack him or break his story. He insisted that he never carried a knife, had often seen Conners with that switchblade, and that Conners had repeatedly bragged how he had cut people with that knife back home.

I then paraded practically everyone in the division that could walk, starting with Conners' division officer, then his chief, then each petty officer and finally all of the men who worked or slept near him. All testified that they knew Irwin and that he had a reputation in the division as a liar and a troublemaker. Many testified that they had seen Irwin with a switchblade knife that looked like the one in evidence, and all said that they had never seen Conners with one. No one in the division had ever heard Conners utter any type of violent statements or assert that he had ever used that knife, or any knife, on anyone. Finally, the testimony was getting so repetitious that the presiding officer on the court asked me how many more witnesses I had that would give testimony in a similar vein.

"About fifty," I replied, exaggerating a bit.

At that the presiding officer asked me not to bring them and the court would take into account that everyone in the division would give substantially similar testimony. So I rested.

A special court-martial determines the guilt phase first, then the penalty phase. The court was out for almost two hours, the longest Harry and I had ever known a court-martial to deliberate. When they finally came back in, they announced a guilty verdict on possession of the knife but a not guilty verdict on the more serious assault charge.

But that was enough to probably break Conners spirit and ruin a potentially fine enlisted man's career. He would lose his promotion now and would most likely spend time in the brig, which would probably turn him the wrong way forever.

In the penalty phase I again paraded my witnesses to tell what a great enlisted man Conners was and to plead for leniency. The court gave him a light sentence, a month in the brig, but that would automatically kill his promotion, and I was very upset.

During the course of this trial Harry and I fought like tigers. I kept calling Harry an "intellectual mushroom" for not seeing that this kid was totally innocent and this miscarriage would break him, and Harry kept repeating his "bleeding heart liberal" refrain.

After the penalty verdict, Lieutenant Commander Wilson, a chubby engineering officer who had presided over the court, came up to both of us who were standing together with a big smile on his face and said: "You boys both did a great job, and Dick, I don't mind telling you, a couple of the boys on the court voted for acquittal on all charges."

This was a five-man court and it took two-thirds to convict.

"Commander," I replied, "if two voted for acquittal you didn't have the two thirds necessary for conviction, Conners should have been acquitted."

"What are you talking about," he said with a confused look on his face, "isn't three out of five two-thirds?"

As Harry and I looked at him aghast, Bracken, who had overheard the conversation, came running up and said to Wilson, "Shut up if you know what's good for you! Members of a court-martial board are not allowed to reveal their deliberations to anyone (this happened to be true). If I tell the Captain about this he'll have your ass."

At this Wilson turned white and literally ran from the scene. I immediately jumped on Bracken and insisted that he tell the Captain what had happened and call this an acquittal. Much to my surprise, Harry jumped right in and started arguing even more vehemently than I did that Conners was not convicted and should be released immediately and the charges dismissed.

Now it was Bracken's turn to call both of us "bleeding hearts," and he would hear none of it. Harry said that he and I would take this up to the Captain, and Bracken told us that he would deny that Wilson had told them how the balloting had gone, and he would make sure that neither Wilson nor any other member of the court would ever repeat that story.

Harry and I were beside ourselves with anger. Harry liked to win, but he was from Maine and only wanted to win fair. As far as he was concerned, this was a miscarriage of justice and he was too moral a person to sit quietly by and see that happen. The two of us went down to our cabin and immediately started typing up an appeal to the Captain in which we explained what happened and requested that he reverse the decision. We then went to Conners' division officer who gladly endorsed our request and added detail for the Captain explaining that Conners was a terrific sailor.

Then the three of us sent our petition up to the Captain and asked for an audience. Within half an hour Bracken's name was being paged over the 1-MC directing him to go to the Captain's at-sea cabin. About 20 minutes later, the three of us were called to the Captain's cabin.

When we arrived, Bracken was sitting there with a smug grin on his face, and the Captain looked furious. He then proceeded to lash out at all three of us for being "nothing but a bunch of damn bleeding hearts" (that term again) and unprofessional, and accused us of trying to undermine discipline about the ship. He then started a harangue on the importance of strict discipline on a military ship, and ended by telling us that he didn't want to see any more "crap like this" and, if our story got spread around, he would know where it came from and would take appropriate measures.

The three of us walked out of that conference literally shaking with anger and white as ghosts. I had often heard the joke that Naval Intelligence was an oxymoron. Now all three of us came to the realization that, in this case at least, so was Naval Justice.

Chapter 11

ENSIGN CHERRY

Not all the new ensigns who reported aboard the Oriskany were ship's company. Attached to the ship when she redeployed to Westpac in February after our return from Justice School was Rear Admiral Ira E. Hobbs, Commander Carrier Division Three (in Navy parlance, ComCarDiv-3), the admiral in charge of the two-carrier task force assigned to the 7th Fleet. With the admiral came a complete staff, including a number of officers who were intended to augment the Oriskany's own staff in tasks made more burdensome by the admiral's presence. One of these was communications. Having an admiral on board greatly increased the amount of radio traffic, particularly coded traffic, the ship sent and received. The admiral, therefore, supplied several officers to assist the ship's communications staff.

When we reached Yokosuka a brand new ensign reported on board for assignment to the admiral's staff. His name was Paul Cherry, a short, pudgy, effeminate, cherubic young man who spoke in a high pitched whine and whose last name was so appropriate that no one ever called him by his first name or anything else. He had come from the Midwest, attended some small, local liberal arts college close to his home before going to Officers' Candidate School ("OCS") to avoid the draft, and was literally the innocent abroad, or in this case aboard. He had never been away from home before going to OCS and wrote separate letters to both of his parents several times each day, and each of them must have responded in kind. Seldom was there a mail call where Cherry didn't receive his own mailbag, all from his mother and father.

Cherry reported on board shortly after the Oriskany arrived in Yokosuka from Alameda via Hawaii. He had just graduated from OCS, which did not operate on the same June graduation schedule as the NROTC programs and Annapolis, and spit out graduates every 90 days all year long. On reporting aboard he was assigned to the staff junior officer bunkroom, one of several bunkrooms reserved just for junior officers on the admiral's staff when the admiral was on board. It was located on the 03 level immediately adjacent to the Captain's in-port cabin.

The Captain of the Oriskany, and probably the Captains on all capital ships (cruisers, battleships and carriers), had two cabins, one a closet sized room located immediately behind (aft of) the bridge that he used when the ship was at sea, and the other that he used when the ship was in port. His in-port cabin was a large suite with beautiful paneling, lovely pictures of ships in the days of sail, a separate galley and dining room for entertaining, and a luxurious sitting room complete with carpeting on the deck (i.e., the floor). It is here that the Captain, in great comfort, slept, usually ate, worked and entertained when in port.

Immediately upon reporting on board, Cherry, still in uniform, decided to defer unpacking and return to the "beach", as dry land was generally referred to in the Navy, to inspect Yokosuka. Proceeding alone, the first thing he came upon after leaving the gate was the notorious street inappropriately nicknamed "Thieves Alley" by the sailors who frequented the street. It was a misnomer because the Japanese were anything but thieves. You couldn't leave your wallet or forget your change but some young urchin would come running after you for two blocks yelling, "Hey Joe, you forgot somethin'," return the lost item and refuse to accept any reward. If you were done with your newspaper, forget about leaving it on the table with your used coffee cup; the urchin would be chasing you with your paper five minutes later. There were no thieves on Thieves Alley.

But there were hustlers aplenty, selling everything from junky souvenirs to cameras and Japan's then idea of home appliances and electronics. There was one very nice store, the second on the right after you entered Thieves Alley, which sold musical instruments.

Cherry was a musician. He apparently had played the organ in church back home, and the first thing his eyes saw as he passed the music store was a used organ in the window for $25 U.S. What a bargain. He went in and played it, it sounded fine, and he put down a deposit. Then he rushed back to the ship for a work detail to retrieve his purchase.

Now as everyone in the Navy except possibly a brand new ensign out of OCS knows, every capital ship displays honors to visiting dignitaries that come aboard. Each capital ship when in port maintains immaculately dressed young sailors, called "side boys," in readiness on the quarterdeck for just this purpose. If a dignitary comes on board, he is piped aboard by the bosun of the watch blowing his bosun's pipe and enters between two phalanxes of erect side boys saluting for the duration of the whistle. The importance of the dignitary determines the number of side boys. The President of the United States or any other head of state would require eight, but as neither the President nor Emperor Hirohito came on board very often, six side boys would usually do to cover any exigency. They would sit on a bench immediately next to the gangway to be readily available if needed.

Back came Cherry to the ship still in his uniform. When he came off the gangway the officer of the deck was in his office writing up his log and failed to notice him. But Cherry noticed the side boys. "You," he commanded, "Attention!" The side boys stood in an instant at attention. "Right face!" Cherry ordered. They turned right, which put them on a straight line with the gangway. "Forward march!" came next, and march they did.

Now the one thing that is drilled into every enlisted man is that you don't question an order from a superior officer, and this pudgy little man with the squeaky voice was dressed in the uniform of a superior officer. So off the six side boys marched in single file, down the gangway, across the Yokosuka Naval Base, through the main gate and right up Thieves Alley to the second store on the right.

Of course you don't use side boys very often, even on a modern aircraft carrier. Watch after watch will go by with no need for side boys. Some OOD's are lenient and let the side boys read while they are waiting for some important visitor who never comes, but usually they just sit there in a vague, semi-comatose state. There is, however, one thing that any officer that has ever stood OOD in port can almost guarantee; if someone walks off with your side boys, an admiral will come by to visit your ship.

So it was on this bright, fall day in Yokosuka that a three-star admiral, Commander, Naval Forces, Japan ("ComNavJap" in Navy shorthand) decided to come down and visit his old friend ComCarDiv-3, only to find that he couldn't come on board because no one could find the side boys to pipe the admiral aboard. The 1-MC, the ship's public address system, paged them vehemently and often, the Captain and the Oriskany's own admiral, Admiral Hobbs, were screaming at the OOD on the quarterdeck, and it was finally necessary to grab the cleanest looking six sailors that could be found, and they weren't very clean at that, to provide the appropriate honors for the visiting admiral.

ComNavJap was already on board, the commotion had died down, and everyone was just plain limp on the quarterdeck when Cherry and six immaculate sailors hove into view carrying what appeared to all to be a small organ. They marched onto the quarterdeck to an apoplectic OOD, but Cherry seemed totally immune to criticism. He insisted on having his men (he had somehow become very possessory over them) carry the organ up to his cabin; after all, he was on the admiral's staff! And so they did.

The side boys placed the organ at Cherry's direction against the wall next to the bunk that had been assigned to him. It just happened, however, that was the very wall that separated the Staff junior officer bunkroom from the Captain's in-port cabin. The organ stayed there, untouched, until about 0200 hours (2 a.m.) when Cherry, homesick, jet-lagged and unable to sleep, decided that a little organ recital would be just what he needed to put him in a restful mood. Oblivious to at least a dozen other sleeping officers in the bunkroom, Cherry proceeded to start playing some nice restful Bach. Immediately his fellow staff officers started to groan and scream, but Cherry was incapable of comprehending that others would not be as moved by a little Bach at two in the morning as was he.

The problem probably would have devolved into physical force and a small lynching of a short fat ensign, shortening this chapter greatly, had not one of the other officers in the bunkroom come to the realization at about that time that the Captain, on the other side of the wall, must by now be having conniptions. This message was, of course, communicated to all of the other officers who, with smiles on their faces, tried to shut out the sound of Bach with their pillows.

The Captain was, however, a light sleeper, and the sound of Cherry's organ caused him to shoot out of bed and search his suite for the source of the offending noise. He finally narrowed it down to one wall, but could not for the life of him conclude what the noise was. One thing for sure, the Captain had never heard Bach, at least not Bach filtered through a steel bulkhead at 0200.

So the Captain called Damage Control Central ("DCC"), the gnomes of the ship that fix anything in an instant or less. Twenty minutes later the Captain had retreated to his at-sea cabin and a virtual army of technicians was tearing his in-port cabin apart trying to find the offending pipes that were making that disturbing noise.

Each morning the technicians would leave, convinced that whatever the problem was had been solved, and the Captain would return.

Each night Cherry would again serenade his rapidly diminishing bunkmates with an organ recital. And each night, the Captain would call Damage Control Central and move back to his at-sea cabin. And each night, DCC would again have its army of gnomes tear the Captain's cabin apart without finding anything.

By the third night, several things had been accomplished. For one, Cherry now resided alone in a Staff junior officer bunkroom big enough for 12 officers. The others had all moved out into other junior officer bunkrooms throughout the ship, including the one I had inhabited before moving in with Harry, which is how I first heard the story. For another, the Captain was now in one continuously terrible mood from lack of sleep and anger at DCC for not being able to control the noise in his pipes.

"If you can't find one lousy noise," he was overheard shouting at the Chief Engineering Officer, "how the hell do you expect to keep this ship afloat if we ever take a hit?"

The third thing that had been accomplished was that the ship was involved in one giant conspiracy. Everyone on board the ship knew about Cherry's post-midnight organ recitals except the Captain, the Chief Engineering Officer, and the DCC personnel, and the other officers weren't so sure that the Chief Engineering Officer and DCC personnel weren't in on the whole thing, too. The Exec may have been kept out of the loop as well, but that is pure conjecture.

The Captain never learned the truth, and for the entire time that the admiral's staff was on board he was denied the use of his in-port cabin for sleeping, and at times that "mysterious noise" would even drive him out during the day.

Cherry, of course, was assigned to communications. The "of course" is because it must have been obvious to anyone with eyes that Cherry was the biggest security risk on the ship, and all the ship's secrets were in the Communications Department. All it would take would be a Russian Mata Hari (who in this case might not necessarily have to be female) to get Cherry into the pad, get his picture in pari delicto, then threaten to show it to his mother or, better yet, the Chaplain, and Cherry would crack.

Not that it really made any difference. Cherry never learned much about communications. His days were filled practicing his organ for his Sunday recitals during church services or reading, when he ran out of letters from home, a good book. Actually, *The* Good Book. Anyway, he could usually be found carrying a bible with him wherever he went.

Cherry was not on the Oriskany very long. Halfway through our tour in WesPac the admiral announced that he intended to move his headquarters to the Hornet, the Oriskany's sister ship which was cruising with her. Admirals are given the prerogative of locating their staff on any ship they wish, but if his carrier division consists of a larger carrier and a smaller carrier, he almost always places his staff (and of course, himself) on the larger carrier. With two identical carriers to choose from, the admiral would usually divide his time.

This presented a logistic problem for Cherry; how was he to get his organ over to the Hornet? He presented the question to me one night while we were working in crypto. I jokingly suggested that Cherry go to the carpenter shop and ask them to crate the organ up and paint the box olive green, the color used on crates of cryptographic equipment, then label the crate "TOP SECRET—CRYPTOGRAPHIC EQUIPMENT," stick an imaginary serial number on it, and address it to the Communications Officer on the Hornet.

"Even when he opens it he'll just think it's a piece of ultra-top secret cryptographic equipment and keep it until the admiral arrives," I told him. Of course, I was kidding.

Cherry's world started to unfold around him shortly before the admiral's move to the Hornet. To celebrate the end of their stay on the Oriskany, the admiral's Chief-of-Staff planned a big party for all of the admiral's staff officers and some of their ship's company counterparts at a notorious strip joint in Yokosuka named the Tradewinds. All the ship's company communications officers, including me, were invited and all who were not on duty went. I, as well as almost all of the other officers on the ship, had been to the Tradewinds—and it was there that I for the first time had seen strippers take it all off. No G-strings or pasties for these wholesome little Japanese girls at the Tradewinds, no sir!

Cherry went to the party, but he had no idea what kind of entertainment or female anatomy lessons the Tradewinds provided homesick sailors. But he learned. The next day he went to see the admiral, who had not been to the party, and was let past the Marine guard who recognized him as a regular communications messenger, which he was.

Once inside the admiral's cabin he told the admiral all about the terrible party that the Staff had held the night before and how the Chief-of-Staff had been present and had appeared to enjoy the entire event.

"Ensign," said the admiral, "I wasn't there so I can't judge whether that party was a good party for morale or a bad party for morale, but I will say this, it sounds to me like you wouldn't be too interested in any party like that, so why don't you not go next time."

When Cherry started to argue, the admiral simply told him "That's all, Ensign!" and dismissed him.

The story didn't die there. Cherry started complaining to everyone on the ship that would listen to him, starting with the Chaplain and working down. As he worked down from the Chaplain, however, sympathy was hard to find.

It just happened that the night the Oriskany pulled out of Yokosuka and steamed south to meet up with the Hornet and transfer the admiral and his Staff, I had just finished reading *"Mr. Roberts."* It also just happened that I had been drinking with Harry Richardson in our stateroom and we were both three sheets to the wind. Somehow the scene in *"Mr. Roberts"* where they threw the Captain's palm tree overboard came to mind, and I thought of Cherry's $25 organ. A light bulb went off. Cherry was on watch just then, so why not throw his organ overboard. That would solve Cherry's problem of how to get it to the Hornet—it could float there! To make it totally fair, we reached into our wallets and put together $25 to leave in place of the organ.

We gathered a few other conspirators, who thought the idea high camp, and off we went. We found the Staff junior officer bunkroom without any problem, and as Cherry had driven out all of the other occupants with his nightly serenades, the room was empty. But there was no organ! It was gone. I later discovered that Cherry had it packed as a piece of crypto gear, in an olive green crate with a fictitious serial number on it, and it had been sent over to the Hornet with the rest of the admiral's equipment several days before, just as I had, in jest, suggested.

The Hornet's Communications Officer was in for a big surprise!

Once Cherry left, Damage Control Central was able to fix the noise in the Captain's in-port cabin permanently, and life returned pretty much to normal, or at least to Navy normal, on the Oriskany.

But not so on the Hornet, where Cherry's career was brief and memorable.

It seemed that their first port of call after reporting to the Hornet was good old Yokosuka, and to celebrate the beginning of their stay on board, the admiral's Chief-of-Staff planned another big party for all of the admiral's staff officers and some of their new ship's company counterparts at that same notorious Tradewinds where the previous party had been held. Included was my old friend Tom Timberlake from whom the remainder of the story derives.

With the build up Cherry had given the last party, this time the admiral went, too.

But in spite of the admiral's warning to him, so did Cherry.

The following morning, communications clip board in hand, Cherry charged past the Marine guard in front of the admiral's cabin and interrupted the admiral in the middle of a conference with the Captains of both carriers and the commanders of the cruiser and destroyer divisions that made up the balance of the 7th Fleet.

With tears running down his face, Cherry let fly at the admiral: "Admiral, I could not believe my eyes last night. After I warned you about that last party at the Tradewinds, you went to this one. I saw you laughing and applauding at those awful, disgusting girls when they took off their clothes. I used to respect you, but I'll never be able to respect you again. You are a disgrace! How do you expect me to be able to salute you now? How could . . . ."

Before he had finished the admiral was across the room and to the door. He hurled it open and yelled at his Marine guard, "PRIVATE, GET IN HERE AND DRAW YOUR GUN; I WANT YOU TO PUT THAT MAN UNDER ARREST, IMMEDIATELY!" pointing at Cherry, and getting red as a beet.

The Marine came in immediately with gun drawn and grabbed Cherry by one arm. He then requested permission of the admiral to call the sergeant of the guard to assist with the arrest, which the admiral immediately gave.

Within minutes the sergeant of the guard arrived, and seconds later the ship's legal officer, who had been alerted by the sergeant, followed him. They took a limp and sobbing Cherry away, and he spent the next several days in the ship's brig while the admiral and his Chief-of Staff tried to decide what to do with him. Finally, everyone agreed that court-martialing Cherry would accomplish little, and he was given a medical discharge as being "unfit for Naval Service."

There wasn't a junior officer on board the Oriskany that couldn't have told the admiral that the first day Cherry arrived on board.

Chapter 12

PASS THE ICE CREAM & CRACKERS

LTJG William Joseph "Billy-Joe" Beauregard, "No regard" as he was known to his "friends," was Louisiana's contribution to the officer corps aboard the Oriskany via the NROTC program at the University of Oklahoma. He had graduated the year before me, and claimed to have been a quarterback at Oklahoma, a claim that seemed far-fetched in view of his relatively small size and general ineptitude. He was a journeyman gunnery officer and, while certainly never up to the fiascos that Kincaid had performed in his short but memorable stint aboard the ship, he had his own reputation to live up to.

One was his craving for ice cream. He loved ice cream, and could never get enough of it. This, of course, was well known to the Filipino stewards who waited on the officers in the Ward Room. Thus it was that each time there was ice cream for desert, each officer at Beauregard's table would receive two huge scoops, but Beauregard would get only one. He would then go ballistic, demanding to see the Chief Steward to complain. The Chief Steward would immediately send their table steward back to investigate and "take care of Mr. Beauregard!" The steward would see the offending dish of ice cream and whisk it away to the kitchen while Beauregard sat looking very important and *very* annoyed. Ten minutes would pass while the rest of the officers at the table finished their ice cream. Then the table steward would return with a piece of yesterday's cake or pie or what-have-you.

"WHERE THE HELL IS MY ICE CREAM!" Beauregard would scream.

"So sorry, Mr. 'Blowregard' (actually, the steward could speak perfectly except when he talked to Beauregard), all out of ice cream; bring you cake, instead."

Beauregard would go ballistic, but the ice cream was, indeed, all gone, even the scoop that he sent back. They were also never able to explain what happened to that scoop, except that it ". . . was now gone!" Beauregard would have nothing left but his cake or pie or what-have-you.

If it happened once, it would be funny. That it happened over and over again when they served ice cream left most of us wondering where Beauregard was when wit was passed out, and how the hell he ever could have memorized a play-book as quarterback at the University of Oklahoma.

The other problem with Beauregard was his general level of intolerance. There was one black officer on board, a career pilot stuck with his stint of sea duty named Bill Washington. Bill was very popular with all the junior officers with the exception of Beauregard, and he was also very tall. So tall, in fact, that he was in danger of hitting his head whenever he passed through one of the watertight hatches that separated compartments and proliferated on a carrier. To protect his head, therefore, he almost always wore a battle helmet when walking around the ship, and you could hear him coming from half a ship away by the constant clank-clank-clank of his helmet hitting the overhead of each hatch.

Even the fellows from the South, like Sommers, liked Bill, but Beauregard had the most unusual habit of never sitting down at the same table as Washington in the wardroom, which had open seating for everyone except the Exec. As Beauregard was not held in much regard by most of us junior officers, and thus his nickname, we were quick to seek out Bill and sit with him if he got into the wardroom first. It was insurance against having to listen to Beauregard regale us with tales of his football heroics at Oklahoma.

—————

My family was nominally Jewish, although my father prided himself on being a practicing agnostic and we seldom had any formal affiliation. I had no religious training and had never had a bar mitzvah.

However, I never denied my religious heritage and was one of several Jewish officers on the Oriskany, some of whom were quite open about their religious affiliation and others were very circumspect about it. I went out of my way to let people know I was Jewish; if they had a problem with that I would have preferred to know it sooner rather than later.

A capital ship, such as a carrier, usually had two chaplains on board, a Catholic chaplain and a Protestant. On the Oriskany the Protestant Chaplain was a lieutenant commander and the Catholic Chaplain was a much younger lieutenant, Father Ryan, who was Boston-Irish to the core and the brogue.

Father Ryan was a great boon to morale and took charge of all of the intra-mural sports on board and conducted an evening radio broadcast in his crisp Boston-Irish accent over the 1-MC. He would read the news off the wire services and give the ship's company a thumbnail sketch of what was going on back home and in the world at large.

On one of these broadcasts Father Ryan announced: "Ah, and here is a report from those fine, democracy loving people of Dublin, Ireland. They have just elected their first Jewish mayor, Bobby Brisco, now isn't that wonderful, now!"

That night after the broadcast Father Ryan happened to sit down at my table directly opposite me.

"What is this I hear about the people of Dublin electing a Jewish mayor, Father?" I asked.

"Ah, Dick," he replied, "it's true, it's true; but it could never happen in Boston!"

The table broke up in laughter, but I, who had lived in the Boston area for part of my life, knew the Padre was probably right, at least in the 1950s.

One day shortly after that exchange with Father Ryan, an enlisted man approached me and asked me if he could ask a personal question.

"Ask away," I replied, "but there is no assurance I will answer it."

"Are you Jewish, Sir?"

"Yes I am, but what business is it of yours?" I replied.

"Well, sir, so am I, and so are about 50 other enlisted men aboard, and we need an officer to sponsor a Passover dinner. If you would sponsor it, the rabbi at Yokosuka can get us all the trimmings for a real Passover feast aboard. It would include matzo, gefilte fish, matzo ball soup, chicken, the works—even Manischewitz wine."

"Well, I'm Jewish, but I'm not very observant," I replied, "and while I certainly have attended a number of Seders, I don't know anything about leading one."

"You don't have anything to worry about, sir, we have a steamfitter from Brooklyn that is as good as a rabbi and he'll do the whole deal for us; all you have to do is sponsor it."

So sponsor it I did, and with the help of Father Ryan and the Protestant Chaplain on board, Lieutenant Commander York, we made arrangements with the Jewish Chaplain at Yokosuka to provide the ship with a complete Passover service package.

When it comes to attending to religious concerns, the Navy performs like a champ. Within two weeks of putting in our request, they flew onto the ship on one of its regular COD flights boxes full of Kosher chicken soup with matzo balls prepared by a delicatessen in Manhattan, gefilte fish from the same source, cases of Manischewitz wine, cases of frozen chickens, everything kosher for Passover, over 50 Haggadahs, the Passover prayer books used for the Passover service, and complete instructions to the ship's cooks on how to prepare and serve everything in accordance with Jewish tradition.

Never one to miss on opportunity, I decided to invite some of my friends to the dinner if they wished to attend, and they all did. I also invited the Captain, Exec, CAG, and all of the department heads and Squadron Commanders on aboard. I felt that it wouldn't hurt if they witnessed a Passover celebration, and I did have fond memories of the Passover celebrations at my grandmother's house when I lived in Boston as a small boy. In addition, two other officers asked if they could attend, and of course I extended them an invitation. It wasn't until many months later that I discovered that both of them were also Jewish.

The service was held in the ship's library, which was under the control of the ship's Chaplains. The Navigation Department was called upon to give us the exact time of sunset for our longitude and latitude, and on that very minute the festivities got underway. The steamfitter from Brooklyn, Kramer, was as good as his reputation and presided over the services most efficiently, i.e. he got through the service quickly and the assembled sailors and officers got down to the eating and legal drinking as quickly as possible. While Navy Regs prohibited drinking aboard ship, there was a specific exception for alcohol used in religious observances. Thus, the Manischewitz was legal even though it was still Manischewitz. However, when even Ripple is illegal, Manischewitz that can legally be consumed can taste awfully good, and we all had a great time.

In spite of all my additional invitees, there was plenty of food left over. The rabbi at Yokosuka must have thought that the Oriskany was part of the Israeli Navy, and everyone took food back to share with their friends or to eat later.

Harry, who was invited, came and participated in the litany of the Haggadah with gusto. When the service and dinner ended, he grabbed several boxes of matzo as he and I were leaving and told me, "Dick, I'm going to make a good Jew out of you if it has to kill me, and for the next eight days you're not eating any leavened bread; its matzo time for you, my friend."

Next morning, good to his word, Harry grabbed a box of matzo as we headed into the wardroom for breakfast. As luck would have it, Washington had the duty and Beauregard sat down at our table, right across from Harry. When Harry took out the matzo, Beauregard turned ashen white. When Harry buttered up a big square for himself and started to raise it to his mouth, Beauregard became convulsive and reached across the table, grabbing a surprised Harry's wrist.

"DON'T EAT THAT, HARRY," he screamed, "THAT'S JEW FOOD!

The sad part was, he meant it. Harry, meanwhile, loved it. As Beauregard protested, Harry started eating the matzo. As he ate he rolled his eyes, extolling how delicious it was (it of course wasn't).

"Want some, Lieutenant?" Harry asked politely after several bites.

Beauregard didn't reply, but just shook his head. At that, everyone else at the table insisted on trying some matzo. As they broke off pieces and started eating, Beauregard leapt up from the table, left his half eaten breakfast, and literally ran from the wardroom.

After he left Harry turned to me with a huge grin and said, "Now that really was a religious experience. God knew what he was doing when he instructed us to eat matzo!"

Chapter 13

HARRY THE HUCK HUNTER

Marine PFC William Small was, in fact, small. His nickname in the Marine Detachment and on the signal bridge, where he took to hanging out when not on duty, was "'Ittlebit," and he was definitely one of the smallest Marines I had ever seen. He must have worn elevator shoes when he enlisted, and then the corpsman that measured him for his physical must have been myopic.

I first came upon him on the signal bridge where I continued as assistant signals officer even after my short tour as Legal Officer expired. At the time, Small had been in the Marines for eight years and had never risen in rank above a PFC, but kept grousing that had he joined the Navy instead he would by this time have been a 1st class petty officer. He kept threatening that on his next "re-up" he was transferring to the Navy. My only thought on that recurring theme was "God save the Navy!"

When I later started rooming with Harry, 'Ittlebit's boss, I would often mention to Harry the apparition of the miniature Marine that haunted the signal bridge, and Harry would just shrug and give me that Maine granite look. Harry could do a great shrug and an even better stony-faced stare.

In May of 1956, the Oriskany pulled into Subic Bay, a United States Navy base on the Philippine Island of Luzon for some much needed repairs and a little R&R for the crew. Unfortunately, there was little to do at the base itself. Rest was possible, but recreation, at least legal recreation, was hard to find. It was constantly hot and muggy, even at night. The officers' club at Subic Bay wasn't air conditioned, and the Oriskany's officers were really better off sneaking beers aboard ship (horrors!) and drinking them in their cabin. At least the portions of the ship occupied by the officers and the crew had air conditioning.

There was a town of sorts outside the gates that was called Po City, although that was probably just an appellation created by the sailors and airedales that tended to frequent its haunts. Against Harry's more experienced advice, I made a quick surveillance and found it a filthy hovel of shacks, bars and whorehouses, with hardly a paved street to be found. The only reliable thing about the citizens of this area was that the boys all appeared to be pimps with accommodating sisters and the sisters all had the clap. Sick call was no joy when the ship left Subic Bay, but except for the more adventure-some flyboys, most of the junior officers stayed clear of the beach.

But as mentioned, 'Ittlebit was a Marine, part of the detachment that served as the honor guard and the "police" on the Oriskany.

Captain Anderson, Harry's boss, decided that no good would come from giving his 69 man Marine detachment liberty in this hell-hole, and opted instead for a little beach exercise of a different kind. With the Captain of the Oriskany's permission, he borrowed some landing craft from the base and a couple of medics from the medical staff and decided to play real Marine and bivouac for a few days on shore on the opposite side of the bay from the Base where the Oriskany was tied up. A few reliable Marines, of course, were left on board to continue guarding Admiral Hobbs, and the Captain, Exec and the special weapons spaces aboard the ship, but Ittlebit did not fall into the category of "reliable."

'Ittlebit and the rest of the detachment collected some tents and K-rations, oiled their guns, and the day after the ship arrived at Subic Bay they threw nets over the side of the ship and the Marines scrambled down into the landing craft. Screaming gung-ho Marine type screams, off they sped for the beach on the opposite side of Subic Bay.

As Harry told me afterwards, when they landed Captain Anderson, Harry, and the rest of the Marines charged out of their landing craft shooting their bullets into the palm trees and undergrowth that made up the jungle in this part of the Philippine archipelago and continuing the gung-ho Marine type screams.

Oh, they had a grand time for the rest of the afternoon, pretending that every coconut they saw was a communist soldier and shooting up every coconut tree in sight. By the end of the afternoon the jungle was damn near uninhabitable from so much coconut milk pouring out of the trees, so they made camp in a small clearing near the beach, set up their tents, built campfires and sat around singing old Marine songs, eating

K-rations and, for all anyone would admit, toasting marshmallows. The Naval officers aboard ship were not privy to the mysteries of what it meant to be a Marine or what went on at a Marine bivouac. One facet of Anderson's and Richardson's little troop was, however, quite apparent; this was not your usual fighting force.

The next morning they rose bright and early for another day of fun and fighting. To ensure that no one would steal anything from the camp while they were out in the brush playing soldier, they decided to leave an armed guard behind to protect the camp. For this rigorous duty they selected 'Ittlebit, and armed him with a loaded 45-caliber handgun that was damn near as big as he was. He apparently didn't get an M-1 because they didn't have enough to go around. As mentioned, this was one hell-of-a fighting force! Then they dashed off into the underbrush for some more shooting.

At noon they stopped shooting long enough to have some K-rations for lunch. As soon as there was a lull in the firing they heard it. A cry, coming from the direction of the campsite: "Help! Help! Medic!"

Then they saw it: from the direction of the cries there was a pillar of black smoke.

The troop rushed back with Anderson, Harry and the two medics in the lead. They found the tents pulled down and piled into a huge bonfire. At the bottom of a small ravine was 'Ittlebit, lying face down, stark naked and badly cut and bruised. Neither his gun nor his uniform were anywhere to be seen. When they turned him over, he looked up at Anderson and said:

"Hucks! They jumped me!" And he passed out.

The Hucks were communist guerrillas that had plagued the Philippines since the end of WWII, but Magsaysay, the then enlightened President of the Philippines, had waged what was believed to have been a very successful war against them in the early '50's and, according to all reports, they had been wiped out. Real Hucks, this close to the U.S. Naval Base at Subic Bay, was big news indeed.

Captain Anderson had twenty of his best men load up with all of the real ammunition that his squad had left and went off into the brush to hunt for real live communists; no coconuts this time. Harry and the rest of the troop were ordered to return immediately to the ship to report the incident and get 'Ittlebit emergency medical attention.

While the news Harry brought back to the ship may have been big, it certainly wasn't welcome. When Harry reported the incident on his return to the ship, the Officer of the Deck must have groaned, "Why did this have to happen on my watch?"

When Harry and the OOD went and reported it to the Captain, the Captain must have thought to himself, "Why did this have to happen on my ship?"

And when Harry, the OOD and the Captain went to report the incident to Admiral Hobbs, ComCarDiv-3, who was then stationed on the Oriskany, Hobbs must have thought, "Why did this have to happen in my Carrier Division?"

Hobbs immediately called ComNavPhil (Commander, Naval Forces, Philippines) and reported the incident. ComNavPhil probably thought, "Why in my archipelago?" The story hit the headlines in every paper in the Philippines and most papers around the world.

"PHILIPPINE HUCKS ATTACK U.S. MARINES," read the headlines in the English language Manila papers the next day. Under that appeared the sub-head: "ONE MARINE GRAVELY INJURED," and they somehow got their hands on an old picture of Marine PFC William Small in his dress uniform. The picture actually made him look full size

President Magsaysay, of course, condemned the incident and announced that they would strike a medal for the courageous injured American, who was now safely tucked away in the Oriskany's sickbay. In the meantime, he announced an immediate search and destroy mission would be undertaken.

To help America's Filipino allies, the ship immediately offloaded its entire compliment of AD-6 propeller driven airplanes to the Subic air base and they, the Oriskany's helicopters, and the 250 planes and helicopters permanently stationed at Subic Bay were in the air immediately searching the jungle. The 500 man Marine detachment at Subic went off into the brush almost immediately to find and assist Captain Anderson's small and, most likely, outnumbered band, and by later that afternoon the first truckloads of the 10,000 Filipino Marines assigned by Magsaysay to flush out the offending Hucks were beginning to arrive.

Magsaysay didn't play around when Huck's were involved!

The following day the whole area was alive with Philippine troops, helicopters and warplanes. That morning Harry and I stood on the signal bridge of the Oriskany watching the soldiers arrive by the truckload to be ferried across the Bay to the site of the attack. The airport was immediately adjacent to the carrier pier, and the sound of planes taking off and landing was constant. It was high excitement, and 'Ittlebit was the hero of the day.

But I had an uneasy feeling in my gut. Harry and I had smuggled some San Miguel Beer aboard in some used ammunition cases, but by late in the day that was long gone and we were now resorting to mixing the vodka we kept in our personal safes with some orange juice from the wardroom conveniently just across the hall. The two of us were alone in our room when I first broached the subject of my concern about our wounded warrior

"Harry, has it ever crossed your mind that 'Ittlebit might be a compulsive liar?"

"I never have liked the little twit," said Harry, "and he's weird, all right, but nah, no one could make up a story like that."

There was then one of those long silences that become memorable years later. Finally, Harry broke the silence and said, "But maybe you and I should go down to sickbay and check out his story."

That is what we preceded to do. We found 'Ittlebit alone in sickbay, which was not that unusual. A ship with over 3,000 men on it almost always had a number of people in sickbay at any one time until it entered port. Then the sick and the lame would suddenly be miraculously cured. Ah, for the power of positive thinking and a good liberty port. Well, actually, any liberty port.

Sickbay was located in the bowels of the ship, well aft of officers' country, and when we found him 'Ittlebit was dressed in a white hospital gown and covered with only a sheet, as even the air conditioning had trouble coping with the Philippine combination of heat and humidity. While I took notes, Harry questioned the wounded warrior.

"Now Small, tell us just what happened out there yesterday."

"Yes, Sir, Mr. Richardson. When you and the others left, I did just what you told me to do. I put out all the fires and policed the area real good. I could hear you all firing off in the distance, so I knew I had plenty of time until you got back, so I took out some instruction materials that I had with me to prep for the next promotion exam. Then I realized it was almost lunch time and I was gettin' hungry, so I took out my rations and was eating and reading that promotion stuff. I guess I was studying so hard that I didn't hear them sneak up behind me. The next thing I know they conked me on the head and I went out like a light. I don't remember anything else until you all found me."

"How many were there?" Harry asked.

"About 20 that I saw, but there could have been more."

"What kind of weapons were they carrying?"

"Oh," answered 'Ittlebit, warming to the subject, "they had Russian or Chinese guns, not M-1's or carbines like us, and they had flame throwers which they used to set the tents on fire and some anti-tank rocket launchers of a type I never seen before."

"Who was their leader?"

"He was a big, wiry guy with a handlebar mustache, kinda like Pancho Villa had in that movie we saw last week on the hanger deck. Yea, he looked a lot like that guy, but thinner."

With this much information, we two experienced trial counsel retired to our room to refill our Vodka screwdrivers and contemplate the significance of this information. 'Ittlebit had already been questioned by some representatives from the base Naval Intelligence Unit, but Harry and I had no idea what he had told them. The only thing that was clear was that there were certain inconsistencies in his story. If they snuck up behind him and knocked him out, and he remembered nothing after that, how could 'Ittlebit have so much detail about his attackers, their weapons, and how they had demolished the camp? Furthermore, no one had ever seen 'Ittlebit reading anything except possibly a porno magazine or comic book, and certainly not material for a promotion exam. The smell was not going away.

So, after we refreshed ourselves with some more orange juice and vodka, we staggered down to sickbay to again confront the diminutive hero. Again, Harry did the talking and I took notes.

"Now Small, let's go thought the entire story again."

This time the story changed in a number of important details. His description of the leader was different. There were now about 50 of them, and they included some women soldiers, and they all had a kind of uniform of sorts. They also now had machine guns, and got the drop on him from the front before he could fire his "piece". This time they jumped down from the trees while he was walking guard duty; there was no mention of studying for a promotion exam. Furthermore, Harry had in the meantime remembered that the promotion exam had just been given and there wouldn't be another for six months.

Harry and I now started to hone in on the inconsistencies. With each new question he changed his prior version of the story, until finally, after looking back and forth between the two of us, he turned to Harry with tears in his eyes and said, "Mr. Richardson, will I get in a lot-a-trouble if I tell the truth?"

At this Harry exploded. As may have been mentioned, Harry was a large man and extremely strong. 'Ittlebit was a *very* small man. And all those beers and vodka screwdrivers had given Harry a hell of a load on by this time.

He pulled off 'Ittlebit's covers and grabbed the front of his nightshirt in both of his granite like hands and swung 'Ittlebit right off the bed. Then, with 'Ittlebit's arms and legs flailing and panic written all over him, Harry swung him back and forth so his head came within inches of the steel bulkhead and said: "Tell the goddamn truth you little bastard or I'll splatter what few brains you allegedly have all over these pea green walls!"

And the truth came tumbling out.

After the troops left, 'Ittlebit concluded that there was no use rushing with his chores, and decided to take a little swim first. He took off his clothes and swam around in the bay for a while until he noticed a lot of smoke coming from the campsite. When he got out of the water he saw that one of the campfires that he had neglected to put out had burned out of control and one of the tents was now on fire. Unfortunately for 'Ittlebit, it happened to be the one tent in which he had placed his uniform.

Knowing that he would be in trouble for not putting out the fires as Captain Anderson and Harry had told him to do, he came up with the idea of the Hucks jumping him. How he happened to remember that there even were such things as Hucks was just Harry and Anderson's bad luck, because 'Ittlebit's general knowledge of world affairs had to be limited at best. But with that brilliant master stroke firmly in mind, he gathered up all of the tents and equipment and added them to the fire. Then he dug a hole and buried his 45. Stark naked, he looked for a small ravine to roll down, but didn't realize how rocky the soil was around there and managed to actually do a pretty good job of cutting and banging himself up.

Harry and I listened to this new and obviously truthful version of the story without interruption. When Small was finally through, Harry uttered his first words.

"No shiiiiit!" he exclaimed, "How are we going to explain this?"

Our first stop after leaving sickbay was to find Captain Anderson, who had returned by now with his 20 sharpshooters. His response to our revelations was much the same as Harry's.

Next, the three of us went to the OOD to report it to him and ask permission to go see the Captain. "No shiiiit!" I heard the OOD exclaim, why did this have to happen on my watch?"

Then we went to see the Captain. He became furious when he heard the news, and proceeded to shout at everyone, first singling out Anderson, then Harry, then the OOD and finally me, who by now sincerely wished that I had gone ashore that day, air conditioning or no.

"What have I done, Captain," I interceded, "except be here?"

"YOU'RE HERE," he shouted, "That's enough!"

When the Captain finally got control of himself, he sent the OOD back to the quarterdeck and the four of us remaining went to see Admiral Hobbs. Hobbs sat there in his swivel chair, rocking back and forth and puffing on his pipe as Harry related the story. He said not a word, but the expression on his bulldog-like face got steadily more grave and disgusted as the narration went on. When Harry finished he gave Harry, Captain Anderson and me one of those looks that told you he felt the Navy should reinstitute keel hauling, or at least the cat-a-nine-tails, picked up the phone on his desk and asked his secretary to call ComNavPhil and hung up while we all waited for the call to go through. The Captain avoided his stare by sitting as far away from us as possible. Hobbs continued to glower at Anderson, Harry and me without uttering a word, rocking back and forth in his chair, while we waited for almost five minutes.

Then the phone rang and Hobbs picked up the receiver, gave his visitors one last glower, then bursting into laughter yelled into the phone, "CHARLIE, WAIT 'TILL YOU HEAR THIS ONE!"

The next day the Filipino newspapers reported that a small bandit village, not really Hucks, had been discovered and destroyed in the vicinity of Subic Bay. The brave Filipino Marines retired from the scene and the airplanes all left or landed. Nothing more was said of the medal for the brave American Marine that had been attacked by the Hucks, and 'Ittlebit was given two APC's (a combination of aspirin, phenobarbital and codeine that was the Navy's response to everything short of cancer) and thrown out of sickbay.

Of course there was the question of what to do with 'Ittlebit. The undaunted Lieutenant Bracken wanted to give him a special court-martial and had the indictment drawn up and assigned to the five man court on which I was trial counsel, but I demurred. I went to Bracken and explained that there was no evidence against 'Ittlebit as his confession had been obtained by coercion and I had been one of the coercers. If he hadn't confessed, Harry would have killed him.

Bracken then withdrew the charges with his usual accolade that I was a "damn bleeding heart" and tried to get Harry to try the case. He also demurred, not only on the grounds that he forced out the confession, but also on the more obvious grounds that Harry was a key witness to the events. Next Bracken had the Captain give 'Ittlebit a summary court-martial, and assigned it to Lieutenant Commander Ed Farrell, the "Hangman" mustang who had so handily taken care of Schrader, my airman with $180, when I had been Legal Officer. As noted, Farrell was tough as nails on any miscreant that came before him for a summary court-martial and his record was still in tact; each defendant that had come before him had received the maximum penalty that he could inflict: 30 days in the brig, 45 days loss of two-thirds pay and loss of a rank. Of course, in 'Ittlebit's case there was no rank to lose. As only the Captain reviewed a summary court-martial, reversal or reduction of a sentence never happened.

As previously noted, the longest summary court that Farrell had ever held had lasted less than 15 minutes before he hit the accused with the verdict, which was the book. It was always the book! He was a favorite of Bracken.

But this time it was to be different. The trial of 'Ittlebit lasted the better part of three hours as 'Ittlebit told Farrell the entire story, or several versions of the entire story. Try as he could, Farrell could never get 'Ittlebit to shut up long enough to give him his standard lecture.

Finally, the exhausted Farrell came out of his stateroom where the trial was being held with 'Ittlebit in tow and announced his verdict: "Not guilty by reason of insanity!"

'Ittlebit was sent off to the beach to a Naval hospital for observation, and Harry and I later heard that he was given a medical discharge. I suspected that he eventually re-enlisted in the Navy and was probably a signalman apprentice someplace complaining about how if he were still in the Marines he would be a top sergeant by now.

And Harry decided to give up his career in the Marines. He never could live down the nickname that might be appended to him wherever he went. Harry "the Hoss" Richardson was in danger of becoming Harry "the Huck Hunter" Richardson. He saw the writing on the wall; a nickname like that would kill his career. So, as his latest tour was up when the Oriskany returned to the States, he quit and went to Hastings Law School, part of the University of California but located in San Francisco instead of Berkeley.

Chapter 14

HOMEWARD BOUND

In August of 1956 the Oriskany completed its latest tour of WesPac and headed back to Alameda with a final stop in Hawaii. The homeward bound sailors were euphoric. They smiled much more, swore much less, and worked like hell to clean up their act. A number of the fly-boys may have been running around looking for their wedding rings as Turner had done at the end of the last cruise, but I certainly was well beyond being shocked by that, and pictures of wives suddenly appeared on the desks of officers who I had thought were single.

Exercise also suddenly became a hot item. Drinking had been a favorite pastime in WesPac, exercise had been almost non-existent, and everyone was just that little bit heavier as a result. Harry, in particular, decided that he needed to get back to "fighting trim," before getting out and going to law school and insisted that I join him at least once a day in the ship's small gym. The gym was located off a catwalk in a small cubicle immediately below the flight deck and open to the sea, which kept it cool from the wind while you worked out. It had some free weights, a boxing bag, a primitive exercise bike, mats on the floor and a medicine ball. Harry loved the medicine ball, which is why he insisted that I work out with him. He would put his 225 pounds into every throw, which I would try, not always successfully, to stop with my 150 pounds of mass. One day I had enough. We were standing along the catwalk throwing the ball back and forth on a hot summer day and each time Harry would hurl the leather sphere I would shout, "Not so hard!" That just seemed to pump up Harry more, and the next throw would be harder still, and my return shout would be louder yet. Finally, my voice was giving out, so I took the ball and threw it at a right angle to Harry, right over the catwalk and into the sea. Harry just stood there, toes pointing inward in his usual pigeon-toed stance, staring at me with a look of complete disbelief. Finally he said, "Why did you do that?"

"Whoops, I missed!" was my reply.

Harry had a case of apoplexy.

———◦◦◦———

From that point on, the trip back to Hawaii moved uneventfully at a steady 15 knots until the evening before our arrival at Pearl. We were due to arrive at 0600 the following morning and tie up at Ford Island inside Pearl Harbor, and the ship was jubilant in expectation of its arrival at its first United States port of call in six months. But the night before our arrival at Pearl I was spending my normal watch duty in the crypto shack when a SECRET message came in addressed to both the Exec and Captain. The first words that I decoded read: "For Executive Officer and Captain's Eyes Only".

Of course, neither the Exec nor the Captain knew how to operate the decoding machines, so I had no choice but to decode the message. If I could have done so without reading it, law-abiding citizen that I was, I probably would have, but it was literally impossible. If I made a single mistake in decoding a message it garbled. Therefore, I had to keep reading it as I decoded it to see if it was garbling

It didn't garble, and the message ordered the ship to anchor outside the harbor until investigators from the Customs Service and its Alcohol, Tobacco and Firearms division could come aboard and search the ship. The Customs people had received word from an informant that an enlisted man aboard the ship was attempting to smuggle drugs into the country.

This was big news, and had significance to the officers on board even though the message was specific that the suspect was an enlisted man. It happened that there was a bottle shop immediately adjacent to the Yokosuka Officers' Club that sold liquor by the case to officers at unbelievably low prices. Ballantine Scotch was $25.20 for a case of twelve, and gin and vodka was a fraction of that. Immediately adjacent to the Officers' Club liquor store was a carpenter shop that specialized in packing cases of whisky and cases of whiskey (the spelling being dependent on whether you drank Scotch or Bourbon), or any other alcoholic beverage, in wooden crates marked "Noritaki China." The cases could not be distinguished from the real thing except for a slight "swishing" sound if you shook the cases and listened carefully. As Noritaki china was a very popular gift for naval officers to bring home to their wives, mothers and sweethearts, the officers' section of the ship was loaded with china boxes. Unfortunately, many more than half of them swished when shaken. In our stateroom alone, not only did we have our own "Noritaki" china boxes, there were at least half a dozen more belonging to our friends. Our room was against an outside bulkhead immediately below the hanger deck and the natural outward curve of the ship at that point provided a substantial storage area.

It was clear to me from this message that our shipment of "china" was in jeopardy. However, as a cryptographer I was sworn to secrecy. In the Navy you were told repeatedly that the secret of keeping something SECRET was limiting its distributions to those with a need to know. In this case, however, the definition of "need to know" had some fascinating nuances. I immediately delivered a copy of the message to the Captain and the Exec. The Exec, who himself was somewhat of a man of the world, had his own crates of "Noritaki china" stored around his stateroom. He looked at me with those pool blue eyes of his that at that moment had certain moistness to them and asked in his Southern drawl, "Dick, who do you think we should tell about this?"

"Well, Commander," I replied, "I would certainly think that you would want to notify the officers so they could be alert to any suspicious behavior by any of their enlisted men when the Customs people come on board tomorrow."

At that moment the commander and I both turned our gaze at one of the "Noritaki china" boxes that the commander was then using, literally, as a cocktail table in his cabin.

He then turned back, his face lit up with a grin from ear to ear, and he replied, "You know, Dick, I think you're right. I don't think we should call a meeting, however, that would alert everyone that something was up. I think I'll just mosey down and tell all the division and squadron commanders and just leave it to their discretion to tell the other officers so they can be on the lookout."

At that I left to tell Harry that we were about to have the biggest tea party since Boston, and this time it was going to be on Noritaki china.

That night, case after case marked "Noritaki china" was thrown off the fantail, including all the cases that had been resting in our cabin.

The impending joy of our arrival in Hawaii had been literally dampened, and the next day when Customs came on board they found nothing. Whether there was a smuggler who was successful in hiding his contraband on a 48,000 ton ship, or the smuggler was alerted by all of the activity on the fantail the night before, or their was no smuggler, the only thing accomplished was to increase the alcohol content of the Pacific Ocean by a fraction of a percent and delay the ship's arrival in Hawaii by over six hours.

But the incident certainly had a sobering influence on a number of the officer's on board.

Chapter 15

DREAMGIRL

After we left Hawaii and just prior to arriving at Alameda the officers of the Oriskany had one important thing to do: submit their new Duty Request Form. The DRF was required of officers annually and asked for their first three choices of duty in the event the Navy, in its infinite wisdom, decided to send them someplace else. For most NROTC and OCS types on a two or three year tour of duty, this was an exercise in futility because they weren't going anywhere except with the ship to which you were originally assigned. A normal tour of duty in the Navy was three years. However, for the officers of the Oriskany this form had real significance as the ship was being taken out of commission and was going into Hunter's Point Navy Yard for an angled deck before its next return to WesPac. This meant that everyone would be getting orders within the next six to seven months, and the Duty Request Form would give BuPers some idea of where they wanted to go so BuPers could be sure not to send them there.

Take me for example. I filled in my first DRF while still at Stanford. My first choice had been the Rhine River Patrol, a fleet of small, motorized gunboats that the Navy at that time maintained on the Rhine River in Germany. My second choice had been any Capital Ship, Atlantic. That meant a big ship, i.e. a cruiser, battleship or aircraft carrier, with a homeport on the Atlantic seaboard. That meant cruises to Europe. My third choice had been any ship or duty on the East Coast. I was willing to serve on a destroyer escort if it meant I could be on the East Coast and have frequent tours of duty to Europe. Thus I got the Oriskany, an aircraft carrier with a homeport within 35 miles of Stanford and two tours of the Far East where I had no desire to go.

So, with my destiny once more poised at the end of my pen, I filled in my latest Duty Request Form, knowing that once more it had some real meaning. Deciding that the Rhine River Patrol might be a little off the wall and dilute my chances of getting on a Capital Ship, Atlantic, I selected "Capital Ship, Atlantic" as my first choice. I relegated the Rhine River Patrol to second choice and stuck with any East Coast sea duty as my third choice.

But that was before I fell in love. Within two weeks after my return I was fixed up on a blind date. As the girl, Charlene Mencoff, came down the stairs, the first thing that I saw were two perfectly shaped legs in very attractive spike heals. As she walked into the room in a tan sheath dress, her naturally thick and wavy hair in the ponytail that was then so popular, I said to myself, "This is the girl I'm going to marry!"

That first blind date was in Los Angeles where I was on leave visiting my parents after returning from WesPac. I was fixed up by an old friend from high school, a girl named June Bennett who then lived in Mexico and was up visiting for the summer and staying with her aunt, who was a good friend of my parents. She was coming to our house for dinner on Sunday and I was calling her to give her the time for dinner when she told me about these two girls from San Francisco who were staying with her at her aunt's house. Apparently their parents were also friends of June's aunt. She insisted that I would really like the older one, who she insisted was 21 (not true). I was reluctant to go out with someone June selected as she had fixed me up once before and it had been a disaster, but agreed after much cajoling by June to at least talk with Charlene, the older sister

Charlene sounded very nice on the phone. This was a Saturday and I offered to come over and take her out for a beer or ice cream so we could get to know each other, but she and her sister had just come back from Hawaii and she told me that she had promised herself that she would sunbathe that afternoon as she didn't want to lose her tan. She had Tuesday night available if I was free, but otherwise she was pretty much booked up while she was down in Los Angeles. Tuesday night was the only night of my leave left when I didn't have a date, so I agreed that Tuesday it would be and I would pick her up at 8:30.

That first date was a disaster. It was spent in a Chevrolet agency while a friend of mine negotiated the purchase his new car. Charlene thought she was going out for a late dinner. No one told me that, and Charlene was starving. After spending several hours exhausting the subject of the merits of the new Corvette, I said: "I'll bet this probably isn't the most exciting date you've ever had."

Charlene looked at me and, with a "Mona Lisa" like smile, replied: "If I knew you better, I'd tell you exactly what I think of this date!"

I loved it—an honest girl!

When my friend finally completed the car purchase it was too late to do anything but go out for a hot fudge sundae. Much to my surprise, Charlene had two. Bad as the date was from Charlene's perspective, she still gave me her telephone number and told me that she was off to Yosemite for two weeks.

When I returned to the ship I told Harry that I had met the girl I was going to marry. I called another woman I knew from Stanford with whom I had been dating prior to going South on leave and told her that I just wanted to be friends as I was very interested in someone I had met.

I would have been a bit chagrined had I known what was really going on with Charlene. For the past year she had been dating two men, one her high school sweetheart who was then at Boalt Hall studying law at the University of California in Berkeley and the other a resident at the University of California Medical School in San Francisco. The doctor was from Madison, Wisconsin. She liked them both and had been very confused.

Charlene's mother, when I got to know her better, reminded me of "Auntie Mame." In her early '40s, like her daughters she was very beautiful and a total character. When Charlene before that Summer explained her quandary to her mother, her mother immediately had a solution: "Not to worry, Charlene, we'll go visit Madam Olga, my fortune teller; she'll tell us which one is right for you."

This they promptly did, although Charlene was literally dragged there by her mother, and after having her palm and tea leaves read, Madam Olga announced with great solemnity that Charlene was not going to marry either of these men. "Instead, I see June and water, June and water; you will marry someone connected to June and water, and it is neither this law student you tell me about nor this doctor. Just remember June and water."

Armed with this sage and indisputable advice, Charlene easily convinced her mother that she and her sister, Carol, should spend the summer attending the University of Hawaii. There they could spend most of the month of June on the beach at Waikiki watching the boys get out of the water. Charlene would wear her Alpha Epsilon Phi ("AEPhi") sorority pin around her neck to make sure that she would meet Jewish college boys. It sounded like a plan, and while her father protested, there was little he ever could do when the three women in his life ganged up on him.

So Charlene and Carol spent the summer in Hawaii, watching the boys leave the water on Waikiki beach, but never finding Mr. Right. In the meantime, the doctor was calling Charlene almost daily from San Francisco, a big deal in 1956, and in one of those calls proposed to her. Charlene's quandary was even bigger, now. She was pretty sure that she didn't love the law student any more; they had been going out for over five years. As for the doctor, he was seven years older than she and came from a very prominent family in Madison, Wisconsin. But Charlene had a gnawing feeling that he really didn't respect women and just felt it was time to get married.

She decided that she had to see the doctor on his home turf around his mother and sister before she could ever consider accepting his proposal. Another call to her mother and it was agreed that she would return home via Los Angeles to attend a wedding with her sister at which the law student would be present so that she could end that relationship for good. Then she would go on to Wisconsin for two weeks and test the doctor. In other words, she had no intention of going to Yosemite!

Now she found herself in Los Angeles staying at the mutual friends of her parents and my parents. But as Wisconsin wasn't yet written in stone, she did not want anyone to know anything about her intentions—or at least her possible intentions. She therefore couldn't let her hostess or her niece, June, know about where she was off to after the wedding or why. And, of course, she certainly couldn't tell me. Anyway, if she came back without a ring, hadn't I said something about there being over three hundred officers on my ship?

—∞∞∞—

Charlene Mencoff was five feet tall, weighed 97 pounds, had a perfect figure, and in my eyes was the prettiest girl I had ever seen. Needless to say, I was smitten big time.

This was not the first time I had fallen in love, of course. It was, however, the first time I had ever met the girl with whom I had become so enthralled. My introduction to love at first sight had occurred about three years before while driving across country returning from my senior NROTC cruise. I had stopped in Denver and visited the University of Colorado with a friend from Stanford who lived in Denver. My friend had a girl friend that was an AEPhi at Boulder and while we were visiting with her in the living room of the AEPhi house, a fantastic looking girl came into the room. She was wearing a sweater, the long skirt that was then in style, and had her hair cut perfectly straight in a 1920's flapper style, much as my mother had worn her hair when I was a young boy and my mother was, literally, a flapper. I had always loved the way my mother looked in what I called her "flapper haircut."

"Introduce me to that girl," I asked my friend's girlfriend.

"No way," was her reply, "she has a boy friend back home and won't give anyone a tumble. I've tried to fix her up before, but it's been a disaster. I wouldn't fix her up now or introduce her to you for anything."

"I don't want to marry the girl," I replied, "I just want to meet her!"

But my window of opportunity closed rapidly. The girl of my enquiry walked across the room to the mail table, took her mail, turned and left. She was gone before I could get another word out or a chance to meet her.

Except in my dreams. I started dreaming of the girl with the flapper haircut from the AEPhi house at Boulder. Every dream was the same; she was dressed in a blue taffeta dress that was off the shoulder and we were dancing to "When the Deep Purple falls over Sleepy Garden Walls." When the song and the dance ended, I would wake up.

I knew that the dream was Oedipal, and that the girl from Boulder just reminded me of my mother, but as I had been having that dream for over three years, and it was the only recurring dream I had ever had, needless to say it was never far from my thoughts.

I was very impatient for Charlene to return from "Yosemite." I couldn't understand how anyone could spend two weeks there unless they were having an affair with Yogi the Bear, so I started calling Charlene's home after a week had passed. I spoke first to her grandmother who assured me that she was in Yosemite and would be home in a week. Four days later I called again, this time speaking with Charlene's mother who responded that she would return home "from Yosemite" in three days, the following Wednesday to be exact.

That following Wednesday afternoon I called and finally got to speak to Charlene and ask her out, but she was busy that night. She was free the following night, however, and we made a date to meet—this time for dinner. I was well aware of the dinner fiasco on the first date.

I was so anxious about this second date that I got two traffic tickets on the way to pick Charlene up. After I dropped her off that evening I was stopped a third time within half a mile of the entrance to Alameda, NAS, where the Oriskany was tied up. I was so shaken up by this time that instead of giving the officer my temporary driver's license (my real one had expired while I was overseas), I gave him the receipts from the two previous tickets. The officer looked at them, and then at me, and then at my Navy ID that was in my wallet and asked, "How long have you been gone?"

"Six months," I responded, "and I think I'm in love."

"In that case I think you've had enough tickets for one night," said the officer. "Follow me and I'll escort you to the base. We have to get you back safely for that young lady."

So a love struck ensign in his turquoise and ivory 1955 Chevy hardtop had a motorcycle escort back to the gate at Alameda NAS.

Charlene was a senior at San Francisco State College and lived at home with her parents in the Richmond District. I hadn't the foggiest idea how to get to the address she had given me and came over side streets that were the most direct on the map, but far from the fastest route. Her home was very typical of homes in the Richmond District with a garage and play room on the ground floor and the main house on the second floor. I climbed the steps to her house and met her parents. First I got a once-over from Charlene's father, who grimaced somewhat at the thought of his daughter dating a sailor, even if he was an officer. Then a very attractive young woman came down the hall toward me and I was perplexed; was it her mother or her sister? Then she reached out her hand and said: "You must be Dick!"

"Mrs. Mencoff, it is so nice to meet you." I replied. This very young looking beautiful woman was Charlene's mother, and the sophisticated way she greeted me gave her away.

I had nothing planned for the evening, but this was definitely a dinner date so I asked Charlene where she would like to go. "After all, you're a native of the area, I'm just a visiting sailor."

"I know a wonderful place in the City," she replied. "It's not cheap, but it's not very expensive, either, and has a great atmosphere."

"Great!" I replied, "Lead the way; just tell me where to turn and I'll get us there."

With that we climbed into my Chevy and Charlene directed me to a spot high on Telegraph Hill where we pulled up in front of the Shadow's, a German restaurant with which, as I mentioned earlier, I was very familiar. Harry and I were both regulars at the Shadows, which had a spectacular view, and we universally took our first dates there for dinner. Afterwards we would hit the show at the Hungry-I or Purple Onion, each of which had a one-drink minimum, and would finish off the evening and our wallets at the Top-of-the-Mark. Not infrequently we would go out on dates independently without comparing our respective plans and wind up in the same place at the same time. Depending on circumstances, we might then join forces. Or not! However, on this occasion I did not have the heart to tell Charlene that this was one of my regular haunts.

Instead, I gave the car to the attendant and the two of us started hiking up the 45 or more steps that it took to reach the Shadow's front door. At the top of the steps, I turned and looked out at the bay and harbor below and exclaimed, "What a great choice, this is terrific!" Which, of course, it was. However, it did imply that maybe I hadn't been there before.

While the view might have been spectacular, what happened next wasn't. As we walked in the front door, the hostess looked up and said, "Good evening, Mr. Maltzman, I didn't know you were coming tonight, but I think your favorite table is available."

With that Charlene gave out a gasp and fled for the ladies room.

"Oh my, I hope I didn't say anything wrong," said the receptionist with surprise, "that wasn't your wife, was it?"

"Not yet," I replied.

When Charlene returned to the reception area, she was very quiet. She told me much later that she had gone into the bathroom and stared at herself in the mirror and said, "Look, Charlene, you only have to put up with him for one night. Just get over it!" Then she put on some lipstick and returned.

Once we were seated I admired her earrings. She didn't have pierced ears and proceeded to yank them off.

"Why did you do that?" I asked.

"Well," she replied, "everything you tell me is the opposite of the truth, so I guess if you tell me you like my earrings you must hate them!"

That didn't sound very promising to me, but I was dedicated to the task of not making this my last date with this beautiful girl. From dinner we went to hear Mort Sahl at the Hungry-I, this time with my acknowledging that I had been there a number of times before, and Charlene introduced me to a new place for a nightcap, the Alta Mira Hotel in Sausalito. We sat out on the terrace on a great Bay Area August evening watching the fog lick at the City and we finally really started talking. We didn't stop until they closed the bar and they kicked us out.

When we got to Charlene's house I walked her to the door and tried to kiss her good night.

"Nice girls don't kiss on the first date," she said, as she gave me a little stiff arm to push me away, "and nice guys don't try."

"But this is our second date!" I said.

"L.A. was no date!" She replied.

So I asked her out for either or both of the next two nights, but she was busy on both nights. Just as I was about to consider this the shortest of my many relationships, Charlene did something that changed my life.

"What are you doing Sunday?" she asked. "Come for brunch, I'm sure my parents would love to get to know you. Bring your bathing suit and we can go out afterwards to Hamilton Air Force Base and go swimming. They have a great pool there at their officer's club and I know you can get in an Air Force Base's officer's club as a Naval officer."

I could, and immediately accepted. I didn't realize, of course, that the only reason I got the invitation was because it was Summer in San Francisco, complete with the fog, and Charlene hated the Fog. Hamilton Air Force Base was in sunny and warm Marin County.

On our third date I discovered that Charlene had transferred to SF State from the University of Colorado after her sophomore year. We were back from Hamilton AFB by this time, it was late in the afternoon, and we were sitting in the front room of here home in front of their Meisner HiFi console listening to Frank Sinatra records and talking. Actually, we hardly ever stopped talking. So when she told me she had gone to Colorado, I told her the story of the girl that I never met but kept dreaming about from the AEPhi house at the University of Colorado. I acknowledge to Charlene that this was probably something Oedipal as my mother had worn her hair the same way this girl had when I was a young boy, and I always liked my mother's hair that way.

"I'm sure a psychiatrist could have a field day with that one!" I added.

"If that was September of 1954 and she was an AEPhi, she would have been one of my sorority sisters. I was also an AEPhi. Could you recognize her? I have my yearbook here."

With that Charlene ran to her room and returned a minute later with the 1955 *Coloradan* opened to the group picture of her Sorority in the first Semester of the 1954-1955 school year. To that point I had not mentioned to Charlene what type of haircut this mystery girl that I kept dreaming about actually had. Just as she was about to hand me the book, I said:

"I would recognize her anyplace from her "flapper" haircut—very short and straight with bangs."

Charlene almost dropped the book. There in front of me was the picture of Charlene's sorority her freshman year at Boulder. There was only one girl in the picture with what could be described as having a "flapper" haircut, the third girl from the left in the front row. She was in the front row because of her height, and her name was Charlene Mencoff!

Charlene and I kissed for the first time in front of the Meisner, listening to Frank Sinatra.

For a brief period of her freshman year at the University of Colorado, Charlene had spent hours every day brushing her naturally thick wavy hair to straighten it, and she wore it then very short with bangs. She now had long, wavy hair worn in a ponytail.

After that kiss in front of the Meisner, I stopped dreaming about the girl from the AEPhi house. Instead, I spent every duty hour thereafter writing Charlene poetry and every off-duty night with Charlene.

Chapter 16

LOVE AND THE ORDER
OF THINGS

It was a great fall for me in San Francisco in 1956. The weather was terrific, Stanford had a football team that was exciting, but still lost the Big Game, the restaurants were great and cheap, the supper clubs such as the Hungry I and Purple Onion had wonderful entertainment like Mort Saul, Phyllis Diller and the Kingston Trio for the cost of a drink, and I had literally found my dreamgirl. Those were wonderful, carefree days.

The day after my return to the ship after meeting Charlene in Los Angeles, I ran to the Captains Office to amend the Duty Request Form I had just sent in on our return from WesPac. My new choices: First, any shore duty in San Francisco; second, any capital ship out of San Francisco/Alameda; and third, any ship out of San Francisco/Alameda.

But I had other resources. Admiral Hobbs and his staff had returned stateside for a year's rotation and were stationed at Treasure Island, right in the heart of San Francisco Bay. Commander Wallace, the admiral's Communications Officer, knowing that the Oriskany was going out of commission, contacted me and offered me the post of Assistant Communications Officer on the admiral's staff.

This was a billet normally reserved for a full lieutenant and I would not even make lieutenant junior grade ("JG") until December. Cdr. Wallace insisted, however, that with the admiral's muscle he could get me the orders. This would mean duty at Treasure Island until June. Then I would spend my last year in the Navy in the Far East.

That sounded pretty good to me. Charlene was a senior in college and, if I could convince her to marry me, we could get married right after her graduation. We could then have a year-long honeymoon in WesPac while she followed the ship around. This was not too common, but I had known of other officers whose wives had done the same, and with the strong dollar it was not impossible on a JG's salary.

Commander Wallace was as good as his word. In early October I received orders to report to the admiral's staff the following January, and I was ecstatic. On receiving my orders, I promptly proposed to Charlene, who just as promptly broke out laughing. She thought I was kidding. Sometimes having a sense of humor can be a curse. I persisted that I wasn't kidding, however, and she finally agreed to at least give the idea some serious consideration.

And so things stood for a number of weeks. Having made the plunge, I told Charlene that I wouldn't mention it again, but I assured her that she would come around and accept my proposal and marry me. I was that confident, and while I knew I loved Charlene, I also knew that she loved me, even though she hadn't admitted it yet even to herself.

One fall day while walking the streets of the City, we passed a newsstand and saw huge headlines announcing the British and French invasion of the Suez Canal. It was November 5, 1956.

I pointed out the article to Charlene. "I'm glad I'm not in the 6th Fleet!" I exclaimed, "I don't like the looks of this. The Russians are not going to like their client state, Egypt, being attacked by Britain, France and Israel."

But geopolitics was not high on my priority at that time. I was in love with Charlene, in love with my new orders, and everything else was way on the back burner. Of course I didn't keep either my love for Charlene or my new orders a secret, and it had become a regular prank for some of my "friends" to joke with me as I passed in the halls or when they ran into me in the Wardroom by telling me that my orders had been changed.

"Oh, sure!" I would reply, they would laugh, and that was it.

When in port, the officers and enlisted men on the Oriskany had the duty one day in every four, even when the ship was Stateside. But the Captain had a young wife, and liberty sounded early on the Oriskany, usually at 1300 (1 p.m.). That meant that when the liberty bell went off, those with the duty, i.e., one-quarter of the crew, had to stay on board. However, if an officer didn't have an actual watch to stand, he could usually find someone who was neither married nor in love to take his duty.

On a beautiful day in early November I had the duty, but didn't have a watch until 2000 (8 p.m.). One of my friends agreed to take my duty for the afternoon as long as I was back before six so my friend could go out on his date. With the afternoon to kill, I went hunting for Charlene and found her studying in the library at school. We spent the afternoon together while Charlene studied and I read Anna Karenina while glancing at Charlene between every paragraph. At 5 p.m. I drove Charlene home, we smooched for a few minutes, and I headed back to the Oriskany.

When I walked up the gangway, Wrecker was the duty OOD waiting for me on the quarterdeck. But instead of his usual smile at meeting his friend he looked very disturbed. After I saluted and requested permission to come on board, Wrecker put his arm on my shoulder, looked me square in the eyes, and said:

"Dick, this is no joke, your orders are changed, you better get up to the Captain's Office on the double."

I started to go with my "Yuk, yuk" routine, but something was different. Wrecker was too serious, and jokes weren't his style, in any event. That and his body language impressed me that he wasn't kidding.

"You're not joking, are you?" I asked.

"I wish the heck I was!" he replied.

With my heart someplace between my stomach and my feet, I ran to the Captain's Office. I couldn't believe that Wrecker wasn't kidding, but my gut told me something had gone very wrong.

Wrecker called the Captain's Office when I left the quarterdeck and the duty yeoman was waiting for me in the office with my new orders in his hand and regrets written all over his face. Everyone knew how thrilled I had been with my old orders, and I wore my heart on my sleeve when it came to Charlene.

My prior orders were canceled and I was ordered to report to the commanding officer of the U.S.S. Lake Champlain, CVA39, another Essex Class carrier, at Jacksonville, Florida, on or before January 4, 1957, for duty as Communications Traffic Officer and Crypto Security Officer, two very responsible jobs, thank you very much, but no thank you. I stared at the single sheet of paper and it was as official as I had ever seen a piece of paper.

"Its a joke, isn't it?" I asked the yeoman.

"I wish it were, sir, but its official. It arrived about 1400 and we looked all over for you until we discovered you were on the beach. We knew you wouldn't be happy, but it's official. I've run off a dozen copies for you."

"Thanks a bunch," I replied, as I picked up my orders and stormed out.

I went right to my cabin and changed into my khaki uniform for dinner, but I couldn't eat. I was sick. Everyone in the wardroom knew what had happened, and no one was joking now. All my friends had met Charlene and liked her tremendously. They knew how I was feeling, and in spite of the occasional nickname of "Smiley" pinned on me by Harry, I certainly wasn't smiling now. Jim Cotton, another communications officer, came up to me and told me how bad he felt and offered to take my duty that night if I wanted to go see Charlene. I gratefully accepted his offer, put down my fork and walked out of the wardroom and off the ship, still dressed in my uniform, which I hardly ever wore on the beach stateside. Officers, unlike enlisted men, usually wore civilian clothes when they left the ship unless they were on official business, but I was in no mood to change and anxious to be with Charlene.

When I rang her doorbell and announced my presence, she pushed the release on the door to let me in. As I walked up the stairs, the spring in my step was gone. I came up the stairs slowly, sounding more like a doomed man being led off to his executioner than a young Naval Officer on his way to see the love of his life.

Charlene probably could tell that something was wrong from my pace going up the stairs. When she saw me in my uniform, she knew immediately that something was *very* wrong.

"What is it?" she asked, and I reached into my pocket and handed her a copy of my orders. Gregarious as I usually was, and never one to be at a loss for words, I was too choked up to speak. She read my new orders and looked at me with tears running down her face.

"Does this mean you have to leave?" she asked.

I nodded. It was the only response I was capable of at that instant. Then she was in my arms and both of us were crying.

Several weeks later we flew down to Los Angeles for the Stanford-U.S.C. game and to introduce Charlene to my parents. On the plane, 35,000 feet up in the air without a parachute, Charlene accepted my proposal. We were engaged.

Chapter 17

SHIPPED OUT

Nothing could take my impending departure off my mind. First I tried to reverse it. I contacted Commander Wallace to see if he could find out what happened. Wallace called the JG Desk at the Bureau of Naval Personnel ("BuPers") and the officer in charge told him that it was just bad luck. The Suez crisis had caused the Pentagon to decide to send a second carrier to the Mediterranean to join the 6th Fleet and the Lake Champlain got the call. Apparently it desperately needed an experienced communicator and had notified BuPers that without one they could not operate effectively in a forward area. They certainly knew the right buzz words to get BuPers to move. Their cable crossed the JG Desk while Wallace's letter extolling my alleged virtues as a communicator was still fresh in the mind of the officer in charge of that desk. The result was my change of orders and two broken hearts.

Armed with that information, I called the JG Desk. A real human being answered the phone first time and knew who I was immediately. He apologized for any inconvenience the change of orders might have engendered, but noted my previously expressed desires on my prior Duty Request Forms for a Capital Ship, Atlantic, and thought he was doing me a favor.

"But I changed my Duty Request Form last September and requested shore duty in San Francisco or a ship out of San Francisco," I replied.

"Yea, I saw that, too," said the voice on the phone, "but its pretty hard to give everyone what they want."

"But you gave me what I wanted when you put me on Commander Wallace's staff," I pleaded. "I'm engaged to be married to a San Francisco girl, and I don't have any desire to leave now."

"Well," said the voice, "find me someone as qualified as you with orders to a San Francisco ship or shore duty that is willing to exchange duty with you and we'll see what we can do. However, the Lake Champlain's homeport is Mayport, Florida, and that's not quite as popular as the San Francisco Bay Area."

He didn't need to tell me that—I had already figured that out.

Over the next several months I tried to find someone who would meet the specifications from the JG Desk without avail, and finally became resigned that I was leaving Charlene. We talked about getting married before I left, but her family felt strongly that she should finish college first, and I couldn't disagree with that decision. She would graduate in June, the Lake Champlain, which was due to deploy right after my arrival, should be back in six months, which would be mid-June, and we could plan a June wedding and a honeymoon at Martha's Vineyard on Cape Code before going down to Mayport or Jacksonville to set up house-keeping.

In the meantime, we had a constant round of parties. First there was a big bash for all of the ensigns in my class on making lieutenant junior grade, or "JG". As Shakespeare said: "And some have greatness thrust upon them." Making JG was automatic if an ensign can last in the Navy for 18 months, and it is the only automatic promotion you get.

Next there was the farewell party for Harry. He had resigned his commission in the Marines and was off to Hastings College of Law. Finally, just before New Years of 1956, the Mencoffs threw a huge engagement party for us at the Presidio Officers' Club. It was essentially the last hurrah, at least for the time being, as it was just a few short days before I would have to leave. The activities kept Charlene and me so busy we hardly had time to grieve for our impending parting.

Then it was time. I had a ticket in my hand for Jacksonville, Florida, and the plane was about to leave. All the way to the airport we held each other and my jaw was sore from holding back the tears. After all, Naval officers didn't cry, did they? However, I certainly wanted to, particularly when they started calling my flight and I knew that I was about to board a Super Constellation for Dallas with connections to Atlanta and Jacksonville. A year and one-half before I had been lined up to board another Super Constellation to report to the Oriskany. That time they called me off the plane, but no one was calling my name this time. I was leaving, and then I was gone.

Part III

The USS Lake Champlain
(CVA-39)

Chapter 18

A CARRIER'S BRIDGE

The Lake Champlain sat like a great, grey colossus, parked at the pier at Mayport, Florida. As I climbed the gangway that January evening in 1957, I was exhausted from the all day flight from San Francisco with multiple changes of planes. I saluted the fantail, saluted the OOD, and handed him my orders. The USS Lake Champlain was a sister ship of the Oriskany and was identical in every respect. Well, almost every respect. Shortly after reporting aboard I was heading from one emergency radio room to another on the opposite side of the ship. Both radio rooms were immediately below the flight deck and there was a catwalk on the Oriskany that took you across the hanger deck about 40 feet below. But I was on the Lake Champlain, and confident that I knew the ship like the back of my hand from my experience on the Oriskany, I headed for the hatch that led to the catwalk. There was a sign on it that I didn't bother to read. I spun the wheel that disengaged the watertight locks, swung the door out and stepped out—into thin air. They had removed the catwalk for some reason on the Lake Champlain. Fortunately, I was still holding onto the wheel with my left hand and grabbed it literally for dear life as I swung hanging from the door until it opened 180 degrees and slammed against the bulkhead. I then kicked the door back with my feet and fell over backwards into the hatch I had just so ungracefully passed through. From my position on my back on the floor, with my feet still hanging out of the hatch, I finally read the sign. In large print it read:

"CAUTION—THIS DOOR DOES NOT LEAD ANYWHERE. IT IS 40 FEET STRAIGHT DOWN TO THE HANGER

DECK. DO NOT OPEN—SERIOUS INJURY OR DEATH COULD RESULT!"

To hell it led to no place, it almost led to my death.

—✦✦✦—

Carriers are like no other ships. They are literally floating cities with a complement of more than three thousand sailors and almost four hundred officers when the air groups are on board. However, even with all those people, a carrier can be a very lonely place. On small ships there is a camaraderie that sweeps in all but the misfits. On a carrier, there is room to be aloof. There will be friends to be made, but it is like a large club where you have to be introduced. Once the introduction is made, and once you prove yourself, you are a member in good standing and accepted by all. But first must come the introductions and the proving.

On the other hand, the "new guy" comes with a leg up that you don't have in civilian life; every Naval officer will be that "new guy" many times over as he wends his way through a Navy career. So they want to accept you and you want to be accepted. All that it takes to bridge the gap is a little patience and a lot of work.

The work part comes in because on a carrier, everyone has a job, and a lot of people depend on you. A ship's company officer does not have a difficult job. It will probably be one of the easier jobs he will have in life, but if he does it well he will be recognized and befriended, and if he does it poorly, or begrudgingly, he will also be recognized, but never accepted and will find it difficult to make friends.

Eighteen months before I had been another "new guy" on the Oriskany, and had learned from that experience. It took several months and a new class of ensigns before I had my first real circle of friends, but after I had proven myself, everyone who appreciated the responsibility we all had was my friend. There were always a few who hated the service and considered it a waste of time and a delay in their life. For them, the time dragged, respect never came, and they had few friends.

When I reported aboard the Lake Champlain, I moved slowly. I met the people in communications, where I was assigned the number three job in the department, Crypto Security Officer and Communications Traffic Officer. I met my new roommate, and was lucky to find that there was a vacancy in the same room I had shared with Harry, next to the Exec's cabin and opposite the wardroom. Then I just watched and observed. In particular, I watched the wardroom interaction, looking for the people with whom I might have the most in common, and searching for my next bridge partner. In those days, I was paid to be a Naval officer but lived to play bridge and get myself safely back to Charlene, not necessarily in that order.

The ship deployed to the Mediterranean shortly after I reported for duty, and it had a full compliment of officers on board, including the fliers from the various squadrons. For the first several weeks after reporting on board, I gravitated to the outer wardroom in my off-duty hours where there usually were a number of card games going at any one time, everything from bridge, poker and hearts to a Navy concoction called "smoke." I just stood around observing.

Having spent a disproportionately large amount of my waking hours in college playing bridge, I was determined to find on the Lake Champlain, as I had on the Oriskany before it, a good bridge partner with whom to pass the time and protect my wallet. In those first two weeks, I narrowed the eligible candidates to three and finally to one, an airedale lieutenant commander named Ed Wolf, an Academy type with an impressive analytical mind and the kind of personality and creativity that made his play fun to watch.

Ed's squadron, VF-71, was temporarily attached to the ship for its Med Cruise. VF-71 flew the Panther, a tired old warhorse of a jet and veteran of the Korean War, but a great looking airplane with its dark blue paint and slightly slanted thin wings behind the bubble canopy. It looked sleek even if it wasn't supersonic, and Ed had been one of the first to qualify in the plane after its introduction. In fact, he had been one of the first Naval aviators to qualify in jets after WWII, was clearly a very fine pilot with the nerves of steel that it takes to land a modern jet fighter on an axial deck carrier, and had over 5,500 hours of flight time without a mishap.

Although he was quite a few years my senior, Ed and I rapidly became friends once I was able to infuse myself into the bridge game, and we soon gravitated to a perpetual partnership when I wasn't on duty or Ed wasn't flying. At the stakes for which we played we were not going to get rich, but we quickly established ourselves as the team to beat. But more about Ed later. First we were off to the Med with our first stops at Gibraltar and Valencia!

Chapter 19

MY COW IS IN VALENCIA

"Lets go to Madrid!"

The speaker was Joe Cranston, my new roommate on the Lake Champlain, and the time was approximately 0345 in the morning. Joe was coming off his midwatch in crypto and I was just going on. In the boredom of the midwatch (midnight to 0400), Joe had been reading up on available tours for the ship's company when we docked in Valencia, our first port-of-call in Spain. He handed me the literature and I read about the trip on my watch. So it was that the die was cast that led to my life of crime in Generalissimo Franco's Spain in early February of 1957.

It was a spring-like day when the Lake Champlain pulled into Valencia on the East Coast of Spain, approximately 150 miles south of Barcelona. This was the Lake Champlain's second port of call on that 1957 Med cruise, and a group of approximately forty officers, with Joe and I among them, had signed up for the five-day American Express tour to Madrid that left as soon as the ship docked. It was scheduled to arrive back just in time to catch the ship before its departure for our first stop at what was to be the Lake Champlain's homeport in the Mediterranean, Naples.

When the ship tied up, a Pegasso bus was waiting at the end of the pier to take our group on the 350-kilometer trip to Madrid. All the officers wore our civilian clothes, which officers were allowed to do, and almost always did, on "the beach." In my hand tailored Hong Kong tweed sport coat and slacks, I looked every bit the American tourist of the fifties, and not one wit a sailor. Today you might be able to tell the difference by the haircut, but in 1957, crew cuts were all the rage.

Our five days in Madrid went very quickly. Joe and I literally shopped 'til we dropped, and I bought mantillas for every woman in both my present and soon-to-be families. We, of course, took the mandatory trip to Toledo with its magnificent cathedral and spent a whole day roaming the halls of the Prado, Spain's great art museum. Our nights were spent searching out the best flamenco bars in town, and enjoying our first taste of true European culture, as this was Joe's first tour to the 6th Fleet as well as mine.

Our hotel, the Menfis, was a good four-star hotel in its day, but has long since seen the wreckers' ball. The Avenida General Don Antonio, on which it was situated, was fashionable and very central to all the activities in which we were interested: the shopping, the Prado and the flamenco bars. We ate tapas in the late afternoon, sat at the sidewalk cafes around the Plaza Mejor, and I had great fun practicing my high school and college Spanish; or what was left of it.

Actually, I was not much of a linguist, which disappointed my father who spoke six languages fluently and my sister who had majored in French at Stanford before me. I had stumbled through Latin and Spanish in high school but flunked the language proficiency test when I got to Stanford and took Spanish again from scratch.

But now I was in Spain and practicing my Spanish on the natives with gusto. The Spaniards are great if you are a novice with their language. Unlike the French, they are very patient with anyone willing to attempt to speak their tongue and will work with you and speak slowly. I seldom had trouble being understood, and my companions were very impressed. But then, I came from California and most of them were from the East or the South. To them, California was essentially a Spanish colony that had somehow come under U.S. protection.

Everything went well until it was time to leave. There was a large plaza with a fountain behind the Menfis at which we were told to congregate at 1300 (1:00 in the afternoon) of our fifth day to board the bus for the return run to Valencia. Alone among my fellow officers, I arrived on time. But this was Spain, and everything moved in Spanish time, or mañana. There was no one there but the bus. Even the driver was still at his siesta.

Then I heard the singing. It was coming from what was obviously a large group of people, and, as the music was rapidly getting louder, they were clearly coming my way. Then I saw them. It was a huge crowd, carrying placards and banners and Spanish flags and marching into the Plaza from one of the many streets opening into it.

"Wow," thought I, "local color!"

When the Oriskany was in Japan, I had splurged and purchased the latest model Nikon S-2 35 mm camera. It had set me back $139 at the PX at Yokosuka, and was an impressive looking machine with its huge f1.4 lens, rapid rewind lever and stainless steel body. Instinctively, I took it off my shoulder to photograph the "local color."

Then all hell broke loose. From every other orifice leading into the square, and there were many, came the roar of trucks and motorcycles, as literally hundreds of soldiers and riot police in green uniforms came roaring in. First were the motorcycles with sidecars that looked like leftover props from an old World War II movie, then the trucks. Before I could gather my thoughts, the green clad soldiers or policemen, I never learned which they were, had jumped from their vehicles and charged into the crowd swinging nightsticks as they went. They were cracking skulls everywhere, and the "local color", which turned out, of course, to be demonstrators in a Spain where Franco did not allow demonstrations, were running in every direction to get away from the melee.

As I mentioned, the Nikon had a rapid winding system, one of the first of its kind, and I kept clicking off shots until the Plaza was totally cleared. Nothing was left except empty trucks and motorcycles, and dozens of bodies lying strewn everywhere. While I watched in amazement, and continued clicking off pictures, a number of ambulances roared into the square. Orderlies jumped out and the injured were whisked away with an impressive efficiency.

Once more I was left alone. About fifteen or twenty minutes passed, and still there was no sign of the others in my group or the bus driver. Then I heard more noise and commotion, this time from in front of the Hotel on the Avenida General Don Antonio. Being curious, I ran across the Plaza to the corner of the Hotel and around the Hotel to the front to see what was going on.

When I got to the front of the Hotel, I could see nothing as the street was mobbed with spectators standing eight to ten deep watching something taking place in the street. Then I looked up and noticed a TWA office on the second floor of the Hotel and figured that, as an American company, they of course would allow me, an American Naval officer, to look out their window and take pictures of what was happening. So I ran up the stairs, only to find that there were no Americans in the TWA office, and the Spanish employees were not about to let me or anyone else anywhere near a window.

Frustrated, I returned to the street, but still could see nothing. I looked at my watch and saw that it was now close to 1400 and became concerned that the bus would leave without me. So I took out my camera, hoisted it as high over my head as possible, and clicked off about fifteen shots in a panorama in the hope that my camera would record that which I could not see. Then I snapped my Nikon into its case, looked again at my watch, and started to run around the Hotel to get back to the bus before it left.

As I turned the corner of the Hotel and entered the Plaza, I realized that I had done the right thing to rush back. Everyone was milling around, obviously waiting for me. They certainly were all looking in my direction as I ran up. But as I approached, two of my friends gestured over my shoulder, and asked in unison: "Who are your friends?"

At this I stopped and turned. There they were, the Keystone Cops, spread out for 100 yards behind me and chasing me at full tilt. They caught up with me as soon as I stopped, two uniformed members of the Guardia Civil, the Spanish police with their great cloaks floating out behind them, grabbed me by either arm, a third grabbed my camera and pulled it off my shoulder, and a fourth man, mustachioed and dressed in a civilian trench coat with a broad brimmed hat, and looking every bit like Adolph Menjou at his shabby best, whipped out a piece of Toledo steel that was supposed to pass for a badge and said in Spanish, and this I understood: "Police, come with me!"

They then started literally dragging me off with half of the officers from the ship in hot pursuit.

"What should we do?" one of my friends shouted.

"Call the American Embassy, quick!" I yelled back as they carted me out of the plaza.

At this stage my first concern was for my camera. It was my pride and joy, after Charlene, and I was very concerned about getting it back. I also knew this had to be some huge mistake, because Spain was an ally of America and the Americans and our aircraft carriers were here to keep the communists from taking over Western civilization and to make the world safe for Democracy and Spain safe for Franco. So I decided that I had better talk to "Adolph Menjou."

"Es un mistakio (when I didn't know a word, I just used its English counterpart and put on a Spanish ending and prayed that it would work), soy un officina en la Maritima de los Estados Unidos de Norte America. Me barca es en Valencia. Me barca vay a mañana a Napoli."

Adolph responded by assuring me that they had a translator at headquarters. But I did not want to go to headquarters. This was all some big mistake. Again I assured Adolph: "Soy un officina en la Maritima de los Estados Unidos de Norte America. Me barca es en Valencia. Me barca vay a mañana a Napoli."

Now, for those of you who are not as conversant in the Spanish tongue as I thought I was at the time, what I was telling "Adolph" with my "Soy un officina en la Maritima de los Estados Unidos de Norte America" was "I am an office (an officer would be an "official") in the United States Navy." I added the "North America" in because I seemed to remember from something I had read that there might be another "Estados Unidos" someplace. Anyway, I knew the words for North America, at least, were right.

I thought that being an office in the Navy of the United States of North America would impress a Spanish policeman in 1957. It apparently didn't.

Possibly some of the fault for Adolph's incredulity might lie with me, or at least the series of what must have been incompetents that attempted to teach me Spanish. Because my next two sentences contained a rather fatal flaw that I proceeded to amplify by repeating it at on no less than five-minute intervals for the rest of the day, whenever anyone would listen to me. What I was trying to say with: "Me barca es en Valencia. Me barca vay a mañana a Napoli" is that "My ship is in Valencia. My ship leaves in the morning for Naples." Unfortunately, I did not learn until much later, when telling the story to my father, who spoke those six languages, one of which was Spanish, was that ship, in Spanish, has a masculine ending, and is "barco", not "barca". But what was worse was that there is no word "barca" in Spanish, but the word "vaca" is pronounced identically and translates "cow". Thus, for the better part of that day, and to whomever would listen to me, I, in my brown tweed sport coat, kept insisting that I was an American Naval office with a cow in Valencia and my cow was leaving in the morning for Naples. At times I would even emphasize that it was a very large cow. Unfortunately, however, I never found a sympathetic policeman with an interest in animal husbandry, even large animal husbandry.

Adolph and the keystone cops took me back to the front of the hotel, the "scene of the crime!" There we met what must have been Adolph's boss. Picture, if you will, the typical Spanish detective if he was trying to go incognito but wanted to make sure that everyone knew who he was. He was wearing a threadbare overcoat that hung down to his ankles, a torn shirt and shabby hat pulled down over his eyes. His nicotine stained fingers held a cigarette that he pulled on constantly, and his features were literally hard to see through the cloud of smoke he emitted. He was about five and a half feet tall, about fifty-five years old, with stooped shoulders and a stocky build. His necktie preserved pleasant memories of some great feasts of the past, splattered at random.

Adolph showed "the smoker" my camera and said something to him in Spanish that was beyond my understanding, at which he grunted "Si!" Then he indicated by a grunt and a tug at my sleeve that he wanted me to come with them.

I tugged back and said, "Se habla Vd. el Ingles? (Do you speak English?)"

Smoker said no, and I said "Vayame (show me) su credentials, por favor!"

I guessed that "credentials" is the same word in Spanish, and apparently I was right, as Smoker grunted again and proceeded to take out his wallet and show me some official looking card with Smoker's picture on it, the word "Policia" emblazoned in an impressive bold type, and a seal with ribbons attached.

Having established who he was, as if I had any doubt, I now once again tried in vain to establish who I was. As I went through my litany about being a U. S. Naval office with a large cow in Valencia, he grunted what sounded like "Si!" at my every pause for breath.

Then I pulled out my Navy ID card. Another grunt. Next I handed him my Geneva Convention Card (supposed to guarantee military personnel the liberties of visiting servicemen in foreign countries). His grunt this time was one of puzzlement.

While this dialogue was going on, we were walking away from the noise and crowds. After several blocks we turned a corner and there stood what was undoubtedly the better part of the Spanish army and what must have been all of the Jeeps in Spain.

The Smoker then said something to "Adolph" and left. "Adolph" and several of the Guardia Civil then whisked me away to the main police headquarters in an ancient and battered miniature Seat station wagon with real wood sides.

141

At the Policia Estacion, I was ushered into a room on the second floor with the title "INSPECTOR" on the door. The word is apparently the same in English and Spanish. The room was large, with six large desks lined up two by two and a row of benches surrounding the room. In the rear was a second door marked "INSPECTOR" followed by an unpronounceable name. A civil servant sat at each of the six desks, and a constant stream of observers kept entering the room and taking their place on the benches to observe "el bandido Americano" that "Adolph" had managed to apprehend.

The person at the first desk proceeded to ask me: "Donde viva usted en Madrid? (Where do you live in Madrid?)"

I promptly answered: "Viva en el Hotel Menfis, pero me barca es en Valencia. Me barca vay a mañana a Napoli."

Next he asked: "Como se llama usted? (What is your name?)"

I then gave him my full name, but added, "Pero soy un officina en la Maritima de los Estados Unidos de Norte America. Me barca es en Valencia. Me barca vay a mañana a Napoli. Me barca es muy grande!"

And so it went. They kept asking me simple questions, and I kept telling them the answer and elaborating on my distinguished Naval office and my by now famous cow, which was very large, and was somehow leaving in the morning for Naples.

Finally they got around to asking me for "identificación." "Identificación" is a very important thing to a Spaniard. If you have it, you are somebody, and they cannot understand the concept that you might not have it.

First they asked me for my "passaporta."

"No tengo una passaporta," I answered, "tiene una Geneva Convención Carta," and I handed them the green Geneva Convention Card I had tried to use earlier to impress my captors.

Same result. Next I tried my green plastic Navy ID card, complete with my picture and signature. This, too, was worthless to them. It couldn't, in their minds, be official as it did not have a seal. In Spain, all official documents came complete with a seal.

This was long before the days of credit cards, and I dug into my wallet looking for something that might satisfy them. I showed them my California driver's license; they threw it to the ground. My international driver's license got the same treatment. The pictures of my fiancé, Charlene, at least got a longer look and some raised eyebrows (she was wearing a two piece bathing suit which was rather risqué by Franco Spanish standards), but nothing caught their attention until I pulled out the last card in my wallet, my life membership in the Stanford Alumni Association, given to me by my parents as a graduation present from Stanford. It came complete with a gold seal and a cardinal and white ribbon on the bottom, which got exclamations from everyone as it was passed around the room with protestations of "Ah, un professor!" Then everyone in the room got in line to come around and shake my hand.

Of course, by this time I was near panic. How was I going to get to Valencia? While I no longer had that dreadful fear of flying, I wasn't sure how I would feel in a Spanish airplane, and wasn't even sure if Spain had anything comparable to a commercial aviation industry. Taxis were cheap, but a taxi to Valencia would have cost me more than my meager savings could tolerate. Then there was my tour bus; would it still be waiting for me? I realized to my chagrin that I was putting my popularity among the officers of the Lake Champlain to a very severe test.

Finally the Inspector came out. He had a shaved head a la Kojack, but Kojack had yet to be created. Or maybe he was trying to win a Yul Brynner look-a-like contest. In any event, the room immediately became as quiet as a tomb, and all eyes were on the Inspector. He approached me, came within a foot from my face, and said, in a slow, deliberate voice, "Where-do-you-live-in-Madrid?"

Instantly, everyone else in the room announced at once that their prisoner could speak some Spanish, but the Inspector would hear none of it. He bellowed at the top of his lungs to the crowded room: "CÁLLATE! CÁLLATE! (BE QUIET! BE QUIET!)." He then repeated, in the same slow, deliberate fashion, the question he had just asked.

Two could play at this game. "I-live-in-the-Hotel-Menfis," I answered slowly.

Inspector "Kojack" shouted at the man at the first desk, "Escribir eso!" (Write that down!) And beat a quick retreat to his office.

After another ten minutes or so, he returned, again came up to within a foot of my face, and asked in a very loud voice, "What-is-your-name?"

I answered him. Slowly. Again he left.

Of course, there was no translator at the main police station, but the inspector had an old copy of Cassel's English-Spanish dictionary in his office and was piecing the questions together one word at a time.

The questioning went on like this for a short time longer until "Adolph" returned to the office with my camera over his shoulder and a roll of film in his hand. It was the film from my camera. He proceeded to hold the film high over his head, and told the Inspector and the milling throng, "Es Kodakrome!"

I could have told them that without the bother of having to arrest me and possibly cause my large cow to be delayed in her trip to Naples.

The inspector then basically said, "So what!" in Spanish.

"Adolph" replied that Kodakrome could only be developed by Kodak and had to be sent to France for processing. "Reporters use Ektokrome as it can be developed locally."

At that point, the Inspector turned to me and asked, in Spanish but with an astonished tone to his voice, "Son usted un official en la maritime de los Estados Unidos?" ("Are you an officer in the United States Navy?") Apparently my mistaken use of "office" for "officer" had not been fatal after all.

"Sí! Sí!" I replied, "Soy un official en la Maritima de los Estados Unidos de Norte America. Me barca es in Valencia. Me barca vay a mañana a Napoli."

The Inspector and "Adolph" looked at each other, shrugged, and the Inspector grabbed me in his arms and gave me a huge embracio, the bear hug that is reserved in Latin countries for your really good amigos. He yelled for brandy and sandwiches for the American Naval hero and expert in cattle, and I was ushered into the Inspectors office for a repast before they would let me go.

Finally, at about five that afternoon, they released me to an air force colonel who had been waiting for me down stairs for the better part of three hours. The colonel knew all about the demonstration that day, and told me it had been student led and concerned an increase in the streetcar fares. It had been the first demonstration ever in Franco Spain since the end of the revolution, and it was put down very harshly. As "Adolph" had returned both the camera and my film, he asked me for copies of the slides when they eventually were developed if the film had not been exposed.

When the film was finally developed by Kodak and returned to me, it turned out that my captors had not exposed the film, as I had feared, and the pictures came out fine—sort of. Of the fifteen pictures I had panned across the crowd, six were of the sky, five of peoples heads, and the remainder showed some young people, who were probably students, either turning over a streetcar, righting a turned over streetcar, or balancing a streetcar on its edge for the fun of it. Hardly the stuff from which famous spies are made, or the newspaper photojournalist they suspected me of being. I sent the slides to the Colonel.

When I was delivered back to the Hotel Menfis, the bus was still there and my comrades were three sheets to the wind. They had spent the entire afternoon in the bar waiting for my imminent release from captivity. When I walked in I was greeted like a conquering hero and paraded around the hotel lobby on their shoulders. The theme of the day was clear: "Free the Madrid One." Then they held me down and poured at least half a bottle of red wine down my throat so that I could catch up with them, and then we were off to Valencia—and my cow.

Chapter 20

LOST WAGES NIGHT

Shortly after the Lake Champlain left Valencia, the Exec's Plan of the Day ("POD"), a mimeographed sheet that was distributed daily to all hands, started a continuing plea for contributions to the new Naval Academy stadium (later to be known as the John F. Kennedy Memorial Stadium) in Philadelphia.

Commander Eldridge Boulivar, the Exec of the Lake Champlain, was a handsome Naval officer, ramrod straight, tall, with jet black hair only slightly tinged with grey at the sideburns and piercing grey eyes. He was extremely ambitious, and part of that ambition took the form of his dedication to ensuring that the Lake Champlain, his ship, would be the biggest contributor to the stadium in the Atlantic Fleet, if not the entire U.S. Navy. This was, however, a formidable task in view of the dearth of Annapolis graduates among the junior officer compliment of an aircraft carrier. The cruiser Worcester was apparently leading the Atlantic Fleet with a little over three thousand dollars, and each morning over the 1-MC and in the POD there was that cry for funds for the stadium, for the glory of the Navy, the glory of the Academy, and the glory of the Lake Champlain. Never mind the glory of Commander Boulivar; that went without saying.

Each day the POD would indicate the total contributed to date by the ship's officers and men and compare it with totals raised by other Atlantic Fleet ships. In the Wardroom there was posted a giant thermometer with dollar levels along the side to reflect the sums contributed by the ship. The top of the thermometer was the goal, a big $5,000. The total rose rather quickly to several hundred dollars, but then froze there like an immoveable rock. All of the Exec's cajoling was for naught; there were very few ring knockers among the airedales and fewer yet among the junior officers. With no loyalty to Annapolis, they sat on their hands and their wallets whenever a plea came out for the Academy's stadium.

The $5,000 goal didn't appear that awesome. It was less than $1.50 per crewmember. But why on earth would the crew contribute anything from their paltry wages to a stadium for Annapolis? And they didn't. It wasn't even large when considered just against the officers. There were almost 400 officers on board with the air groups, so the goal was only about $12.50 per officer. But they weren't going to get my $12.50, and it appeared that about 350 of the 400 officers on board agreed with my sentiments.

Then one day in the POD there was an announcement of a great party to be held on the hanger deck in two weeks time, right after the ship left its next visit to Cannes and right after payday—"Las Vegas Night!" All kinds of gambling would be available, roulette, craps, poker, you name it. Each day the POD would hype the event. The print shop printed up posters for the event and they were distributed all over the ship. A special short duty watch was designed for that night which ended smack in the middle of the event so that every watch section would have a chance to participate in at least half of Los Vegas Night. The Public Information Office ("PIO"), which was responsible for crew moral and rest and recreation, was contributing substantial prizes for drawings to be had throughout that evening.

"COME ONE, COME ALL—EVERYONE A WINNER—AND THE PROFITS GO TO A WORTHY CAUSE!!!" read the signs posted throughout the ship. And come one, come all, they did; all, that is, except for the officers. On the night of the big event the movie in the wardroom was canceled by order of the Exec, and with nothing else to do most of the officers not on duty, including me, went up to the hanger bay to see what was going on. How the Exec did it no one in my circle knew, but the entire front bay on the hanger deck was filled with roulette tables, crap tables, "21" tables, poker tables, and every other game you could think of. There was only one rub; the odds at each had been dramatically skewered to the house's favor. The odds for each game were cut in half to favor the house and that "worthy cause" to which the posters alluded. Winning at roulette, for instance, paid 16 to one. If you won at the craps table you got back your bet plus fifty percent. In other words, it was almost impossible to be a winner.

The officers took one look at what was going on and clasped their wallets shut. They were nauseated by the gullibility of the enlisted men, who were throwing their money on the tables as if they really had a chance to win. After watching for a while, most of us officers were so repulsed by the scene of all of those enlisted men throwing away their money that we retired to the wardroom for our usual card games, where at least the odds were still the usual percentages. Even if your opponent cheated, the odds were better than they were on the hanger deck.

The next day the POD was exultant. Las Vegas Night had produced over $5,000 for that worthy cause, which just happened to be the stadium for Annapolis in Philadelphia. The thermometer in the wardroom burst its top, and the Exec was one very happy man.

Of course, when the Lake Champlain pulled into Naples two days later the crew was flat broke, which made for a very unfriendly reception by the whores, pimps and street hustlers that greeted the ship whenever it arrived there, which was often as Naples was the Lake Champlain's nominal homeport while with the 6th Fleet.

Chapter 21

THE BIG GUN

Parish was a huge man by anyone's standard, with a deep booming voice that could frighten the devil himself. He was a seaman apprentice with a GCT of 33, the lowest acceptable score for a Navy recruit. He probably never would rise to a higher rank, but he performed his one job, communications messenger, with consummate skill. If you told him to find someone, he would find him, and if you told him to go wake your relief on the mid-watch, he could wake him from the dead.

He would come into my pitch-black room, find my bunk, put his ham sized hand on my arm, give it a shake that could wake the devil, or tear off an arm, and announce in his sonorous base, "You better get up, Mr. Maltzman!" I would be so terrified that I would leap out of my bunk, forgetting completely that I slept on the upper tier, damn near kill myself, throw on my cloths, and rush out into the lighted hall as I tucked in my shirt, thinking for all the world that I was late for the relief of my watch—only to discover that I was an hour early, but Parish happened to be passing by.

He was, in short, a piece of work. Not too bright, but a piece of work.

The Lake Champlain was in Naples and I had the 2000 to 2400 watch in the radio room. It was approximately 2200 when Parish came to the Dutch door that led to main radio with a grin a mile wide and his hat at a jaunty angle.

Obviously just off liberty, he leaned on the door and asked, "Lieutenant, can a sailor own a gun?"

"He can own one," I answered, "that's guaranteed by the constitution, but he can't keep it himself aboard ship. Navy regulations require that if an enlisted man has a gun, he must give it to his officer for safekeeping.

When we get stateside he can get a license for the gun and then the officer will give it to him, but it must be removed from the ship immediately, remain unloaded at all times aboard ship, and cannot be brought back on board. Why do you ask?"

"Well, I bought a 22 caliber Beretta on the beach from this guy for $25," he replied," and its a beauty. Can you keep it for me until we get Stateside?"

Naples in 1957 was an emporium for thieves. On every corner there were hucksters trying to sell you look-a-likes for Rolex watches and Parker pens. The watches would keep time just long enough for the seller to disappear, and the pens would squirt ink from every orifice if you were foolish enough to try and fill them with ink, but otherwise they looked just great. It also wasn't just out-of-work bums who were the thieves; in those days it seemed like no one in Naples was honest. You would take a cab and the driver would run you all over town to build up the fare. Then, while you argued with him about his circuitous routing and were distracted, he would steal your raincoat that you had casually thrown over the front seat.

It thus may not surprise the reader that I was a bit skeptical when Parish related the story of how he had purchased the gun from someone on the street, and was expecting to see a clever mock-up that might have made a nice, realistic toy for some child. But Parish was insistent that he had the real thing, and proudly pulled from his jumper blouse a small, tightly wrapped parcel and handed it to me.

It certainly had the heft of a weapon, and as everyone on duty in the radio room gathered around, I cut the strings and opened it.

It contained a piece of black slate. The thief had shown Parish a real gun, then with slight of hand had palmed it and wrapped up a piece of slate the same size, telling him to keep it under cover or he would get in trouble with the authorities as it was illegal to carry a gun in Italy.

As the radio room exploded with laughter, Parish went ballistic. "I'm going back out there and find that bastard!" he shouted. "I'm gonna kill him when I find him."

"Calm down, Parish," I shouted back, "its after ten o'clock and liberty is over at midnight; you'll never find him and if you do you'll never get back before midnight. You'll just get yourself into a pack of trouble. It's not worth it."

But he wouldn't listen. He had tears running down his face, and this great bear of a man went roaring out of main radio heading toward the quarterdeck to get back on another liberty boat.

I was sure that he was going to end up in trouble, and was very concerned.

At almost midnight, as I was filling in my relief on all the non-events of the last four hours, a great, booming bass voice hit us from the open top half of the radio room Dutch door.

"You said I wouldn't find him, Mr. Maltzman, BUT I FOUND HIM!!!" There at the door stood Parish, again with a huge grin, looking like a giant elf.

"Did you get your money back?" I asked.

"Better than that," he replied, "for another five bucks he sold me an even bigger gun; a 25 caliber Beretta." With that he took from his pocket another, larger, tightly wrapped package.

The radio crew all gathered around to see the devastating device as I cut the string and pulled away the paper.

It was absolutely beautiful. Beautiful, that is, if you like black rock.

Parish was now the proud owner of a bigger piece of slate.

Chapter 22

MUSIC TO SOOTH THE SAVAGE BEAST

In mid-cruise, just before a new skipper relieved the Captain of the Lake Champlain, the Exec wandered into main radio looking for me. He had a message that he wanted to go out on civilian circuits to the Fisher Company, a manufacturer of expensive high fidelity equipment, ordering an $1,800 hi-fi system for the outgoing Captain as a gift from the ship's officers. In 1957 dollars, that was real money.

He asked that I keep the matter confidential as he hadn't figured out how to pay for the thing yet, but he wanted it sent out immediately to the Captain's home with directions for the Fisher Company to bill the ship directly with attention to LTJG Donald Felt. Felt, was the wardroom mess officer and a friend of mine. The wardroom is really a private "club" run by the officers, who pay for their own food, leather chairs and the like by paying in monthly to the wardroom mess. Everyone pays the same set amount, both ships company and airedales, regardless of rank, and if there is a shortfall in the wardroom mess budget everyone is taxed a few extra bucks to make it up. The Exec's plan was simply to take the money from the wardroom and have Felt put a surcharge on the officers to pay for the purchase.

However, wardrooms are really democracies in miniature, and the members vote on any major expenditures. Regardless of how popular the Captain was, and he wasn't very, the airedales had no particular loyalty to the Lake Champlain. They were only on board for a single cruise and their loyalty was to their squadron and squadron commander, and I had a strong feeling that they would not be happy about this boondoggle.

Of course, I sent the message, but as soon as my watch was over I sought out Don to warn him of what was coming. I explained to him that it was against Naval Regulations to give expensive gifts to senior officers (which it was) and that as Wardroom Mess Officer he was a fiduciary (which was true) and could not use wardroom mess money for anything not authorized by the officers who paid for the mess. I told him that if he gave the Exec the money without a vote of the officers, he could wind up the fall guy.

This certainly got Felt's attention. Without mentioning my name, when the Exec approached him for the $1,800 check to the Fisher Company, Felt told him he couldn't do it without a vote of the wardroom officers.

The Exec promptly replaced Felt as wardroom mess officer with another officer, but got the same response, particularly after Felt and I talked to him. The Exec was visibly upset and threatened the new wardroom mess officer with replacement, but quickly changed his mind when he realized that the appointment was nothing a junior officer would necessarily relish! The wardroom mess officer got very little thanks when the meals were good but plenty of criticism when they weren't.

Now, forced to the wall, the Exec called all the officers together for a meeting in the wardroom and tried to get a majority decision of the wardroom members to support his plan by voice vote. Everyone sat around in silence as the Exec explained that it would be nice for the officers to give the Captain this great sendoff and, with almost 400 officers on board, it would cost less than $5 per head to do it. Several of the squadron members asked to speak, and suggested in the strongest language that the airedales should be left out of the gift as the Lake Champlain was just a temporary duty station for them and they had no reason to give a gift to the Captain of a ship they were on for less than two months before his replacement arrived. There seemed to be a consensus, all right, but it was clearly going in the wrong direction. If only the ship's company officers had to pay, that would come to about $25 per head, but an ensign made only $310 a month in 1957, and at that level $25 was real money.

The Exec suggested a show of hands of all those against, but someone suggested that it would be fairer if they used a secret ballot. The consensus was clearly in favor of a secret ballot, so they passed out slips of paper and a hat in which to collect them after everyone had a chance to write "yes" or "no." I suspected that there were very few "yes" slips, but the Exec and several of his cronies who counted the ballots never revealed the actual count. They merely reported that there were not enough votes in favor to go forward with the plan and left it at that.

It was always a mistake, however, to underestimate Commander Boulivar. The Captain got his hi fi and the Fisher Company got its money, thanks to Las Vegas Night II—another great event for a "worthy cause." The hype was on, the event went off just like the earlier one, and again the enlisted men were the ones that succumbed to the authorized gambling at stunted odds. Most of the officers didn't even bother to go topside.

This time only $3500 was raised, and the Exec proudly announced that another $1700 was sent to support the Stadium and the rest of the money, exactly $1800, went to other "worthy causes."

Chapter 23

OPEN SESAME

While I was one lovesick sailor, there was nothing to fault that Med Cruise for interesting ports of call. In addition to the ports previously mentioned, we hit most of the ports on the French and Italian Riviera, Malta, Beirut, Athens and Istanbul. This latter port was one that was tremendously intriguing; both because the culture was so different and because the officers of the Lake Champlain could literally live there like kings.

This latter phenomenon came about from a happy set of circumstances which started with the U.S. having an extremely favorable balance of trade with Turkey, Turkey having an arbitrary official rate of exchange of 2:1 to the dollar when the Geneva rate was 13:1, and the U.S. Ambassador to Turkey's desire to make sure that the sailors were fairly treated. To accomplish this, he set up a desk on board the ship when it arrived at Istanbul and exchanged money at the Swiss bank rate of 13 Turkish lira to the dollar instead of the official two Turkish lira to the dollar.

We officers could live like potentates on the beach. Five of us JOs took a suite of rooms at the Istanbul Hilton, then the best hotel in the city, as our base of operations for our five-day stay, and the cost was $10 U.S. per day. Divided by five, that came to exactly $2 each.

For most of us junior officers, living as we were on an ensign's or JG's pay, this little windfall allowed us to do some luxurious things. I called Charlene and talked to her for 45 minutes. The telephone rates were based on the official rate of exchange and the call was less than the cost of a cross-country call in the US. I bought a number of art books published in England and the U.S. for a fraction of their stateside cost—again, the book prices were based on the official rate of exchange based on a treaty between the various countries involved.

When the Ambassador exchanged the money, he advised us to exchange no more than we needed, as he would not be able to change it back. This was not a problem for most of us junior officers, but one of my buddies on board, LTJG Dexter Pike, was a Yale graduate who apparently came from a wealthy family and had a trust fund from which he received several thousand dollars each month. He had a lot of money to spend and had that unique talent of being able to be generous without being condescending. At each liberty port he would usually exchange five hundred to a thousand dollars and use the money to buy presents for friends, eat well, and socialize better. No shrinking violet was Dexter.

Following his usual custom, and perceiving Istanbul to be the fascinating place it was, with some exotic opportunities to spend a little wampum, he had taken up the Ambassador's offer and exchanged $1,000 for 13,000 Turkish lira.

Then he tried to figure some way to spend it in five days. It was not easy. On the fourth day he and I went on liberty with my roommate, Joe Cranston, and the three of us combed the famous Istanbul bazaar looking for promising things for Dexter to buy. Dexter had bought a few rugs by that time and had partied to a fair-thee-well, but he had hardly made a dent in his bankroll. Then, fortunately, the heel of my shoe came off, and we went searching through the back streets of the bazaar for a shoemaker to make some quick repairs.

We found one in an unpromising alley just outside of the bazaar proper. The shoemaker spoke almost no English, which was perfectly fair, as we spoke no Turkish, but we got the idea across easily enough by showing him the shoe and the heel. While the shoemaker went to work gluing and hammering the heel back on, I noticed a beautiful copper Russian samovar on the back wall, complete with the Imperial double eagle that revealed that it was pre-revolutionary.

I nudged Dexter, "Ask him how much he wants for the samovar; my mother collects those things and that's a beauty. Its worth a lot of money back home. Note the double eagle; that indicates it was made in Czarist Russia."

"How much for the samovar?" asked Dexter.

The shoemaker looked very puzzled. He knew just enough English to know that a sale was at hand, but not what Dexter had in mind. Dexter again pointed to the samovar and pointed to a wad of bills.

"Not for sale—my soup," he replied.

"You eat soup, then sell samovar," Dexter parried.

"My soup!" was the response.

"Not buy soup, buy only samovar," repeated Dexter.

"Samovar solamente," was my contribution; I was still under the mistaken belief that I could communicate anywhere with a word or two of Spanish.

Eventually Dexter started pulling large denomination lira notes from the wad he had in his pocket. As he started to deposit them on the counter, the shoemaker's eyes lit up like a pinball machine. When four hundred lira bills were sitting on the table, the shoemaker started to shake his head up and down so hard we thought he would lose his dentures, if he had any, which he obviously didn't but desperately needed.

The shoemaker then started screaming into the back of the shop for a pot. After a minute or so a frightened little girl came out with a large pot and the shoemaker started pouring the soup from the samovar into the pot. It actually smelled pretty good. When the soup was drained, he took his newspaper, wiped out the interior, and started wrapping the samovar in the remaining newspaper. Money changed hands and Dexter, Cranston and I headed back to the ship carrying our "treasure."

The next day was Dexter's last day to spend the remainder of his still considerable bankroll, but I had the duty and was not going to be of any help. Dexter left early with half of the JO's in tow, and I stayed on board. After I got off watch, had dinner and saw the movie, I wrote a letter to Charlene and packed it in for the night.

About midnight the door burst open and Dexter turned on the light, bringing me instantly awake. The Navy tends to do that to you.

"What the hell's going on?" was my less than friendly response.

"Dick, get your butt out of the sack, you've got to see this."

With that, Dexter started pulling me off of my upper bunk. As all the officers slept in their underwear, I threw on a pair of khaki pants and shoes and followed Dexter to his bunkroom.

Dexter and Joe Powell, another JG, had commandeered a staff JO bunkroom as there was no admiral on board. Clearly, if an admiral came on board they would be out in the cold, but the chance of that happening was slight as long as the USS Forrestal, a super-carrier almost twice as big as the Lake Champlain, was its cruising partner in the 6th Fleet. This bunkroom was designed to sleep a dozen staff junior officers, so there were ten empty bunks and ten empty desks in the room, but that was before Dexter's last day of liberty.

When Dexter opened the door, I thought I was looking into the cave of Ali Baba. The ten empty bunks and ten empty desks were loaded with samovars of every conceivable shape and size. There must have been 40 of them if there was one. Copper samovars, brass samovars, copper and brass samovars, and even a few silver samovars. The floor was covered with the oriental rugs he had previously purchased, and possibly one or two more from today's venture, and I marveled at the logistical wonder of how Dexter had managed to not only find and buy that many soup containers in the bazaar, but how he had gotten them to the ship.

The answer turned out to be organization. Dexter told me that he had used up some of the chits he had outstanding from a bunch of the other junior officers and gave them cash and a brief lesson on samovars. They then fanned out into the bazaar. They set up one of the shore-patrol officers to watch the booty as they brought it back to the fleet landing and then got the OOD to send in an extra boat to take back the haul when Dexter finally ran out of money. His average price paid was under 300 Turkish lira, or less than $25 each. Dexter assured us that he was going to make his mother, and a lot of other Connecticut ladies that composed his mother's circle of friends, very happy, even if it was at the cost of a lot of hot soup to the workers in the Istanbul bazaar.

Chapter 24

THE ED WOLF SAGA

I started the story of my adventures on the Lake Champlain by introducing Ed Wolf, my new bridge partner. Ed was married, with a wife and three little girls at Oceana NAS, in New Jersey, where the squadron was stationed when it wasn't flying off flattops. He had attended Annapolis and chosen Naval Aviation as the quickest and most direct route to command and eventually to admiral. He was one of the first career officers that I had met in the Navy with real ambition. I felt he wanted to be Chief of Naval Operations ("CNO") someday, and if possible he was going to fly his way there.

Originally all carriers had axial decks, but after the British invented the canted, or angled, deck all subsequent carriers were built in that format. The angled deck, in effect, created two runways, a short axial runway for takeoffs and plane storage and an angled runway on which a plane could touch down and take off again if it didn't catch a wire. Later they either converted the older carriers to angle decks, as they were then doing to the Oriskany, or used the remaining axial deck carriers as helicopter attack ships, as they later did with the Lake Champlain. But in this winter of 1957, brave men landed fast jets on these bobbing postage stamps, knowing full well that they had to catch the hook first time around or plow into the barrier, and usually through it into the pack of planes on the other side. On axial deck carriers, the landing was literally a controlled crash. Ideally the plane would be on the verge of stalling as it took the wave from the Landing Signal Officer ("LSO"), came down hard on the deck, and caught a wire.

The barrier was a huge canvas webbed fence that was raised prior to each landing, then lowered to allow the plane that had just landed to taxi forward after it caught a wire. The barrier was reasonably affective against relatively slow, propeller driven aircraft like the AD-6's that were then still flown off the Oriskany and Lake Champlain, but no one really believed they could stop a jet, particularly one like the Panther that Ed flew with its swept-back wings. The danger to these aviators was very real. On the Oriskany when I first reported aboard, my duty station had been the signal bridge during air operations, and I had watched with horror as one flier a month was killed, an event euphemistically referred to as "buying the farm."

Angle decks, steam catapults and the then recently developed curved mirror automatic landing indicators that were soon to assist the LSO made the procedure much safer, but in my year and a half on the Oriskany you could literally count the number of fliers likely to be lost on the cruise by the number of months we would be away.

While leisurely heading to the Mediterranean that January, air operations were held almost daily. The weather wasn't always the best, but the Captain and the CAG wanted to get the ship and the Air Group ready for operations in a forward area, which the 6th Fleet was definitely considered to be.

As I mentioned earlier, Ed flew the Panther Jet and had over 5,500 hours of flight time without a mishap. But during one of these operations, Ed had his first mishap ever. He was landing his Panther in rather rough weather, but brought the plane down nicely for a perfect touchdown. But something went wrong. All navy carrier planes have a hook that extends out the rear of the plane on landing to grab one of the series of wires strung across the deck in front of the barrier. Each wire has a mechanism on each of its ends called an "arresting gear" which plays out with a tremendous resistance that brings the plane to a very quick stop. The hook itself has what is called a "dash-pot" at its front end that keeps it at a constant angle and at a constant pressure during landing. Its purpose is to prevent the hook from bouncing when it hits the deck. Instead, the dashpot is designed to hold the hook down with tremendous pressure and force it to scrape across the deck until it catches a wire.

Essex class carriers, such as the Oriskany and the Lake Champlain, had a total of twelve wires spaced approximately five feet apart with the first wire approximately 20 feet in from the rear of the flight deck. Thus, a pilot had less than 100 feet within which to make a safe landing. The great pilots, like Ed, would try and catch the number three wire, which was considered a perfect carrier landing. If you caught the number one wire you were coming in too close to the edge—a few feet less and you would smash into the fantail. The number two wire was still considered too close for comfort, the number three wire was considered perfect, and the number four through the eleventh wires were decreasingly perfect landings, with the number twelve wire the wire of last resort. If you caught that wire you were playing it much too close for comfort.

But of course, any wire you caught was a hell-of-a-lot better than not catching a wire. It was axiomatic that any landing you walked away from was a good landing. At the front of the island in Primary Flight (PriFly) every landing was photographed and graded. Pilots who routinely caught the wrong wire took flack, and those that get close to the last wire took a great deal of flack.

This day as Ed came in his hook hit the deck immediately aft of the number three wire, just as it was supposed to, but instead of digging into the deck as it was supposed to do, his hook proceeded to bounce across the deck. It bounced over all the wires and his Panther plowed into and through the barrier. Fortunately for Ed, his was the first plane landing that day, none of the planes in front had been fueled, and there was no fire or explosion. Ed took out two other planes in addition to his own, but walked away from the crash. The barrier had probably served some purpose as it obviously absorbed momentum and slowed his plane sufficiently to prevent disaster.

When the ship arrived in Gibraltar it was met by a phalanx of representatives from the Navy Department and Northrop, the manufacturer of the Panther, to investigate the incident. Everyone agreed that hooks can't bounce, and certainly not over every wire on the deck, but the movies of the landing, and all landings were photographed in those days for just this reason, clearly showed the hook bouncing over each wire.

In early May of 1957, towards the end of a long and rather boring exercise, the Lake Champlain was on its way to Palma de Majorca, a beautiful island several hundred miles off the coast of Barcelona in the Mediterranean. It was far enough south to have good weather year round, and by May the weather and the swimming were expected to be excellent.

However, there was a strong damper on the ship's moral. Two nights before, during night air ops, a newly commissioned Marine pilot had been killed. This had happened on one of his first missions. He had been flying the Banshee twinjet ground support fighter-bomber, had panicked on his approach, had been waived off by the LSO, and came around again for a second try. Again he was too low and the LSO again waived him off for a third try. Around he came again, and still it wasn't right. Once more came the waive-off, but now he panicked. He yelled over his radio, "I CAN'T COME AROUND AGAIN, I GOTTA COME IN NOW, I'M COMING IN!!!" With that he cut his engine and just missed the flight deck, crashing into the gun turret on the fantail. The 40 mm gun speared the plane, it didn't explode, and for some crazy reason it didn't fall back into the sea. It sat there like a giant olive on two steel toothpicks. The young pilot might have walked away from an accident like that, but he landed just wrong, being the opposite of "just right," and he was killed. They didn't announce how he died, but rumor had it that he was impaled on one of the guns.

On my two tours on the Oriskany, one pilot a month, on average, bought the farm, but we had been luckier on the Lake Champlain, this was only the second death for the cruise, but you could depend on the gloom that descended on the ship when any such incident occurred.

Just two days after this accident, Ed Wolf was taking his turn to fly. Again, the weather was clear, everything had been uneventful, and it was Ed's turn to circle around and come in for the controlled crash they call a landing on axial deck carriers. Coming in this time was strictly routine. Great weather, plenty of fuel, good wind across the bow, a sober LSO, Ed Wolf at the controls of his Panther; what could go wrong?

Ed came in at the perfect height and the perfect speed. He got the cut from the LSO at the correct time and turned off his engine for the controlled crash that was going to collect the number three wire as he almost always did. Then something happened at the end of the ten feet of free fall; his right landing gear collapsed as his plane touched down and his right wing, instead of his hook, caught a wire. This caused the entire plane to spin around like a top and smash into the island, the large superstructure that rises up on the starboard edge of every American aircraft carrier. He crashed immediately aft of PriFly, which was always loaded with personnel during air operations, and missed it entirely. The plane exploded on impact into a huge fireball that momentarily blinded everyone looking at the landing.

It looked like nothing could have survived the crash, but the cockpit of the Panther was designed to break away from the fuselage in an explosion, and the design worked. Ed's cockpit, with Ed in it, rolled across the flight deck like a loose football and rolled off the port side of the ship, but fortunately got caught in the port side catwalk right side up and didn't fall into the sea. Ed snapped up his canopy and leaped from what was left of his plane in front of two frightened airmen holding fire extinguishers, snapped to attention, saluted, and asked permission to come on board. After that performance, his reputation was made. Ed was a legend, but the legend wasn't finished.

On June 26, 1957, the Lake Champlain was on an extended exercise with its NATO allies. In this operation the Italians were the Lake Champlain's allies on the "Blue Team" along with part of the 6th Fleet's cruisers and destroyers as her escorts. The enemy "Red Team" consisted of the super carrier, USS Forrestal, with its assigned allotment of cruisers and destroyers and a country called France. Early on that Wednesday, the Lake Champlain was cruising to the west of Italy with its mini-task force approximately equidistant from Naples and Palermo. Ed Wolf was flying carrier air patrol, or CAP, with his wingman at 30,000 feet plus when the Lake Champlain's Combat Information Center ("CIC") spotted Forrestal jets heading toward it. CIC contacted Ed and his wingman and vectored them to the Forrestal jets. Ed spotted the "bogeys" from above and to the right and made a big, swinging arc to the right to come upon them from the rear and above, with his wingman behind him on his right.

Unfortunately, the Italian's air defense center at Naples had also seen the Forrestal jets and had vectored in two of their F-86's to intercept them as well. They came in at the same altitude Ed was flying but from the left, and the lead Italian made a big, swinging arc to the left to also come upon the two Forrestal jets from the rear and above. Neither Ed nor the Italian ever saw each other. They crashed belly to belly, and the resultant fireball filled the sky. Both wingmen saw it, as it happened, but too late to send a warning. Neither one could prevent the disaster that resulted. The Forrestal jets were no longer enemies now, and the four planes, two from the Forrestal, Ed's wingman and the Italian's wingman, circled the one red parachute that emanated from the explosion and opened at 27,000 feet.

The F86, unlike the Panther, had red parachutes and automatic ejection systems, but all four pilots reported that there was nothing on the end of the 'chute that could possibly resemble a man.

Of course there was still the procedures to follow. For the rest of the day and through the night they searched the area for traces of the wreckage or possible survivors, but nothing was found. So mid-morning of the next day the task force left, to continue their deadly game of playing at war.

Ed's loss hit me like a thunderbolt. It didn't seem possible. He had been back at the bridge table the night after both of his previous accidents, joking about them. Now he was gone. I had seen a number of pilots die in the previous two years, and now Ed was part of that deadly statistic of one pilot a month. Up to now we had been lucky on the Lake Champlain, except for the Banshee crash two days before Ed's last mishap we had still not lost any other fliers, but this time we had lost my favorite flier. Never before had one of the unlucky ones been such a close friend.

I was terribly depressed, and wrote a long, rambling letter to Charlene trying to make some sense out of this tragedy and why all these wonderful, brave young men had to die. Of course, I wasn't alone in my grief. Ed had been very popular and the entire ship was like a morgue. Whenever someone died the ship got quiet and depressed, but it seemed even more so with Ed's passing. He had been very senior, one of the earliest Navy pilots to qualify in jets, and took great pleasure in helping the younger men. It was clear to everyone that he was a real comer. Guys like Ed were just not supposed to die so needlessly. They were supposed to survive and become admirals, maybe even CNO.

As Communications Traffic Officer, I had to review all messages coming to or from the ship. Thus, I had to read the messages from Ed's Squadron Commander and from the Captain to Ed's wife. They talked about his bravery and patriotism, and the great loss it was for the country as well as his family. The upsetting part was that it was all true.

On Sunday we held memorial services for Ed aboard ship and similar services were to be held in Oceana where Ed's wife and children lived, but we were seven hours ahead of Oceana. I had the duty that Sunday morning but, as Ed was such a close friend, the Communications Officer gave me permission to secure the watch and go to services, which I did.

On my return to the radio shack, the senior petty officer on the watch, a Radioman First-Class, was standing at the upper half of the Dutch door that separated main radio from the outer office and asked: "Hey,

Lieutenant, wasn't that guy who got killed last week named Wolf? What do you think of this?"

He then handed me a "Class Easy" (for Class E) message. These were civilian messages to military ships and came in from the telegraph companies in Morse code. This message was purportedly from the police in Messina, Italy, was in plain English, and read:

"LIEUTENANT EDWARD WOLF FROM YOUR SHIP WASHED ASHORE THIS MORNING ON ISLAND OF SALINA STOP WEAK BUT OTHERWISE UNINJURED AND UNDER MEDICAL TREATMENT AT MALFA STOP PLEASE ADVISE STOP"

Salina was a small rock of an island to the north of Sicily about equidistant between that island and the little island of Stromboli of Ingrid Bergman fame. Malfa is a tiny fishing village on the north coast of Salina and didn't even appear on the Lake Champlain's charts.

My first reaction was incomprehension. Next I thought it might be a sick joke from a Communist ham radio operator in Italy that had seen an article about Ed's crash in the Italian newspapers. Everyone in the Navy was a little paranoid about Communists in 1957. But I remembered that Ed made lieutenant commander just before the ship left and his flight jacket still had his old rank of lieutenant on it. I had seen that flight jacket many times, and on the back of the jacket was Ed's name and the statement "I am an aviator and an officer in the United States Navy; please lend me every assistance possible" or words to that effect, in about ten different languages. I was convinced that the message must be true, and whoever had sent it got the information about Ed off his flight jacket, not off a newspaper article.

I immediately called Ed's Squadron Commander with the news and quickly drafted a message to the police in Messina for confirmation of their prior message. Then I grabbed my message board and started out the door to bring copies of the original message to CAG and the Exec, but I never made it out of Main Com.

The passageway was filled with members of Ed's squadron led by his Squadron Commander, and everyone was shouting for details. They had gathered in their Ready Room after the Memorial Service and had all heard the report the instant I phoned it in. I gave them all the copies of the message I had, and by then the Exec, CAG and most of the other senior officers had heard the news and they were fighting their way through the throng.

There might have been a little skepticism, but it was overwhelmed by the buoyant optimism of the crowd that had gathered inside and outside Main Com. The senior officers present insisted on waiting in Main Com until we had a reply from Messina to my follow-up message, and the others in Ed's squadron would not allow themselves to be frozen out. About fifty of them tried to squeeze into the compact main radio area waiting for the reply and, fortunately for all of our respiration, it was not long in coming.

Within twenty minutes we had the confirmation from Messina; ED WAS ALIVE! When I read the message, the place went wild, with so much cheering and shouting in that tight little area that its surprising damage wasn't done to more than one eardrum.

When the commotion died down long enough for Ed's Squadron Commander to think, he shot off an immediate message to Ed's wife at Oceana and to the CO there, just in case Ed's wife had gone off to visit family in her grief. We notified the admiral on the Forrestal, and he immediately dispatched one of the Lake Champlain's destroyers to proceed to Malfa at top speed and bring Ed home.

The news quickly spread throughout the ship, and there was euphoria. The Exec thought it would be a good idea to raise some money and give it to the people of this small island that had apparently rescued Ed. The ship quickly passed the hat and had over $3,500 raised in no time, and without the need for a Los Vegas Night. Ed was apparently a lot more popular than a stadium for Annapolis and we wired the destroyer en route to Malfa to give the money collected to the islanders. But our generosity was for naught. When the destroyer arrived, the islanders would not consider accepting any money.

On its return to the Lake Champlain with Ed aboard, the destroyer sent him across in a "bosun's chair," on the "high wire," a device for sending people and cargo back and forth between two ships traveling parallel courses to each other at identical speeds. The passenger sits in the bosun's chair that is suspended from wires strung between the ships. It was a rather rough day when the destroyer arrived with Ed, and for a while as I watched him bobbing up and down between the two ships from the signal bridge, I had an awful feeling that we might lose Ed this way. But he made it aboard, slightly drenched but in one piece. Ed had never been a big man, but he had lost fifteen pounds at least in the ordeal and looked like a sun burnt survivor of Auschwitz. His uniform just hung on his gaunt frame. The sun had scorched him terribly, he had a huge shiner, and he was still very weak from his ordeal.

I was one of the very first to talk to Ed after he got back on board and relayed to him the effort we had made to contact his wife and family to advise them that he was alive. He filled me in on exactly what happened and how he had survived.

That previously mentioned breakaway cockpit on the Panther Jet had saved Ed for the second time from the immediate impact of the explosion. He certainly felt the explosion, which blew off his canopy and the suction pulled off his helmet and oxygen mask, which probably gave him the black eye he now had. Without oxygen at that altitude he probably lost consciousness, but when he came to his first instinct was to pull back on the stick and try to pull out of the dive. When he did so he got no response! He looked out and saw that he had no wings. Then he armed his ejector seat and pulled his ejector curtain, a screen that pulls over the pilot's head and offers some protection as the cannon shell under his seat propels him through the canopy and clear of the tail structure. In Ed's case he had nothing to concern himself with on those counts; he had neither a canopy nor a tail left.

When ejecting you are supposed to pull your feet back and put them into stirrups made for that purpose to protect your legs from being sheered off in the ejection process, but Ed told me that he had no recollection of having done that, but as he still had his legs it must have been automatic for him.

Free of the plane, Ed started spinning head over heals from the impact of the firing mechanism that had propelled him into space. He realized that he might have been unconscious for a spell and didn't know what his altitude was. He remembered that in high-altitude bailouts it was important to use the auxiliary oxygen that was under his seat or he could pass out. Ed reached down, pulled out the oxygen bottle and took a big swig. Then he thought about how high or low he actually was. It is impossible to tell altitude over open water and as Ed didn't know how long he was unconscious, he had no idea how high he was. He was also still spinning like a top. Discretion, he reasoned, suggested that he should pull his parachute now and risk that he might have a long way down. He did. The parachute inflated and the next instant his feet hit the water. Ed had been a microsecond from death once more, and had once again dodged the bullet.

Initially, the shock of his instant landing caused him to panic but he quickly unstrapped his chute and swam clear. Then his wits came back to him and he realized he had forgotten to get out the life raft and the emergency survival kit, which were tucked side by side under the seat attached to his parachute. He swam back, took off his life jacket that he had inadvertently inflated, and dove down. He was able to hit the inflation device on the life raft, which freed it from its position under the seat as it inflated and floated to the surface, but he got entangled in his parachute webbing and was unable to extricate the survival kit.

On the surface he realized that the wind was blowing hard and pushing away his life raft. If he dove down again to try and find the survival kit, he might not find the raft. His wits were still about him, and he swam after and grabbed the raft and climbed on board. All he had with him was some red dye marker, a very pistol with some flares, a waterproof map and a Hershey bar tucked in the pocket of his flight jacket.

That night the weather was rough and he was thrown out of the boat six times. He was terribly exhausted, and by the third time had to convince himself to try and crawl back in. Each time he managed to climb back in with ever greater difficulty, exhausted as he was from his ordeal and exposure to the elements. He also was almost run down by one of the search destroyers and fired all of the flares in his very pistol, but no one noticed the flares, or him, because everyone knew that there was nothing out there to see, the weather was bad, and there had been some lightning that could be confused with the flares.

Ed's cockpit had dropped like a bomb from the fireball that engulfed his and the Italian's planes. No one had noticed it and no one conceived that anyone could have survived the terrible collision and contemporaneous explosion that had been described by the returning pilots.

The next day Ed saw no more smoke from the searching ships and realized that they had given up the search. He inventoried his remaining resources, which consisted of the waterproof map of the area and that one Hershey bar in his jacket pocket. He vowed he would save that until he really needed his strength. Ed was a good navigator, knew were he was reasonably well, and decided that Salina was the closest point of land that he could possibly reach based on what he knew of where he was and the prevailing wind direction and tides. In fact, it was only about 65 miles from the crash site.

Unfortunately, there are no sails on life rafts so, based on his knowledge of the tides and prevailing winds, Ed told me that he felt his only hope was to be spotted from the air, found by a fishing boat, or float to Stromboli, Salina or one of the other small islands north of Sicily on the prevailing current. So off he floated, as he had no choice.

He was on board that life raft for three and one-half days without food or water. Regrettably, after that first night it never even rained. When he got back on board he told me that after the second day he started hallucinating that he had someone with him on the raft. He would talk to him and get his approval of any decision he was tempted to make, although there weren't any real decisions available to him without a sail.

Very late in the afternoon of the third day he finally saw Stromboli off to his left and Salina directly in front of him. At about sunset of the third day, he floated into the protected bay of the little island of Salina, right below the village of Malfa, only to find that there was no sign of life near the water line that he could see from the raft. The island rose out of the water on stark cliffs, and there appeared to be but one small trail cut in the rock from the boat landing below. His only hope appeared from the number of small boats tied up to the island. Ed looked at the narrow path and the steep climb, and finally ate his candy bar to give him the strength to paddle his small boat in against the prevailing current and wind with the one small paddle with which the raft was equipped.

When he arrived at the landing it was already dark and he realized for the first time just how weak he was. He pulled himself from the boat, tried to stand and immediately fell. He got up again, took a few steps, and fell again. He realized he could not walk for any distance. If he tried to walk up the path to the town, he knew he could fall off the narrow trail into the sea. He had not come this far to die falling off a cliff.

So he crawled. Inch by inch, foot by foot, up the narrow trail. The moon came up to give him some light, and he felt his way along the path, always hugging the cliff and staying away from the sheer drop. Intermittently he would pass out from exhaustion, only to force himself awake to continue his crawl. By the morning he had made it almost to the top when he finally passed out, but was soon discovered by some fishermen on their way to their boats. He easily convinced them that he was a United States Naval pilot and that his plane had crashed at sea. Of course, his leather jacket, which he was still wearing, and his physical condition, fully supported his claim.

Malfi had about 2,000 inhabitants and that one doctor, and Ed's arrival was probably the event of the century. The doctor was immediately called, and he gave Ed emergency treatment. When he was sure Ed was out of danger and he had been moved to the small clinic in his own home, he reported the incident to the police at Messina.

—◦◦◦—

If the story had a happy ending, it had a tragic epilogue. The admiral was so overjoyed with the news of Ed's return that he dispatched the Lake Champlain and two destroyers from the exercise we were on to a special five days of liberty at Marseilles, but not before the Lake Champlain detached one of its destroyers to go back to Malfa with a portable X-ray machine, a refrigerator full of antibiotics and a diesel generator as a gift for the island's doctor, a gift the ship knew he could not turn down, and he didn't. The destroyer also brought with it a supply of ice cream for the island's children and instructions to put on a party for the islanders when it arrived. This they did, and reported that it was a great success.

When the Lake Champlain and its two escort destroyers arrived in Marseilles, the destroyers tied up at the pier, but the carrier was too large for any available berth and anchored out in Marseilles Harbor. As aircraft carriers carry all the vehicles and small boats that they need for liberty purposes, a French barge came alongside the starboard side of the ship to receive its buses and cars that were to be offloaded. There were seven Frenchmen and five Lake Champlain sailors on the barge, and one of my radiomen, the same First Class that had delivered the message to me about Ed Wolf's resurrection, was climbing down a rope ladder to the barge when the OOD noted an oil slick on the starboard side. Aircraft carriers have numerous fuel storage tanks to store both bunker fuel, which is not particularly explosive, and high-octane aviation fuel, "avgas," which is. They also have literally miles of piping to carry the various fuels from one location to another for proper ballasting of the ship, for damage control purposes, or for just plain convenience.

It is not that unusual to occasionally spring a leak, and you frequently don't notice it until you stop and the fuel has a chance to accumulate on the surface of the water. The OOD followed standard instructions when a leak is discovered and announced on the 1-MC: "The smoking lamp is out throughout the ship while investigating a fuel leak on the starboard side."

I was asleep in my bunk at the time, heard the announcement, and promptly turned over to go back to sleep. At that very instant, one of the sailors on the barge apparently yelled to a Frenchman on the barge who was smoking, "Hey! No Fumare!" The Frenchman took his cigarette out of his mouth and threw it overboard.

I didn't roll over for long. The OD was yelling over the 1-MC, "FIRE, FIRE ON THE STARBOARD SIDE, FIRE ON THE STARBOARD SIDE, THIS IS NO DRILL, THIS IS NO DRILL! ALL HANDS TO FIRE STATIONS IMMEDIATELY!"

Words like that are electrifying on a ship and get people moving. I was at my fire station in main radio within a minute, but before arriving I had a glimpse of the hell outside. There was a wall of fire running the entire length of the starboard side of the ship that was almost fifty feet higher than the flight deck. The heat was so intense and the fire so close to the ship that there was no way to get near the edge of the ship to play water down on the fire.

All twelve men on the barge were incinerated; we weren't even able to recover all of their bodies. My radioman was half way down the rope ladder when the fire erupted and immediately reversed direction as the fire started to burn the ladder out from underneath him. He barely got one hand on the deck as the ladder literally evaporated in flames. Another sailor risked the flames that were already shooting up higher than the flight deck and grabbed him and two other sailors put out the fire on his uniform and saved his life. He suffered second-degree burns, but none were life threatening, and he was the witness to what had happened on the barge in the seconds before the explosion.

Thus, the odds caught up with the Lake Champlain. While only two pilots had been killed on this cruise, we now had lost five enlisted men. We would be away on this cruise seven months. One a month continued to be the rate at which brave young men died on axial deck aircraft carriers in the peacetime Navy.

Fortunately for the ship, the Gun Boss, who wanted to use that space to clean boats, had removed the airplanes that usually are stacked along the starboard side of a carrier's deck when it comes into port. When stacked on deck, the wings of the planes extend over the side with their wing tanks. Had the planes been there, the fire could have ignited the residual fuel in their wing tanks, causing a chain reaction that could have spread throughout the ship.

The French fireboats came out to fight the fire, but they refused to get close enough to play their water on the fire. It appeared that they had been recently painted and wouldn't come too close to the fire for fear of ruining their new paint jobs. Whatever the truth was, the sight of them sitting out there spraying their water into the air and back into the water, splashing a good hundred yards from the nearest flames, was especially galling. Or would that be Gaulling?

The ship would have been in real trouble had it not been for its destroyers. They still had steam up in their boilers, and pulled out the minute they saw the fire. One of them came out dragging 100 feet of pier when the French pier crews were too slow untying the ship for the Captain.

They stormed into the fire with every hose they had on their ships blazing away and with no regard for their own safety. Within a half hour they had the fire under control, but not before it did 55 million 1957 dollars worth of damage to the old girl. As the island was on the starboard side, all of the starboard radio rooms except main radio were out of commission. The ship's antennae were twisted like pretzels. The Lake Champlain was one sick ship.

Later that day I rode in on the officers' motorboat with Ed. He was on his way in for transportation back to the United States on the USS Mississinewa, an oil tanker that took three weeks to get home. He had refused to fly home, even on a commercial flight, and had turned in his wings that morning to his Squadron Commander. "Three times is the charm," he told me, "if you keep flying after that, you're a damn fool."

"Ed, can you still have a career in the Navy without your wings?" I asked.

"I'll have lots of time to think that problem through on my boat ride home," he replied. "It'll take me three weeks to get home, and I need the time to put some weight back on and get back in condition. When I'm feeling better, I'll think better. In the meantime, I would hate my wife and kids to see me looking like this."

"Ed, I'm sure they would be thrilled to just see you. I can't imagine what it must have been like for them to think that you were dead for the better part of a week and now find out you're alive."

The sight of Ed standing there talking to me on the bridge of the officers motor boat with his uniform now several sizes too large, that terrible black eye, his skin blackened and dried out by the sun, and with the scarred wreck of the Lake Champlain's starboard side behind him, would be etched in my memory for life.

Chapter 25

STAR CROSSED

Two days after Ed's second accident, the Lake Champlain sailed into Palma de Majorca. With its deep-water port, the Lake Champlain could tie up at the pier, making liberty much easier. All you had to do was walk down the gangway instead of taking a boat. It was a beautiful sunny day, and as Majorca had a well-deserved reputation for beautiful beaches, lovely Mediterranean water and plenty of sun, it looked to me like it was BEACH PARTY TIME!

The Lake Champlain's Communications Officer agreed with me when I suggested that a beach party for the communications division was a jolly good idea, and with his permission I set up a beach party for our group on the afternoon of our arrival. The ship actually carried all of the accouterments for a beach party, i.e., beer and balls of the foot, base and volley variety, and with the appropriate requisition we obtained ten cases of beer, several of each type of ball, a garbage can for policing the beach when we were done, and one of the ship's busses.

Leaving a skeleton crew in main radio, we took off to San Pablo Beach with our supplies; everything necessary for the perfect beach party except one small item: Ice for the beer.

We forgot the ice.

Now warm beer may be acceptable in England and even in the Royal Navy, but in the heat of Majorca it left a little to be desired for the crew of a U.S. Navy ship, even with the thirsty lot with which I had to contend. Being resourceful, we scoured the area around San Pablo Beach for some place that sold ice. No one did, or if they did they didn't sell it in the mom and pop markets which proliferated around the beach area. Finally, an idea came to one of the other officers in the group. While it was hot and sunny, it was still only May and the water was on the chilly side. The garbage cans supplied by the community on the beach, unlike the Navy issue galvanized steel cans, were open wire. We could take one of the wire garbage cans, weight it down with rocks, put in our beer, and sing songs and play a little ball while waiting for the beer to cool.

That is exactly what we did. We figured it would take an hour to get the beer cold, so out came the footballs, baseballs and volleyballs and we started having BEACH PARTY!

Unfortunately, it was shorted lived. After about half an hour some of the others and I noticed people walking down the street next to the beach carrying six-packs of American beer. At first we thought nothing of it—after all, why shouldn't Majorcans have every right to buy American beer—even Schlitz, the beer that made Milwaukee famous. But nothing but Schlitz?

"CARAMBA, THE BEER!" Several yelled in unison. A bunch of sailors then ran into the water and raced out to our "beer locker" where our store of beer was supposed to be cooling, but all that they found cooling there was a garbage can full of rocks. The beer was gone. The Majorcans must have seen what we were doing and, as soon as we planted the beer locker, they swam out to retrieve the beer. Of course, we still had football and baseball and volleyball, but balls of the foot, base and volley kind do not a beach party make for 60 sailors who have been at sea for 21 days without even sacrificial wine to quench our thirst.

The last laugh was on the Majorcans, however. Forced to retreat again to the local markets and buy local beer to continue our party, we rapidly discovered that the local brew was a hell-of-a-lot better than that which had made Milwaukee famous. And it was cold!

—◈◈◈—

Beer, or the lack of it, was not the only problem to confront me in beautiful Palma de Majorca. The Lake Champlain was tied up in Palma next to a very well known sailing ship; a big, black three mastered sailing schooner named the *Black Swan*. It had been in Cannes when we were there and appeared to be following us around the Mediterranean, which of course it was not. Its fame, however, was not so much from its looks, which were spectacular, but from its owner, Errol Flynn, who was reported to be living aboard with his teenaged wife and their new baby.

Very early one morning several days later, Joe Cranston, Bob Pollack, a JG from engineering, and I were returning from a night of reveling. Bob was a large, indeed a very large, jovial guy from Georgia Tech with a wonderful sense of humor. He was kind of a cross between Lou Costello and the Goodyear blimp. The three of us had first gone to a reception thrown by the Mayor of Palma for the officers of the Lake Champlain and from there to the local taverns to round off our evening. We had more than rounded it off; it was damn near flattened by the time we tried to maneuver back to the ship.

As we staggered down the pier singing old college songs, out of the Black Swan came none other than himself, Errol Flynn, old (to our young eyes), drunk, fat, dressed in nothing but his boxer shorts and waiving a belaying pin, one of those wooden bats used to tie down ropes on a sailing ship when it wasn't being used as a club to fight off pirates or threaten drunken sailors. My friends and I had apparently awakened the great man from his reverie, whatever that might have been, and he did not have time to dress for the occasion. He was a sight. He was tremendously out of condition, with a huge gut that hung out over the waistband of his boxers and a puffy face swollen from a life of too much excess. In a few years his life would be cut short by this excess, but all the three of us could tell at the time was that he was fat, drunk, showing way too much flesh, and furious.

"YOU'VE AWAKENED MY WIFE AND BABY, YOU (really bad expletive deleted) SONS-A-BITCHES!" he shouted.

"I'm terribly sorry," I replied for the three of us, "we were just singing college songs and weren't thinking. We'll be quiet from now on." This was an easy promise as we were only several hundred feet from the Lake Champlain's gangway.

"YOU'RE GOD DAMNED RIGHT YOU'LL BE QUITE, YOU (another really, really bad expletive deleted)—DO YOU KNOW WHO I AM?" If he was concerned about waking his wife and child, he seemed unconcerned about his own voice, which was operating at several decibels louder than one of the Lake Champlain's jets.

Of course we knew who he was, but this was high camp, and we replied as close to unison as an ad lib could get, "No, sir, who are you?"

"I'M ERROL FLYNN, THAT'S WHO I AM!" he shouted, waiving the belaying pin over his head in a staggering effort that almost made him fall over. It was obvious that the great one was drunker than we were.

"Nah," said Pollack, "you couldn't be Errol Flynn; you're too fat to be Errol Flynn."

Flynn exploded with that, and started screaming every expletive in his very extensive vocabulary of expletives. In the Navy, I had heard quite a few expletives, and some that were obviously of the same genre, but Errol Flynn knew some that were new even to me. Probably old pirate expletives. He also now started waiving the belaying pin around in earnest, but it was true, he was too fat to be Errol Flynn; too fat, too drunk, and too slow. He couldn't hit a thing. He staggered after we three musketeers for about twenty feet as we retreated down the pier laughing, but gave up and just stood there watching and continuing his stream of expletives as we boarded the ship in hysterics.

—◊◊◊—

The next morning I was paged on the 1-MC and directed to report to the Exec. When I got to Commander Boulivar's cabin, he was sitting at his desk looking at a dispatch. He gave me that long look he had over his bushy eyebrows and said, "Lieutenant, you wouldn't know anything about a little incident this morning at about 0200 between three allegedly drunken JG's from the Lake Champlain and Errol Flynn, would you?"

"Well, Commander, I do know a little about it, what's going on?"

"Well, we received a message this morning from BuPers relaying a message that they received from Mr. Flynn complaining about the behavior of three of our officers. Seems that they made a lot of racket while returning to the ship in a high state of inebriation, awakened Mr. Flynn's family, and then insulted Mr. Flynn."

"What makes you think that I had anything to do with it, Sir?"

"Well, Dick, it sounds like you and the description fits you. He never told me what that description could have been, but nevertheless I replied, "Any thoughts on who my companions were?"

"No, Lieutenant, but I know you'll tell me."

"I'd preferred not to, Sir, at least on the record."

"We're not on the record, haven't been for this whole session. Tell me what happened, then I'll see if I want to know who else was involved."

So I relayed to the Exec the exact events described above. Commander Boulivar laughed so hard I was afraid he might fall out of his chair. I didn't have to tell the Exec who was involved, he guessed that, and certainly guessed that Pollack was the one who had come up with the great one-liner.

The joke was that Pollack was the fattest officer on the ship. He, if anyone on board, would know one when he saw one.

The Commander then directed me to take a message to BuPers:

YOURS OF 0742 ZULU STOP UNABLE TO IDENTIFY OFFICERS FROM DESCRIPTION GIVEN BUT AM CONTINUING TO INVESTIGATE STOP PLEASE ASSURE MR. FLYNN AND HIS FAMILY THAT THE SHIP AND ITS OFFICERS AND MEN ARE GREATLY TROUBLED BY THE INCIDENT AND WISH TO EXTEND THEIR APOLOGY ON BEHALF OF THE OFFICERS INVOLVED AND THE ENTIRE SHIP STOP IF OFFENDING OFFICERS ARE LOCATED ASSURE MR. FLYNN THAT APPROPRIATE STEPS WILL BE TAKEN STOP BOULIVAR EXECUTIVE OFFICER USS LAKE CHAMPLAIN END

"What do you think, Dick, will that appease the fat bastard?"

"Well, Sir, it might—but what would you think of adding to the end of the message something along the lines of:

'UNFORTUNATELY WE DID NOT RECOGNIZE THE OWNER OF THE BOAT IN QUESTION AS ERROL FLYNN—WE THOUGHT MR FLYNN WAS A THINNER GENTLEMAN!'"

"Now you're really pushing. I won't say I wouldn't like to do it, but I won't, and neither will you. This is one message you don't change on me, understand Lieutenant."

I gave the reply taught me long ago by another Exec on another ship: "Aye, aye, Sir!"

Chapter 26

CROSSING THE CHAPLAINS

Busy as I kept myself on the Lake Champlain, my mind was never very far from San Francisco where Charlene awaited my return. As soon as I arrived home we planned to get married, but I soon discovered that planning for a marriage required at least some small amount of cooperation from one's employer, particularly when that employer is a 600 pound gorilla named the United States Navy.

The first shocker came when I discovered that, unlike the Pacific Fleet with its six-month tours of rotation to WesPac, the Atlantic Fleet brass thought nothing of keeping the Lake Champlain in the Mediterranean for seven months or more and then rotating the ship back to Europe only six weeks after its return. That was to be the fate of the Lake Champlain when it returned to Mayport. It was scheduled to have six weeks of R&R and then off on a NATO exercise and a tour of "showing the flag" in Northern Europe. This, of course, was all before the fire.

This caused Charlene and me all sorts of logistic problems. What could Charlene do after we were married. If we could afford to have her follow me over to Europe, that would make a great extended honeymoon, but if not, Charlene would have to set up housekeeping by herself, far away from her friends and family, very far away from me, and someplace convenient to Mayport, but no place was convenient to Mayport.

Furthermore, the Exec had announced that no one, *for any reason*, would be granted more than two weeks leave prior to the ship's redeployment. He contended that he needed two-thirds of the crew on board at all times to prepare for the next sailing, and that left everyone with just two weeks leave—no exceptions! While that may have been logical from the Navy's standpoint, for a lovesick sailor who had to fly 3,000 miles across country to get married, then drive out to the East Coast with his new bride and establish housekeeping, two weeks seemed impossible.

So I went to Commander Boulivar and asked the Exec to make an exception for me; after all, I was one of the very few officers on board, if not the only one, that was neither from the South nor the East Coast, was about to get married, and just had too many things that had to be accomplished before redeployment. I needed more than a two week window.

Boulivar turned me down flat.

Meanwhile, the Navy was having great fun making the planning for the wedding almost impossible. The Lake Champlain left Mayport on January 6, 1957, for what was supposed to be a six-month tour of duty. But then the Lake Champlain's replacement carrier had mechanical problems and was delayed in coming to its relief and our date to return kept getting extended and extended. Initially we were due back on the 4th of July. Then the 15th. Then the 20th. Then the 30th. Then "sometime in mid-August."

Meanwhile, back in San Francisco, Charlene and her family were constantly frustrated in trying to plan a wedding. Charlene, also Jewish, had been affiliated with the same temple her entire life, but the rabbi there finally told her parents that he could not hold an indefinite date; too many others were demanding the time slots that Charlene and her parents kept blocking out as the Lake Champlain's schedule kept changing.

I finally suggested to Charlene that she contact the Jewish chaplain at Treasure Island. The Navy, at least, had to have sympathy for the indefinite schedule of a Naval officer. This they did, and found a young JG, Rabbi Joshua Burstein, who was extremely excited at the prospect of conducting a wedding at the chapel at Treasure Island. Apparently it was his first wedding since being ordained and commissioned. Charlene and her family found Rabbi Burstein, at least, very understanding of the Lake Champlain's schedule and he was prepared to make whatever adjustments were necessary to make sure that Miss Charlene Mencoff became Mrs. Charlene Maltzman at the earliest possible opportunity.

There was one hitch, however, and the following chain of events was relayed to me through Charlene's letters. After finding the Jewish Chaplain so accommodating, one day, on entering Treasure Island to discuss details of the wedding with the Chaplain, Charlene's mother looked up and for the first time took a good look at the Treasure Island Chapel where the event would be held. On top of the Chapel, which was the only house of worship on the Base, was something that was not on top of Congregation Sherith Israel, the family's reformed synagogue in San Francisco's Pacific Heights; they had placed a large cross at its peak.

Now Charlene's mother certainly understood that we are essentially a Christian nation and was not surprised that there was a cross on the only chapel on the base, but she did express her concern for the feelings of her parents and some of their older Jewish friends to the rabbi. Rabbi Burstein, being a creative person, to say the least, immediately suggested a simple solution; construct a giant Star of David that would clamp on to either side of the cross so that, on the day of the wedding, the Chapel would have a Jewish star on its top instead of a cross. This sounded like a very good idea to Mrs. Mencoff who, unfortunately, failed to recognize the significance of the rabbi having only recently been ordained and commissioned.

So Rabbi Burstein called the Treasure Island carpenter shop and ordered them to climb to the top of the Chapel, measure the cross, and construct a Mogen David, as the Star of David is called in Hebrew, that would fit over and clamp on to the cross.

Naturally, an order from someone as important as a Navy chaplain would be obeyed.

Thus it was that two weeks later the Mogen David was completed and, immediately prior to another visit from Charlene's mother, Chaplain Burstein had the new appendage to the Chapel installed so she could view it when she drove onto the base. Installation was completed at 1315 Navy time.

Mrs. Mencoff arrived on the base forty-five minutes later. Imagine her pleasure as she made the turn for the Chaplain's Office and passed in front of the Chapel, now crowned with the symbol of her Jewish faith.

Fifteen minutes later, the Protestant chaplain, Commander Stroud, entered the base after a fine lunch at Jack's in the City. As his driver made the turn after passing the guard house at Treasure Island onto the street facing the Chapel, imagine his reaction as he looked up to admire his wonderful house of worship.

I suspect he exclaimed some significant protestation as he stared in disbelief at the sacrilege that had been perpetrated on his Lord's house.

Commander Stroud apparently went immediately to Father Brannan, the Catholic chaplain and a lieutenant commander, to see if he knew anything about the sudden change in ethnicity that had taken place at the Chapel. From the window in Father Brannan's office they apparently had an excellent vista from which to view what formerly had been a non-denominational Christian house of worship.

"Lord Mother of God!" Father Brannan probably exclaimed as he crossed himself rapidly, "Who could have done such a thing."

Then in unison they must have looked at each other and exclaimed, "ITS GOT TO BE THE RABBI!"

In any event, regardless of what had transpired in their discussion on discovering the Mogen David, they dashed out of Father Brannan's office and down the hall to the rabbi's office, storming in on the rabbi and Charlene's mother, who were standing at the rabbi's window, which also offered an excellent vista of the recently created non-denominational synagogue, admiring the rabbi's effort.

They turned at the interruption to face a full commander, who's face was beet red, and a lieutenant commander, who's face was purple.

"WHAT THE HELL HAVE YOU DONE TO OUR CHAPEL?" they asked in unison, apparently ignoring that there was someone else in the office other than the rabbi, and that person was a lady.

The recently ordained and commissioned rabbi appeared not the least bit flustered by the assembled superior officers—he apparently felt that there was only one superior officer to whom he had to answer.

"First," replied Burstein, "Let me introduce you gentlemen to Mrs. Mencoff, the lady for whom I conceived the concept of covering up the cross so that we could use the Chapel for a Jewish wedding. What could possibly be wrong with that?"

"It's sacrilege, that's what it is," said Stroud.

"It's desecration of a house of worship, that's what it is," said Brannan.

"It's a Mogen David, that's what it is," said Burstein.

"It's only for my daughter's wedding," said Charlene's mother.

"I order you to get that da . . . , that thing down off of there by the end of the day, *Lieutenant* Burstein," said Commander Stroud, and with that he and Brannan turned on their heels and left the room.

Burstein, shaken by this exchange, was now as red in the face as Stroud. Ignoring Charlene's mother, he reached down and placed a telephone call to the senior Jewish chaplain in the Navy, a full captain. He fortunately got right through and explained the situation. The senior Jewish chaplain in the Navy agreed completely with LTJG Burstein that Jewish personnel have just as much right to put a Mogen David on top of the chapel as Christian personnel have to put up a cross.

"I'm sending you a telegram as we speak," said the Captain to Burstein, "countermanding Commander Stroud's order to you to take down the Mogen David and I will fly out first thing tomorrow if necessary to get this matter resolved."

Within an hour Burstein had his orders from the Captain and took them to Stroud. Stroud's color now went from red to magenta, and he and Brannan immediately placed calls to the respective highest-ranking chaplains in each of their respective religions. Each supported their co-religionist and responded that they, too, would be out the following day to get this matter resolved.

Thus it was that the following day the three highest ranking chaplains in the Navy, two captains and a commodore (the equivalent of a one-star admiral or general), descended on Treasure Island to observe what probably one of the most junior rabbi's in the Navy had wrought on that base's Chapel for the benefit of Charlene's mother.

The discussion was hot and heavy, and LTJG Burstein and his boss were clearly losing ground. The senior Jewish chaplain, realizing that he was outgunned, pointed out to Burstein and Mrs. Mencoff that after all, we were a predominantly Christian nation, and Commander Stroud and Lieutenant Commander Brannan were quite generous to allow us to use the Chapel at all.

"I must admit," he continued, "we really don't have the right to change their regular house of worship to meet our specifications when we are such a small percentage of the population."

At this, Mrs. Mencoff entered the fray. As noted, she was an extremely attractive woman who looked more like Charlene's sister than her mother. To this point she had left it to the rabbis to present her case. Burstein was obviously awed by the rank of the other officers, and his boss was not standing his ground.

"Wait a minute," said Mrs. Mencoff, "are you suggesting to me that God wouldn't know that the cross was still there if we covered it up for a few hours? We are not asking for any permanent change in the Chapel, only that the sensitivities of Jewish Naval personnel and their families be considered. There is no question of desecration here, Jesus was Jewish and when he prayed, he prayed in a synagogue under a Mogen David, not in a church under a cross. All we are asking is that a young Jewish girl that is marrying one of your fine, young Jewish Naval officers be allowed to get married in her faith in a house of worship that doesn't overtly reflect the faith of any other religion."

"We can't take off the cross, you know," interjected Father Brannan.

"I know that," continued Mrs. Mencoff, "so let us cover the cross for a few hours. It doesn't hurt anything, and will demonstrate that the Navy is equally considerate to all its personnel, no matter what their faith."

The Commodore now took over, as the senior officer present, and said, "You know, Captain Levine, our Jewish sailors and officers may not be large in numbers, but their contribution to our service is greatly appreciated, and we would be small, indeed, if we didn't try and lean over backwards to accommodate someone as delightful as Mrs. Mencoff and her daughter, who I am sure is as lovely as she is. But how about a compromise? How about putting a plaque commemorating the ten commandments with a Mogen David star above it immediately below the cross. Then it will be obvious that the Chapel is there for Christians as well as Jews, and no one should be offended."

He hadn't become a Commodore for nothing, and everyone bought off on the compromise. All further discussion was now unnecessary as the three highest ranking chaplains in the U.S. Naval Service, joined by Commander Stroud, Lieutenant Commander Brannan and LTJG Burstein, fell all over themselves to accommodate Mrs. Mencoff and her daughter who they had never met. They invited Mrs. Mencoff to join them for lunch, and she happily agreed.

After coffee, Commander Stroud even offered to bring in potted palms to cover the stained glass windows of Christ being crucified.

In retrospect, it was an unfair fight—six officers, five of whom were quite senior, against a determined Jewish mother.

Chapter 27

ANNAPOLIS CALLING

In mid May, just when my frustration with Commander Boulivar's refusal to give me more than two weeks leave to get married was at its peak, and before Ed Wolf's final mishap, reprieve came in the form of an offer from BuPers (the Bureau of Naval Personnel) for an appointment to Annapolis teaching communications. The only hitch was that it was a two year tour of duty and as I would only have one year left on my original three year commitment by the time I would have to report to duty on June 27th, 1957, I would have to agree to a one-year extension. But it was a no-brainer for me. In exchange for a one year extension as a Regular Naval officer I would have a marvelous two-year honeymoon at Annapolis, and that sounded a lot better than two weeks to get married and move Charlene to Mayport and immediately redeploy on a new cruise to Northern Europe.

We were in port when the message from BuPers came through, and being in communications it got to me before anyone. Within minutes I arranged a relief and went ashore, heading for the nearest post office to place a trans-Atlantic telephone call to Charlene. In my excitement I forgot the time difference and woke her from a sound sleep, but she agreed with me immediately that I should take Annapolis, even though it meant delaying my return to Stanford Law School by a year.

Later that day I framed a letter of acceptance and sent it off through official channels, as required by Naval Regulations, via the Exec and Captain. But things did not go smoothly. Commander Boulivar insisted on adding an endorsement to my acceptance to the effect that the Lake Champlain was to redeploy to the North Atlantic six weeks after its return from the Med and that it could not perform acceptably in a forward area without a replacement communicator of at least my qualifications. I was apoplectic when I heard about it, but the chief in the Captain's office, where these things were processed, assured me that if BuPers wanted me at Annapolis, "The Exec was pissing into the wind."

Now the waiting started. According to the BuPers offer I would be reporting to Annapolis at the end of June. That meant a mid-June wedding if the plans could be worked out quickly enough. But while Charlene and her parents could try and do the planning, without a firm fix on whether we would be going to Annapolis there was no way they could send out invitations.

Meanwhile, weeks went by and I heard nothing from BuPers. June 1st came and went and still nothing. Finally, on June 15th I shot off a message to the JG desk at BuPers:

"PLEASE ADVISE WHEN ORDERS FOR ANNAPOLIS CAN BE EXPECTED AND WHEN I WILL BE DETACHED FROM LAKE CHAMPLAIN STOP"

Within hours came the reply:

"REGRET UNABLE TO OFFER YOU ANNAPOLIS APPOINTMENT DUE TO UNAVAILABILITY OF ADEQUATE RELIEF STOP JG DESK BUPERS STOP"

Now I was furious. As far as I was concerned, the simple laws of contract governed this situation. Offer and acceptance equals contract, at least at Stanford Law School. In the Navy, apparently not so much! While I knew that all communications with BuPers are supposed to go through the chain of command, I found an obscure Navy Regulation that stated that officers could communicate with BuPers regarding personnel problems without going through the chain of command. Being a journeyman dyslexic (this was true enough), I just elected to read "personnel" as "personal" and shot off a letter to the JG Desk at BuPers to the effect that as a Regular Naval officer about to be married, how did they expect my wife to accept my making the Navy my career when the Navy reneged on its contracts. I pointed out that BuPers had made an offer to me: Extend for a year and the Navy will give you an appointment as an instructor at Annapolis for two years. I had accepted that offer in unequivocal terms. Under any interpretation of Anglo-Saxon jurisprudence, that was a binding contract.

While an insignificant JG had no real power to force the Navy to live up to its commitments, shouldn't the Navy treat its officers in the same manner as the Navy expected its officers to treat it and live up to its commitments?

I sent the letter via regular airmail; I certainly couldn't use the Communications Department, as that would have sent the message up through the chain of command. Meanwhile, Commander Boulivar had been ecstatic at my rejection for the Annapolis appointment, and took pride in telling everyone how he had so much influence at BuPers that he was able to kill my appointment and transfer.

Ten days after my letter left the ship I received orders from BuPers transferring me to the staff of Commander, Naval Training Command, Pacific Fleet (ComTraPac) at the Naval Training Command Center in San Diego, California. My new assignment was as Assistant Communications Officer, with no extension of my required active duty necessary, and I didn't have to report for duty until after Labor Day.

To put icing on the cake, my relief was an ensign just out of Com (Communications) School.

Needless to say, Charlene and I were ecstatic. The fire in Marseilles had already taken place and after that there was no alternative for the Lake Champlain but to limp home immediately. She could do no further good in the Mediterranean. The schedule had been set and the ship was due to arrive in Mayport on July 27th, with or without a relief. Charlene and her parents, with the help of Rabbi Burstein and Mrs. Mencoff's new friends, Commander Stroud and Father Brannan, made sure that the chapel would be available and they set the new wedding date and time as Sunday, August 4, 1957, at 4 PM—a scant week after my return. We would then be able to have almost a one-month honeymoon before having to report to duty at ComTraPac.

Now it was Commander Boulivar's turn to be furious, but there was nothing he could do about it. BuPers had spoken, and so it was writ.

Chapter 28

THE COURT-MARTIAL OF MOORE

Some time before Ed Wolf's resurrection from the sea and my resurrection from Commander Boulivar's grasp by my new orders, during a liberty call at Cannes, the ship was shocked by the revelation in the Exec's Plan of the Day ("POD") that one of the Lake Champlain's enlisted men had brutally beaten an elderly French baker. The incident had apparently occurred outside his shop, in front of his elderly wife, and left the man a cripple for life. The identity of the enlisted man was unknown, and anyone with any information was requested to come forward and save the honor of the ship and the Navy.

To no one's surprise, no one came forward, and we all felt terrible about the incident. The Exec suggested that we raise a collection to help the elderly French baker. This time there was no need for a Las Vegas Night. Everyone was very generous, even I bought into this one, and we raised over $6,500. The Exec then had one of the flyers fly one of the Lake Champlain's planes with one of the Chaplains, Commander Longo, to Italy where Longo exchanged the money on the black market for substantially more French currency than we could have obtained in Cannes. When the plane returned the Chaplain to Cannes, we heard that the Chaplain gave the French money to the baker with no strings attached and urged him to bring a claim for compensation against the Navy, which the Frenchman apparently did.

A nice gesture, although of questionable legality, especially the smuggling of the black market currency part.

I thought nothing more of the incident until one day I heard that the case had been broken. An enlisted man named Parker had been with the culprit at the time of the incident and confessed to Commander Longo.

The Chaplain prevailed on Parker to report the incident to the Exec, which he eventually did after sitting on the problem for almost a week. The man Parker identified was Electrician's Mate 3rd Class James "Jimmie" Moore. Moore was picked up immediately and thrown in the brig, where most of the ship's company thought he should probably stay for a good long time, if not the rest of his life.

I had been totally removed from the military justice program on the Lake Champlain. When I reported aboard I had kept my background to myself and, with the responsibilities I had, I decided to try and avoid the court-martial scene. Commander Boulivar, apparently, neither knew about my background and Naval Justice School experience or by this time had forgotten it.

In any event, the Exec also viewed me as one of "his boys" for reasons that were totally inexplicable to me, except possibly because I continued to do my job well and had the "Aye, aye, Sir!" and the salute down perfectly. Each time we went to sea on an exercise they distributed to each Department on the ship an Operations Manual (Op Manual) the size of the New York telephone directory. In my opinion, Op Manuals were written by geniuses for use by idiots. Everything was spelled out, practically to when you went to the bathroom and how you brushed your teeth. The detail in each Op Manual included a description of every message that was to go out from the ship and each of its departments during the exercise based on what occurred, including the exact time when it should be sent, its wording, its code level, and the action addressees and information addressees to whom it should be sent.

From my first days on the Oriskany, I was fascinated by these Op Manuals, and actually read them. That made me possibly unique on both ships. On both the Oriskany and the Lake Champlain the same pattern developed. During my first exercise of each cruise I would receive a series of messages, usually about various "air strikes," to be sent during the operation. I would compare the messages to the Op Manual and would take it upon myself to make the changes necessary to make them comply with the Manual. Usually that meant completely rewriting the messages, changing the code level and the addressees. Then, after I sent the messages and the watch was over, I would take the revised messages and the original version back to the originating department head. I would then show the department head, usually a full commander, the Op Manual and the revisions I had made to the messages to comply with the Op Manual.

"Commander," I would say, "I hope you didn't mind that I made the changes to comply with the Op Manual without coming back to you first, but I was tied up with the watch . . ."

"No, no, Lieutenant, (or Ensign on the Oriskany)" the senior officer would interrupt, "that's terrific, do it any time."

So I did, and the word quickly got around to all of the other division commanders, and the next thing I knew, when I came on watch during an exercise I would find that there had been no traffic over the previous watch. Everyone was waiting for *me* to come on duty. That kept me extremely busy, but I liked being busy. It didn't take me long to discover that, when you are busy, time passes fast and you're not bored. I liked both facets of that equation.

When you do good work in the Navy, you have no shortage of friends or benefits. I kept getting selected to go off on special duty to places like Rome, Florence, Capri and Venice, and that was a direct result of what I accomplished in the radio shack.

When we arrived in Marseilles, however, I suddenly received a new assignment from the Exec. The Exec had decided not to rely on either of the two established special court-martial boards on the ship for a court-martial of Jimmie Moore and instead formed a new special court-martial board solely to hang poor old Jimmy. A full Commander named Benjamin Salt, a mustang, who was chief engineering officer, headed the court. It included on its panel Lieutenant Tim Mitchell, in charge of the Exec's office and Commander Boulivar's right hand man, and three other senior career officers, all lieutenant commanders and all with big reputations for being disciplinarians. The trial counsel was Captain Dan Phelps, the commandant of the Marine detachment on board, and for reasons that were totally inexplicable to me, I was named as the defense counsel.

The Exec had chosen me, probably, because I was a "short timer" with orders off the ship and about to get married. He did not expect me to give the matter much attention. I, however, had not forgotten the Exec's attitude about my pending marriage and what he did to torpedo my Annapolis appointment, and was about to give this matter a lot of attention.

Initially, I must admit that I had little enthusiasm for this assignment. From the daily reports in the Exec's POD I had been persuaded that Moore was guilty and had behaved atrociously. I was totally convinced that my opinion of Moore was shared by almost everyone on the ship. I was, therefore, surprised and somewhat troubled when they decided to keep

Moore on board and give him a special court-martial instead of sending him to the beach for a general court-martial, which could impose much more severe penalties. Six, six and BCD sounded like soft punishment for someone who had mercilessly beaten an elderly man in front of his wife and left him crippled for life.

However, I was less surprised and more troubled after I talked to Jimmie Moore. The Marine guards brought him in chains to my cabin, a first in all of my experience in dealing with defendants in a court-martial. The Legal Officer told me that I could avoid the chains if I would agree to interview Moore in his cell, but I preferred to interview him in my cabin rather than the brig where there was no privacy. With a Marine stationed outside my cabin door to make sure that the manacled prisoner couldn't escape, we had a long talk.

Moore was a blond man of ruddy complexion and built like a fireplug. Only 5'8" tall, he weighed close to 200 pounds, and none of it was fat. His story, later confirmed by Parker, the sailor who was with him and turned him in, was far different than the version transmitted to the officers and crew through the POD.

According to Moore and Parker, the two of them were returning to the ship in a high state of inebriation when they passed a corrugated iron fence. Moore had picked up a small stick as he staggered along and was running it across the ridges of the corrugated fence when they came upon the baker's shop. The baker, a man named Paul Bouvier, had a coffee and pastry shop along one of the side streets that led to the fleet landing. His wife was his principal employee. The shop was down three stairs from the sidewalk and in front of the shop was a sheet-metal sign sticking out vertically into the sidewalk shaped like a fat chef with the menu printed on both sides of the sheet-metal held out in the chef's sheet-metal arms. Moore slapped the sign as he passed, probably with the stick, but he had little memory of that detail.

Regardless, the slap gave off a healthy twang, which brought Bouvier to the doorway, where he started shouting and swearing at Moore. Moore pushed Parker away and returned to the steps leading down to the cafe where Bouvier was standing. Bouvier, the "elderly French baker," was in his mid-thirties, and we later found out that he had been the former light-heavyweight Golden Gloves champion of Marseilles. He normally would have towered over Moore, but he was standing at the bottom of the steps and Moore on the top. The three steps made a substantial difference, and

Moore, drunk as he was, was looking down on the man shouting back epithets with his arms on his hips.

Parker came over behind Moore and pulled him around by one elbow, saying, "Let's get out of here before we get into trouble." With that he started dragging the drunken Moore down the street, but Bouvier leaped out of the stair well and gave chase. In a few steps he caught up with the two sailors and punched Moore in the back of the head, sending him sprawling. He tried to get up, but Bouvier started kicking him and hit him again and again.

A crowd had gathered by this time, and they were yelling at Bouvier to stop. Finally, several customers and neighbors jumped in and grabbed Bouvier by both arms, pulling him back.

Parker now grabbed Moore, who was semi-comatose from the combination of alcohol and Bouvier's fists and feet, and with the help of one of the Frenchman started dragging him back toward the fleet landing He got about 20 feet, the Frenchman assisting him let go, and Moore seemed to be navigating successfully with the assistance of Parker. Then the Frenchmen holding Bouvier made the mistake of letting him go and Bouvier pulled away and started running after Moore and Parker. When he reached them, he kicked Moore in the small of the back with a huge laugh.

But Bouvier was a *former* Golden Gloves champ, and was not in as great condition as he perceived himself to be. This last move apparently caused his leg to go out from under him, and he fell. Moore, now thoroughly enraged, shoved Parker aside and kneed Bouvier in the stomach. Parker pulled him back and dragged him back to the ship. Moore was cut and bleeding, and was shipped off to sickbay the minute he arrived on board, but no one associated the beaten and bloody Moore with the story in the POD about the elderly old French baker who had been beaten and crippled. Apparently Bouvier's knee had been the source of his fall and it continued to bother him.

With a story like that, I could see why the Exec wanted the trial aboard ship, and wanted to make sure there would be a swift conviction. After all, the Exec had broken a number of laws to pay Bouvier a large sum of money for apparently no reason at all. The only way to check out Moore's story was for me to go back to Cannes and see the situation first hand. Of course, Cannes was also a much nicer place to visit than Marseilles! I also wanted to take the baker's deposition and depositions from any civilian witnesses that I could find.

So, on our third day in Marseilles after the fire and Ed Wolf's departure, the Marine captain who was trying Moore, Dan Phelps, and I commandeered one of the remaining Lake Champlain cars that wasn't destroyed in the fire and a driver and went to Cannes to take the victim's deposition, along with any other witnesses we could find, and view the scene of the "crime." We also took with us a Yeoman 1st Class named Richards from the Captain's Office on the Lake Champlain who was both fluent in French and certified to give oaths, one of the ship's photographers, a 3rd Class Photographer's Mate named Rauen, and my Olivetti portable typewriter. Rauen for this occasion and for what I had in mind for him was allowed to wear civilian clothes.

We arrived at the café and found it exactly as Moore and Parker had described it. Dan wasn't happy about it, but he let me send in the photographer first with instructions not to talk to any of the others but to sit at a table and take surreptitious photographs of Bouvier as he was waiting on tables and serving customers with one of the ship's tiny Minox cameras. This he did, and the rest of us waited a good twenty minutes before we went in ourselves. On this one occasion Dan and I had worn our uniforms, as we were on official business. We went in with the yeoman, also in uniform, and took a table. There was the baker exactly as Parker and Moore had described him and there was no hint of a limp. Unfortunately, I didn't have the photographer bring a movie camera, but surreptitious movies would have been hard to take, especially indoors. We finally told Mrs. Bouvier that we were from the Lake Champlain and had come to talk to her husband about the incident with the sailor. She went to her husband, who looked over at our table, put a grimace on his face, and instantly started limping. He hobbled into the kitchen and came out with a cane. His erect posture had suddenly drooped six inches and a pained look was now on his face. He limped to the table and with the help of the yeoman translator introductions were made.

After the introductions, we told Bouvier that we were there to take his deposition in connection with the court marital of the sailor who had assaulted him. At first he wouldn't talk to us; he was concerned it would affect his claim for compensation. We assured him that this had nothing to do with his claim for compensation and we were taking the evidence solely for the purpose of the court-martial of the sailor involved in the incident. This loosened him up a bit, he agreed to the procedure and was sworn in.

Dan Phelps began the questioning, asking all the preliminary questions. Bouvier's version of how he got hurt was that Moore had kicked him in the knee while he was being held by two of his neighbors. Dan's last question was to ask Bouvier if he had hit Moore after Moore kicked him and he replied that he could not, he was on the ground and his knee was ruined permanently.

Next it was my turn at the questioning. After some more preliminary questions to flesh out his background, I asked him, "Monsieur Bouvier, we have found the sailor who assaulted you, and he is not a large man. I would estimate that he is a good 15 to 20 centimeters shorter than you. Is it your testimony that this small sailor assaulted you and beat you up?"

His Gallic pride would not permit any such interpretation of the events. "Mon Dieu, No!" he exclaimed. "He never landed a blow on me when we were fighting. I knocked him down each time he got up. But it was after the fight that I was injured when he attacked me and kicked me when my compatriots were holding me back. No, no, monsieur, your little sailor was no match for Paul Bouvier! I am former Golden Glove champion for all of Marseilles! Light-heavyweight division for three years right after the war. Even with my injured leg I would like to get him in the ring with me now. I would show him a thing or two."

Bouvier confirmed that Moore had first been brought to his attention when he banged the sign in front of his shop.

"He hit it with such force that it could be heard throughout the café. I came right out, and he had bent the sign, he hit it so hard. I told him that he had to pay for the sign, but he ignored me completely."

"Do you speak any English?" I asked.

"No," he replied, "or maybe a little bit to take orders in the restaurant if an American were to come in, but that seldom happens. We serve mostly our regular customers here."

"So you were speaking to him in French all this time?"

"Yes, of course, but many of the words that he was using were universal. He called me terrible names," replied Bouvier.

"Why did you hit him?" I asked.

"The sailor tried to run away without paying for the damage to the sign. I am still pretty fast and I jumped up the stairs and grabbed him and showed him how a Frenchman can fight, and he doesn't need any fancy uniform."

"I gave him a good thrashing," the Frenchman added, "and it was a fair fight until others grabbed me and held me. Then the American sailor kicked me in my leg and damaged my knee. Your government will pay me for my injured leg, no?"

"Others will be by to ask you more questions before the payment can be determined," I answered, "but didn't you already receive some money from the ship?"

"No, no, nothing," Bouvier lied.

"Didn't you have a meeting with a Navy Chaplain named Commander Longo?" I asked.

"He tell me that I did not have to say anything about it."

"So you did have a meeting with Chaplain Longo?" I repeated.

"He tell me that I do not have to mention anything about what he did," came the reply.

"What did he do?" I continued.

"The Chaplain tell me that I do not have to tell anyone about it."

"So you are telling me that you did not receive any money from the ship through Chaplain Longo," I pressed.

"That's right," replied the "elderly crippled baker," "I got no money from the ship."

"You mentioned that someone was holding you when the sailor attacked you, who was that?"

"Pierre Latouse, who has the tabac shop next door, he was on one side, and his brother, René, was on the other. It would take two of them; they are not big like me."

"How bad is your injury?" I asked.

"Very bad, I will always have the limp you see the doctor tells me," said Bouvier.

"Funny," I countered, "I didn't see any limp when I first came in."

"It sometimes gets better," wriggled Bouvier with the hint of a Gallic smile, "but it always hurts me."

"Do you have medical bills?"

"Only for the ambulance that first day. Bah, doctors, what do they know except to charge lots of money! I buy a cane and I limp. I have the bill for the cane someplace."

The interrogation went on, but I had pretty much obtained what I had come for. Dan asked him a number of questions on redirect, all of which boiled down to Moore getting in the last punch. He also tried to convince

Bouvier that it was all right to admit that he received the money, but all he would tell us was that the Chaplain told him not to say anything. We left the yeoman with the typewriter in the café to type up the deposition in both French and English and went out to see if we could find the Latouse brothers.

The tabac shop had a sign on it that said it was closed and it would open again at 3:30 p.m. That was less than an hour, so we waited in the café drinking excellent coffee and eating some of the baker's delicious pan-au-chocolate, which we paid for, of course. The yeoman, meanwhile, finished the French version of the deposition and I gave it to Bouvier and asked him to sign it if he agreed with the answers. I knew that they could translate it to English when they got back to the ship.

Bouvier was very reluctant, but on our assurance that it would not affect his claim against the government and would show the United States that he was cooperative, he signed and the three of us in uniform left. I had previously told Rauen to stay where he was until we returned to get him.

The Latouse brothers were not at their shop at 3:30, and we waited around until almost 4 p.m. when the two brothers finally arrived and unlocked their shop.

Our entourage of a Naval officer, a Marine officer and an enlisted man in uniform went up and introduced ourselves. The brothers were very friendly when we explained who we were and they both quickly confirmed Parker and Moore's version of the incident. I then showed them Bouvier's signed statement.

"Paul is not only a bully, he is a liar," said Pierre, shaking his head sadly.

"Yes," said René, "there is no truth to this. The man lies. He also has a bad record for this type of thing. You go to the gendarmes, you will see. They have arrested him many times for attacking people, including his poor wife and his children. He beats them mercilessly."

"Would you give us a statement confirming this?" I asked. "It would be very important for the sailor; he is in very big trouble and is being court-martialed."

"Why?" they both exclaimed at once. "He did nothing. He was too drunk to even defend himself."

"Well," I replied, "apparently the U.S. Navy thinks that it was Paul who was badly beaten, not the sailor. The ship even raised a lot of money, something between five and eight million francs"

This was before the new franc and the devaluation of the old franc by 100:1.

"No!" exclaimed Pierre, "that is outrageous. That man is nothing but a bully! He should get nothing!"

"Will you give me a statement?" I repeated.

The two brothers looked at each other, and then started talking rapidly to each other.

"What are they saying?" I asked the yeoman cum translator.

"I can't get it all, Mr. Maltzman, they are going too fast, but they apparently want to help but are afraid of Bouvier. They are afraid that he will come after them."

"Tell them that Bouvier will never see their statements and they will only be used aboard the ship and given to the officers on the court-martial board. Tell them that we will not tell Bouvier that they made a statement."

Dan shook his head in agreement, and the yeoman relayed our remarks in French. The two brothers then conferred for a few more minutes, and finally Pierre, the older of the two, turned to us and said they would be happy to cooperate.

The yeoman then swore them in and they gave their testimony as had Bouvier earlier. The yeoman typed out their depositions in French and the brothers read the statements, made a few technical corrections that they wrote in by hand, and the brothers signed their respective depositions.

From the tabac shop we went and gathered up Rauen and then proceeded to the police station where the uniforms of a Marine captain and a Navy lieutenant junior grade were sufficient to obtain a certified copy of Bouvier's very long rap sheet, and from there we returned to the ship, via a stop for a very good meal, getting back around midnight.

Two days later the Lake Champlain was ready to sail for Mayport, to the dampened delight of the crew; dampened, of course, by the recent tragedy of the fire. Their trip was also going to be quick, with only a short stop at Gibraltar on the way home. They would meet their relief, the Princeton, en route and be relieved in mid-Atlantic.

The court-martial convened on the day the ship left Marseilles. The Exec felt that the trial was so important that he directed Jeff Halbertson, the Legal Officer on the Lake Champlain, to sit in on the entire trial, as I had done in the court-martial of CWO Hills early in my Oriskany career.

The first thing I did was demand a verbatim transcript of the proceedings instead of a summary transcript. The latter was required only in the instance where the accused received a bad-conduct discharge, but in this instance, as the court had already prejudged the case and believed that Moore would be out of the Navy by nightfall, they granted my request before they heard a piece of evidence.

Next I moved to *voir dire* each member of the panel. This is a procedure where the defense counsel interrogates each member of the court and makes enquiry about their possible prejudice against the accused or their preconceived notions of guilt or innocence. It was a very unusual procedure in a shipboard court-martial, but definitely authorized and, after some quick study time in the UCMJ manual, Halbertson had to confirm that I had this right.

First up was LT Timothy Mitchell, Commander Boulivar's executive assistant and the head of the Exec's Office. It was his office that published the PODs that described the beating of the "elderly French baker." At the onset I entered into evidence the POD's that referred to Moore's alleged crime and the ship's collection of funds for the man. I then walked Mitchell through their content, got his assurance that he believed every word of what they said and that the source of the information was the Exec. Then I moved to have him removed for cause; he had prejudged my client.

I got a blank look from Commander Salt, who eventually turned to Halbertson and said, "What should I do, Jeff?"

Halbertson replied, "Commander, that would be a matter of judicial discretion which you, as the president of the court, must make yourself. I'm afraid that my opinion in this matter does not count, its up to you."

At that, Commander Salt turned to Mitchell and said, "Tim, you can decide this matter fairly, based on the evidence presented, can't you?

"Yes, sir!" was his reply.

"Challenge denied, Lieutenant, what else have you got," the commander said.

"Well, Commander, I intend to challenge each of the other members of the Board, including you, on the same issues. I think that each member of the Board has read the PODs that told of this affair and I think that each of the other members thinks that Commander Boulivar's statements in those PODs were true. I intend to challenge each court member on the same grounds if they respond as Lt. Mitchell has."

"Dick, that won't be necessary. I think all of us read the POD's and each of us believed what was said in there at the time, but that won't affect our ability to decide this matter fairly based on the evidence that is presented before us. Isn't that right, gentlemen?" Salt concluded, directing his last remark at the rest of the court.

All members of the court concurred.

"That ends that, Lieutenant, what else have you got?" asked Salt.

"The Exec has a lot of influence on the Lake Champlain, Commander," I replied, "and I would next like to enter evidence of that influence, after which I will move to change venue and transfer this case to some other jurisdiction where Petty Officer 3rd Class Moore can receive a fair trial."

I then returned to my interrogation of Lieutenant Mitchell and proceeded to take Mitchell through all of the various stratagems engaged in by Boulivar since I had come aboard. That covered Las Vegas Nights I and II, the Fisher hi-fi set for the Captain, and the use of the POD to publicize these events and make them successful. I also covered the use of the Public Information Office's rest & recreation funds to purchase prizes for the two Las Vegas Nights and the gambling equipment used in the Los Vegas Nights.

I next called as a witness Commander Longo, the Lake Champlain's senior chaplain. I took him through all of the various matters that I had covered with Mitchell. Longo, too, certainly believed everything that had appeared in the POD.

Next I went over the fund raising on the Lake Champlain for Paul Bouvier and Commander Longo's part in flying the money to Italy and changing it on the Italian black market. He wasn't happy about my questioning, acknowledged that he had received almost one-third more for the U.S. dollars in Italy than he could have obtained in France, which at that time did not allow its currency to float with the world market. He also reluctantly acknowledged that he knew that it was illegal to smuggle French currency into France.

Then I asked him the $64 question: "Tell me, Commander Longo, wouldn't the Exec be terribly embarrassed if Moore were acquitted by this court?"

The Chaplain didn't have to think about his answer and shot back, "He sure would be!" before Dan even had a chance to object, which he did and the Court ordered the answer stricken.

I now moved to transfer the case to another convening authority in view of the unreasonable publicity and the influence of the Exec over the officers on the ship and his obvious embarrassment if this court-martial board were to acquit Moore.

"After all," I argued, "if Moore was innocent, the officers and men of this ship have given $6,500 to Paul Bouvier for no reason at all, and based solely on the Exec's version of what had transpired."

Salt was visibly upset by my argument and, when I concluded, he asked everyone except Halbertson to leave while the Board considered the motion.

The discussion among the Board in private lasted for almost an hour, which gave me some hope, but when they finally came back in, Salt gave the opinion of the Board.

"Motion denied, the trial will continue."

I finally sat down, and it was Dan Phelps' turn to try and prove Moore guilty of the charges.

Dan called Parker as his first witness and swore him in. He directed his examination of Parker exclusively to the drinking they had done that night, that Moore was definitely drunk, and then asked Parker if he had seen the Frenchman on the ground.

"Yes sir, there was a point in time when the Frenchman was on the ground," replied Parker.

"What happened when the Frenchman was on the ground?" asked Dan.

"Moore pushed me away and kicked him."

"No further questions," said Dan.

Parker was now mine to cross-examine. I took him through the entire evening, and he confirmed all of evidence we had developed; Bouvier was the assailant here, he clobbered the Defendant and Moore had not kicked him in the knee, the knee had collapsed when Bouvier kicked Moore.

From there the trial proceeded quickly. Dan entered the deposition of Bouvier into evidence and I entered into evidence the depositions of the two Latouse brothers. Then I called as a witness Richards, the Yeoman translator, to describe Bouvier as he saw him in the café when we entered and before Dan and I identified ourselves.

"The Frenchman had no trace of any injury or limp that I saw, Lieutenant, and you and I watched him for a good twenty minutes before you identified us to his wife," Richards testified. "Then, when his wife pointed us out, he ran into the back room and came out with a cane and an exaggerated limp."

"Did you feel that the limp was real, or caused by any problem he had with his leg?" I asked.

"Hell, Lieutenant, that limp was as phony as a three dollar bill."

Next I called Rauen, the photographer, who confirmed everything Richards had said and then backed up his statements with several rolls of high-speed black and white photographs he had taken in natural light. They showed Bouvier waiting on tables, carrying heavy trays, joking with customers, gesticulating widely as only a Frenchman can, and in all ways appearing in excellent health and moving about without any visible impediment. Then there were a series of photos of him with the cane when he approached the table where Dan Phelps and I were sitting and in escorting us to the door after we had finished our interrogation.

Then there was the coup-de-grâce. After we had left and he was sure we were out of earshot, Rauen testified that Bouvier gave out a howl, threw the cane across the room to his wife, and did a horn-pipe dance to the delighted amusement of a number of his regular patrons who were apparently acquainted with the scam he was perpetrating on rich Uncle Sam. During all this time, Rauen sat in the corner snapping surreptitious pictures with his Minox camera.

I did not put Moore on the stand. Moore was too drunk at the time to have proven a valuable witness and the depositions I had submitted and the cross-examination of Parker told the story. I closed by entering Bouvier's fat police record. Dan objected on the grounds of relevance, but again I prevailed, as it was admissible to impeach Bouvier's credibility. There was, however, one flaw in the defense; the last blow, the kick by Moore to Bouvier's groin, was not in self defense. Bouvier was already down after his knee collapsed.

Dan Phelps made the most of that flaw in his closing argument, and my counter-argument was that this was nothing more than a fight between two brawlers and Moore, who did not start the fight, should not be punished for happening to get in the last punch. In any event, he was too drunk to have been able to properly evaluate whether Bouvier was capable of getting up and continuing the mauling he had already taken.

"Under all the circumstance of the event and Bouvier's background as a fighter and bully, Moore was justified in whatever he did to defend himself," I concluded.

The panel was out less than half an hour and came back with a judgment of guilty of simple assault. From the beginning it was clear that it would be almost impossible for that panel to acquit Moore in the face of the Exec's accusations against him in the POD. The Chaplain was right;

to do so would have been very embarrassing to Commander Boulivar, and this court-martial board was not about to embarrass the Exec.

The penalty phase of the court-martial went pretty quickly. Moore's chief testified that he was a hard worker and had not been in trouble before. I entered into evidence his service record, which confirmed his clean record, and left it to the Board. Dan didn't even bother to enter any evidence.

The Board was again out for a very short time. The verdict: Moore was sentenced to three weeks confinement to ship, a penalty that could have been imposed by a Captain's mast. This was not even a hard slap on the wrist, particularly since the ship was en route to the States and would not arrive for three weeks. Moore would miss liberty in our short stay in Gibraltar, but he would be free as a bird once we arrived home.

The Exec was not happy, but he was very stoic and treated the verdict as a victory. There was, of course, no publicity except a short statement in the POD that the culprit had been found guilty by a special court-martial. No mention was made of the punishment imposed.

With such a minor punishment there was no reason for a verbatim transcript of the proceedings, but as the order had already been made, the legal officer had no choice but to supply one to me as the defense counsel. I received the transcript several days later. I read through it and it was fine, but I delayed signing it. Had I signed it and returned it prior to the Lake Champlain leaving the 6th Fleet, the automatic review given to all special courts-martial would have been by the Sixth Feet's legal officer, a commander on the Forrestal who was known for his casual review of anything short of a BCD (bad conduct discharge). Instead I held on to the transcript until we arrived at Mayport, where the review would be by JAG in Washington. I did not think that they would take the light sentence already carried out worth reviewing, but I had spiced up the transcript considerably with my attack on the Exec's influence on the ship and his Las Vegas Nights, etc.

So it was that on July 29th, 1957, as the Lake Champlain tied up at Mayport to the joyous greeting of the crew's families, I marched up to the quarterdeck with my orders in my hand, saluted the OOD, and requested permission to go ashore. I handed the OOD a copy of my orders, which officially detached me from the ship. Then I asked the OOD, "Oh, by the way, give this to Jeff Halbertson in Legal will you?" and I handed the OOD the signed copy of Moore's transcript.

With that, I saluted the flag on the fantail, hoisted my duffle bag and V-4 bag, and started down the long gangway for the longer trip to San Francisco and Charlene. My Navy days were not yet over, but my sea duty was finished. My next ship would be a Sunfish in San Diego Bay and my crew would be the lovely Charlene Maltzman.

When I reached the end of the pier, I turned back for one last look at the Lake Champlain. She was tied up starboard side to the pier, and her fire scar was an ugly reminder of how beautiful, awesome and frightening a fighting ship can be, even in peacetime. I loved the Navy, loved both ships on which I had served, and in retrospect knew that I had been very lucky to have shared these experiences with some very wonderful people. I stood there for a long moment. Then I turned and never looked back.

Epilogue

Charlene & Dick's Wedding 8.4.1957

Six days after my return to San Francisco, Charlene and I were married in the new "Synagogue" at Treasure Island (note the plaque over the door and directly below the cross on the roof). Over 350 guests attended, but I had eyes for no one except Charlene. I was married in my whites with Harry Richardson, now a law student at Hastings, as one of my ushers in good, old-fashioned civilian formal wear.

The reception at the Officers Club at Treasure Island was wonderful, but the only thing that I remembered of the event was my first dance of the evening with the new Mrs. Maltzman. Instead of the traditional music usually played for such events, we insisted on dancing to "When the Deep Purple Falls Over Sleepy Garden Walls." Charlene's wedding dress was billowy, white and off the shoulder, and my dream had finally come true.

Dexter Pike (not his real name, of course) was unable to attend the wedding, but sent a beautiful copper samovar as a present. We made it into a lamp and have it to this day.

We had a delightful honeymoon, after which I reported for my next duty as Assistant Communications Officer, Commander, Training Command Pacific Fleet (ComTraPac). This was a very impressive position. I was second in command of a Communications Department that consisted of four officers and 75 enlisted men. There was only one small thing missing—we had no communications equipment except a couple of telephones!

The Navy, in its infinite wisdom, had decided some seven years earlier to do away with the communications capability of ComTraPac. They removed all of the radios and cryptographic equipment and advised the admiral that he could pick up his message traffic at 11th Naval District Headquarters ("Com11"), approximately two miles away. Only they forgot to remove the seventy-five enlisted men and four officers assigned to ComTraPac's communications staff.

Thus, twice each day one of the seventy-five enlisted men would drive a Navy car down to Com11 and pick up the mail and message traffic. Sometimes two would go so they would have someone to talk to as they carried out their difficult mission. Everyone else sat around playing pinochle, except the four officers, who sat around playing bridge and hearts. Once each month one of the officers would have the duty, which required us to stay overnight at the Sonar School.

Fortunately for me, I had only eleven months left of my tour of duty and Charlene to keep me interested.

—∞—

My delay in turning in the transcript of Moore's court-martial was far more effective than I could have ever imagined. I later learned from my friend from the Lake Champlain, Don Felt, who went to law school after leaving the Navy and settled in San Francisco, that JAG sent an investigation team to the Lake Champlain and investigated all of the incidents that I described in that transcript. Hearings were had in the Wardroom for several weeks, and produced a 300-page report condemning, of all people, the Captain for allowing such activities to go on aboard his ship. They also reversed Moore's conviction, so his record was still clean. The Exec, Cdr. Boulivar, got off without even a reprimand and probably eventually made captain and probably retired an admiral, but that is only my conjecture.

I discovered the ultimate irony years later when visiting Washington. I went to the Navy Department and looked at my Navy jacket, the file that contained the entire record of my three years of active duty and five years of reserve status. Boulivar had given me nothing but the highest 4.0 fitness reports, even after the court-martial of Moore.

Another thing I discovered in my Navy jacket was the answer to an inscrutable question that had bothered me for years: why had I never received a permanent Top Secret Clearance? When I first went into communications on the Oriskany I had to fill out the application for a Top Secret Clearance—after all, I was to be a cryptographer—and automatically received a temporary Top Secret Clearance. Just about everyone that I knew of that needed a Top Secret Clearance received a permanent one in about six weeks. I had a temporary Top Secret Clearance for the full three years that I was on active duty and for the next five years while I served in the active reserve—*as a Naval Intelligence Officer!*

My Navy jacket revealed the answer; while they could find nothing suspicious about me other than some bad poetry from my years at Stanford, they were very suspicious of my father. He spoke six languages—What kind of American speaks six languages? He and my mother traveled extensively, once, in 1948, leaving the U.S. for 15 months. And my father was born in—you guessed it—*Russia!* Admittedly he was 18 months old when he arrived in Canada fifteen years before the Russian revolution and about five when he arrived in the U.S., but the Communists loved to get them young, didn't they?

I thought this was pretty hysterical as my father was a life long Republican. The only Democrat he had ever voted for was Lyndon Johnson—he considered Goldwater too radical. So I told my father the story and he thought it was funnier than I did. It seems that in 1948 before he and my mother left on that first 15-month trip to South America and

Europe, my father was contacted by a friend who was a Major in the OSS, the precursor to the CIA. He asked my father, who was a very gifted civil engineer, if he would be willing to report to the OSS if he saw anything in his travels that might help the U.S. in its commerce or defense. My father was more than willing to do so and he was given an "Aunt Edna" in the San Fernando Valley that he should write to if he saw something of interest.

My father told me that he wrote to "Aunt Edna" every Friday with newsy reports that he tried to make innocent looking, but with drawings and details of new types of bridges, buildings, harbors and the like that he saw in his travels. When he returned his friend advised my father that his agency, by that time renamed the CIA, loved my father's reports and wanted to place my father on salary. They would pay him an annual salary and pay all of his travel expenses and his only condition was that he had to travel overseas six months every two years at a time and to locations to be selected by my father and he had to keep writing to "Aunt Edna."

My father responded that if he were paid he would be a spy. If he wasn't paid but elected to write to "Aunt Edna," he was a patriot who loved America for what it had given him, but he wasn't a spy. He wouldn't take the money and wouldn't go on contract with the CIA.

However, between that first 15-month trip in 1948 until he died in 1969 my parents took seven more trips abroad, the shortest of which was seven months long, and my father wrote a newsy letter to his "Aunt Edna" every Friday while he traveled.

When my three-year tour of duty ended, I resigned my regular commission and returned to Stanford to finish my last year of law school. Charlene and I settled in Palo Alto and I practiced tax and business law in San Francisco. Boring stuff compared to my adventures on the Oriskany and Lake Champlain, but I had my Charlene and we had three sons and we literally lived happily ever after. My sons used to insist that I someday sit down and write about all those fascinating adventures I had in the Navy that I regaled them with regularly over the dinner table. Well, I finally found the time.

A Note from the Author

Regrettably, there are very few of the many fine people with whom I served that I kept contact with after I got out of the service, and I have changed most of the names of those with whom I did serve in this book—some of my descriptions of their activities might charitably be described as less than charitable.

One exception was Harry Richardson. Harry finished law school and returned to Maine, where he had a very successful professional career and eventually went into politics. He served three terms in the Maine House of Representatives from 1965 to 1971, the last two as Majority Leader and served in the Maine Senate from 1973 to 1975. He then ran as a Republican for governor of Maine, but lost in the primary by 1,200 votes. It was Maine's loss more than his.

He was a Republican as I mentioned, but a very liberal Republican in the tradition of Maine. The bumper sticker on his car at the time of that last election read: "IF YOU ARE OPPOSED TO ABORTIONS, DON'T HAVE ONE!"

After that defeat he went on to head a very successful law firm in Portland, Maine, and became one of the finest trial lawyers in New England. At one point in his legal career he gave an interview that I found on the internet after he had just finished his nineteenth consecutive trial victory. Of course, in those nineteen cases he wasn't facing me on the opposite side. If he had been, the number probably would have been much larger than nineteen! Most regrettably, Harry passed away several years ago, but he did get a chance to read an earlier draft of my book and was in total agreement that I could never be sued for libel—the book, particularly as it related to him, was obviously pure fiction.

The only mystery about Harry is the name he eventually used throughout his legal career. As a Marine he was Harrison Lambert Richardson, III. As a politician and lawyer in Maine he was Harrison Lambert Richardson, Jr. Something must have been discovered about an ancestor that prompted that subtle change.

Ron Reicher, a.k.a. "Wrecker," (not his real name, of course, but someone with whom I did keep in contact) stayed on in Northern California when he got out of the Navy and established himself as a successful businessman in the Bay Area, just as he had been a very successful officer in the Navy once he got his sea legs and a very successful athlete in college.

Ben Benson (not his real name, of course) probably left the Navy after two years and went into daddy's business. Today he is probably rich enough to buy his own Navy, if he hasn't done so already. He also probably went into politics when the family business was sold and he bought himself a Senate seat, but again, this is all conjecture.

Carlton Kincaid (not his real name, of course) I would have presumed stayed on in the Navy, never managed to run any ship he was driving onto a reef or into another ship, continued to salute impeccably, and would, in my imagination, of course, eventually retire as an admiral. I would also have assumed that Lollie (not her real name, either) would have divorced him soon after his transfer and would wind up dealing blackjack in Reno. I also would have assumed that Carlton eventually remarried his commanding officer's elderly ugly daughter, which would explain the success of his career path in my imagination. But none of that actually happened. With the advantage of things like Google these days you can find almost anyone if you know their real name, it is not too common, and you try hard enough. I found the person I called "Carlton Kincaid," at least his obituary. He also passed away several years ago, and his obituary revealed that he was survived by his wife of over 50 years and a number of children, but left the Navy when his initial commitment was up and settled down to a very successful career in business. Well, he always claimed he did well at the Academy, and he apparently did!

Former Ensign Cherry (not his real name, of course, but a very real character, unbelievable as he might seem) I'm sure returned to his small mid-west town where I would bet anything he wound up living with his parents and later with his widowed mother. He probably became an accountant in my imagination, never married, and played the organ in church, religiously. In that imagination of mine, I see the famous organ from the Oriskany still sitting in his mother's living room. The crypto-green carton in which it was shipped to his home would still be sitting in the garage.

And in that same imagination of mine, no one would know what happened to Billy-Joe Beauregard (not his real name, of course), and no one would care.

Another person whose name I didn't change was Ed Wolf, or more accurately, Lieutenant Commander Edward F. Wolf of VF-71 on the Lake Champlain. While I never saw Ed again after we took him ashore to return to Norfolk on the Mississinewa, I'm sure he had a great deal of time to think about his future on his return. As he had indicated on that boat ride into shore in Marseille that without flying the Navy might not offer him a future, I believe that Ed did what he was contemplating and resigned his commission.

I can just imagine what that reunion must have been like at Oceana when Ed literally returned from the dead. Unfortunately, I have lost track of Ed, who was one of the finest officers and best bridge players I had met in the Navy. I have heard that there was a Captain for United Air Lines by the name of Ed Wolf, but I have no assurance that it is the same man. I have very fond memories of Ed, and I hope he and his family are all still well and prospering. To this day I believe that if Ed had stayed in the Navy he would eventually have become CNO, the top job in the Navy. He was that good!

Certain characters in this work, such as Gary Crosby and Errol Flynn, are historical figures, and to the best of my recollection the events portrayed did take place at or about the time stated with those particular people and as actually described. Furthermore, not all of the characters mentioned have fictional names; only where my memory was wearing thin or their activities that I describe could be considered questionable did I resort to pseudonyms. The story about Ken Schecter (his real name) and the Stanford blood drive, for instance, is totally factual. However, this is a chronicle of events that took place over 58 years ago, and while they are to the best of my recollection, that is all that I can say for it. It is best to just consider this a work based on events that actually happened—like the movies based on events that actually happened but we know events have been modified to fit the need of the film, or in this case, the memory of the author, because a 58-year-old memory can't be very reliable regardless of how unforgettable certain events were.

Except as I've specifically noted otherwise, all of the characters, names, and events as well as all places, incidents, organizations, and dialogue in this novel are embellished by the author's imagination or are used fictitiously for dramatic effect.

Having said that, I was assisted in my research for the book by the 109 letters I wrote to Charlene in the seven months I was stationed aboard the Lake Champlain and some letters I wrote to my parents while on the Oriskany, all of which the recipients kept and gave to me. Even more fun than writing this book was reading those old letters.

Finally, I wish to give special thanks to my good friend Harvey Popell, who like me was a regular NROTC student at the Stanford of the East (they call it Harvard) while I was at the Harvard of the West. Harvey is a professional editor who reviewed this work and gave me some invaluable suggestions that I believe I have incorporated in the book. Harvey, unfortunately, never had the opportunity of serving on an aircraft carrier, and instead spent his three years on a destroyer. In his opinion, a number of my stories were unbelievable, like the race between the Oriskany and its Number One motorboat out of San Francisco Bay, the hunt for the Hucks in the Philippines, and officers keeping liquor in their safes. But the stories he felt were unbelievable were the very stories that I know actually happened, as I was present when they did. I guess life on a destroyer must have been pretty boring.

—Palo Alto, California